Ms. Matched

Kay Keppler

Ms. Matched

Cover design © Patricia Simpson
ISBN: 978-0-9848211-4-3

Acknowledgments

No one writes alone, and I appreciate the help and suggestions of my critique partners and long-time readers more than I can say. Special thanks to Beth Barany; Patricia Simpson, who did her level best to keep my Scottish on track; and Laura McClure, who was there right from the start.

Chapter 1

Maggie Jorgenson struggled down the crowded aisle of the Wee Bite diner with her two-year-old daughter screaming on her hip and her two sons swarming like locusts around her. She was trying to get to the booth that Peg, the owner, had pointed her to. *If we get to the booth, we can eat,* Maggie thought. *When we eat, we can go home, Emily can nap, the boys can kill each other, I don't care.*

She plunked Emily on the booth's tartan plaid vinyl upholstery and straightened to see where the boys were. Eleven-year-old David was spinning his nine-year-old brother Kyle around on a counter stool. They were both laughing as Kyle's flying feet kicked the man on the stool next to him. At the age of forty, Chuck Winkel, Cedarburg, Iowa's financial planner, still lived with his mother. But whatever Chuck Winkel's domestic arrangements, he didn't deserve to be kicked every time Kyle made a revolution on the counter stool.

"Kyle, David, get over here," she said. "And apologize to Mr. Winkel for kicking him."

"Sorry," David said perfunctorily, leaving Kyle in mid-spin.

"Sorry," Kyle agreed, sliding off the stool. He raced his

brother to the booth, bumping into Tom Strodthoff's table, spilling Tom's coffee, and knocking his John Deere baseball cap off the back of his chair. Maggie sighed.

"Sorry, Tom," she said. "Boys, *walk* when you're in a restaurant. Pick up Mr. Strodthoff's cap. Now sit down and decide what you want."

The boys settled in and started to kick the bench, arguing with each other about what they should order. Emily continued to scream. Tom Strodthoff edged his chair away from them. Maggie felt a headache coming on and wondered if somehow she'd made the gods angry.

Peg came over with her order pad and dropped a handful of saltine cracker packets on the table. "Sounds like the little one's hungry," she observed, and Maggie cast her a look of gratitude.

"She is. We all are. Plus, we've had a big morning. Thanks." She tore open one of the packets and gave the cracker to Emily, who grabbed it and stuffed it into her mouth. Mercifully, silence reigned.

"Kyle had a tetanus shot," she told Peg into the sudden vacuum. "He stepped on a rusty nail. Not that I see it hurt him any." She frowned at her two sons, the light of her life, soon to be the end of it if they didn't stop kicking the bench.

Peg smiled at Kyle. "You need a reward after something like that," she said. "You had enough time to decide what you want?"

"I hope so," Maggie said. "Boys, tell Peg what you'd like."

"Hamburger!" shouted Kyle.

"Cheeseburger!" shouted David.

"*Boys!*" said Maggie, her headache throbbing. "There's no need to shout. You just have to tell Peg, not the next county."

Just then Emily dropped her cracker, and in reaching for it as it fell, hit her head on the edge of the table. She started to scream again. Maggie picked her up and cuddled her, kissing her forehead.

"And I'll have a Valium," she said, over the top of Emily's head and her escalating wails. "Make it two. Extra large. Chocolate."

Peg smiled in sympathy.

"The mac and cheese with side salad," Maggie sighed. "And milk for them and lemonade for me."

Peg nodded and tucked her order pad into the pocket of her shamrock-trimmed apron. "Coming right up," she said.

Maggie opened another cracker packet and gave the saltine to Emily, who clutched it and instantly stopped crying, her deep, violet eyes enormous with unshed tears. Maggie grabbed a paper napkin from the dispenser on the table and wiped Emily's cheeks and dripping nose, which made her look somewhat less like a snot bucket and somewhat more like the adorable toddler she knew and loved. Emily munched her cracker, oblivious to all efforts to clean her up, and Maggie thought, peace for another minute. *Thank heaven.*

The lunch crowd at Peg's had thinned by the time the boys demolished their burgers and Emily demolished the table. Maggie hoped that most of her daughter's lunch had gotten into her mouth rather than smeared on the Formica or ground into the floor, but seeing the mess at her feet, she couldn't be sure. Maybe if she didn't bring the kids back here for a while, say ten years, Peg would forget and let them back in.

"Sorry about the mess," she told her as she stood at the register to pay her bill.

"Nothing to it." Peg smiled at Emily, who now drowsed with her cheek against Maggie's shoulder. "Kids are the next generation of customers."

Maggie laughed, thanked her, and herded her two sons out the door and home.

IN A PLACE FAR, FAR AWAY from Cedarburg, Iowa, a cold and tired Venus Victoria Tane swam toward shore. *I've had it*, she thought. *This is the last time I play out this stupid*

Venus-rising-from-the-sea routine for my boyfriend.

The boyfriend in question, Mars Maxwell Huntington-Smyth about the 52nd, was indeed watching for her. His dark hair, long enough to curl over a collar had he been wearing a shirt, rippled in the soft onshore breeze as he gazed out to sea. He was tall and broad, with a powerful chest tapering to a narrow waist and strong, muscular thighs. He wore only a pair of loose cotton shorts, and a dusting of soft hair highlighted his chest and pointed the eye toward his manhood, which Venus had reason to know was also powerful. A soft, pink beach towel lay folded in his strong arms, and other beach accoutrements essential to a goddess rising from the waves were tucked into the picnic basket resting at his feet.

Mars waited with barely concealed impatience. This was always one of the most magical times for him, when his Venus, the gorgeous, the sensual, the magnificent, stood before him, water running everywhere down her luscious curves, her skin as pink as the lightest fingers of dawn, her hair like a gift from the sea, her bounteous breasts bursting from a bikini at least two sizes too small. These were the moments a man lived for, and Mars intended to live them as often as possible. If he had his way, Venus would rise from the sea every day of the week and twice on Sundays.

As he watched, she reached shore, staggering slightly under the force of the frothy surf. He held the beach towel before him like an offering, and as she stepped into the warm and sheltering circle of his arms, he bent his head to take her lips, and he tasted all the longing, all the desire, and all the salt of the long trip that had brought them together. He loved this woman with a warrior's heart.

"I wrecked my pedicure," Venus said, coming up for air.

"I'll make it up to you." Mars wrapped her more securely in the warm towel.

"Damn straight."

Later—much later—Venus told him why she'd come.

"I have to go to Cedarburg, Iowa, and Dr. J says, can

you come with me," she said languidly.

"When?" He'd picked up the sunscreen, ready to stroke the lotion on her perfect skin, but he halted at the news.

"Now, pretty much."

"Let's go, then." Mars tossed the sunscreen bottle into the picnic basket. "We can patch up that pedicure when we get there."

Seated in Peg's diner a nanosecond later, though, Venus had misgivings. "This one won't be easy," she said.

"You've had tougher." Mars slathered butter on his roll. "*Much* tougher. Remember the mathematician in Fairbanks?"

Venus laughed, but Mars was right. The situation was difficult but not hopeless. She was the goddess of love, for Pete's sake. Helping people find their perfect match was her wheelhouse. She couldn't guarantee anything, but she could give people a push. All she had to do was get them together, smile at one, smile at the other, and *boom*. They wouldn't be *committed*, it wasn't a *lock*, but they'd be interested. In fact, her magical smile could make anyone feel interested in anything Venus had in mind.

"And I'm here," Mars said.

Venus stopped checking out the diner and focused on him. Mars had been a part of her life for so long she'd almost forgotten what it was like before she'd met him. He'd gotten her out of countless scrapes, sometimes real danger. He'd saved her life once. He was dangerous, ruthless, ambitious, and rash. He looked like a Greek god. Well, of course, he *was* a Greek god—the god of war—which also made him a kick-butt peacekeeper, and that came in handy in her line of work. Best of all, he was devoted to her, which just showed how smart he was, too. And he could still turn her on like nobody she'd ever known.

"Thank heaven for that," she said.

"I already have." He bit into his sandwich, nodding toward the exit. "We're in motion."

Venus watched Maggie and her children leave the

diner. She frowned. "I don't have to wear flannel shirts while I'm here, do I?"

"I don't think you have to go that far."

She speared a melon ball from her ambrosia fruit salad, eying at Mars speculatively. "Maybe we have time to finish my pedicure, now that I don't have to go shopping for wardrobe."

Mars glanced up from his meal, his slow smile warming his flinty gray eyes until she felt her heartbeat pick up a notch.

"I think we can find time for that," he said.

BY THE TIME MAGGIE dropped the kids off with her ex-husband for the weekend, she was ready for some peace and quiet. She loved her kids, but getting a break now and then was a lifesaver.

She carried a tall glass of sweetened iced tea and the newspaper out to her dilapidated back veranda and lowered herself carefully onto the swing. When she gave herself a push against the porch railing, the nail that held the rail in place pulled out, causing the rail to sag toward the lawn.

Maggie sighed. One of these days she hoped to find the time, the money, and the ingenuity to make all the repairs that her comfortable dump of a house needed. Plan B was to win the lottery and pay someone to make the repairs. Plan C was to fall in love with and marry somebody rich, who would pay someone to make the repairs. She supposed there could even be a Plan D, where she fell in love with and married somebody not rich, but who would have the time, money, and ingenuity to make the repairs for her.

But so far, neither the rich and clueless nor the poor and skillful had materialized as a prospective husband, devoted fiancé, steady boyfriend, accommodating co-worker, kind neighbor, or even casual acquaintance. And when she herself had any spare time, the money and ingenuity escaped her, so the repairs didn't get made and the house stayed shabby. Maggie didn't mind. She needed one hundred percent of her energy for her job, one hundred percent of her energy for her kids, and the ten percent that was left over, she'd rather spend on her porch swing working the crossword puzzle.

This porch rail was dangerous, though. She needed to fix it before the kids hurt themselves on it. Kyle had had a tetanus shot today, thanks to a rusty nail she hadn't seen in the closet; she didn't need worse things happening.

Maggie put down the paper and went into the house, coming back with a tube of Super Glue and a ball of twine. She found where the nail had gone into the column and brushed aside a few slivers of old glue from previous repair jobs. Then she squirted some glue into the hole, pulled the rail back into place, and jammed the nail into the hole. Holding the railing in place, she wound some twine in a figure eight around the column and then the railing uprights. She tied the final knot with satisfaction. There. That should hold for a while. A week, anyway.

When she straightened up from the railing, Maggie saw someone watching her from the vacant house next door. She hadn't heard that the Bentons had sold their place, but she often missed out on neighborhood gossip.

She had a new neighbor, evidently. A tall, beautiful, blonde woman wearing tight, faded jeans, a spotless white T-shirt, and a floppy straw hat with pink flowers on the brim gazed at her from the next yard. Her clothes fit her like they were custom made, and Maggie felt dowdy next to her. Her own clothes were baggy, faded, and stained, and her unruly hair hadn't seen professional help since her fifth college re-union, and that was eight years ago. Just what she needed, Maggie thought with a twinge of envy, a gorgeous next-door neighbor with fabulous clothes. And then she thought, *maybe I can get some pointers.*

"Hello," the woman said, smiling at her. That smile was spectacular—it lit up her whole face, and Maggie felt dizzy in its radiance. The woman was standing on the other side of the fence that separated their properties, a limp and sagging structure that did little to prohibit trespass. The woman's left cheek was smudged with dirt, no doubt a side effect of the turned-over flower beds that Maggie could see behind her.

"Sorry to disturb you," the woman said. "And pardon my appearance, but I've been gardening. I'm a mess."

Maggie blinked. The woman was not a mess. The woman was pristine. Not to mention as quiet as the Sphinx. If it weren't for the smudge, Maggie would have thought she'd dropped out of the sky.

"We've moved in next door," the woman said. "My name is Venus Tane—Venus Victoria Tane. After the queen and a bunch of gods. I think my forebears were looking to give me a powerful aspect."

"Maggie Jorgenson," Maggie said. "After my grandmother. I think my forebears were hoping she'd bequeath me the family farm." She smiled at her new neighbor. "I hadn't realized the Bentons were planning to move."

"I believe Mr. Benton had a sudden opportunity," Venus said. "Would you mind if I joined you? I'm ready to quit work, I'm ready for a drink, and I'd love a little conversation." She held up a bottle of white wine in invitation—a bottle so chilled that even from her spot on the porch swing Maggie could see the condensation trickling down the green glass. "If you could go for something stronger than iced tea, I'd be happy to share."

Suddenly the thought of wine and a new neighbor was irresistible. "Sounds great," Maggie said. "Come on over. I'll get wine glasses." She got up, dropping her crossword on the swing and went into her kitchen, but came to an abrupt halt at her cupboard door. Who was she kidding? Wine glasses? She hadn't seen anything like a wine glass in years except in a restaurant. And she didn't get to many of those kinds of restaurants, either.

"Wonderful," Venus said from her seat on the porch steps when Maggie came out and handed her a Flintstones jelly-jar glass and a bubbled green tumbler, both relics from garage sales years ago and for some reason impervious to breakage.

Venus poured. "Here's to new neighbors," she said, handing Maggie the Flintstones glass filled with the golden wine. They clinked glasses.

"To new neighbors," Maggie agreed. She took a sip of the wine and closed her eyes in shocked appreciation. She had never in her life tasted anything so wonderful.

"This is incredible wine," she said. "Where did you get it? Not around here, I bet."

"Oh, it's something I picked up along the way," Venus said. "Nice place you've got."

Maggie laughed, taking in her glued-and-twined porch rail, the peeling paint, and the bicycles, athletic equipment, and miscellaneous toys stored on the porch. "It's a mess held together with Super Glue. If you can call it held together. Don't, by the way, lean against the railing. I just fixed it." She glanced over to where Venus had been digging in her yard next door.

"You've made serious headway in that garden," she said. Now that she was paying attention, she could see that Venus obviously had been hard at work for some time. The edges of the yard had been turned over for planting, and the earth was rich and loamy, nothing like Maggie's own grayish and lumpy soil. *How could I have missed all that activity?* Maggie wondered. *She must have been out here for hours. Maybe days.*

"Just giving it a little TLC." Venus gazed complacently at the new beds and wilted grass, bare dirt patches, and weeds that constituted the rest of her yard. "I like to garden. I seem to have a knack for it."

Maggie looked again at the Benton's former yard and the changes Venus had brought to it in one afternoon. "I'd say so," she said.

Venus pulled her hat off and her long, wavy, blonde hair rippled down her back. She ran her hands through it, shaking her head, and it fluffed out around her head, creating a bright halo around her face and a soft curtain around her shoulders. She leaned back against the column, stretching her impossibly long and shapely legs before her. Maggie wondered what she'd done to have this vision sitting here on her back porch, and then she thought, *don't be silly.*

"Mars is away on a job right now, so I have lots of time to get some work done and meet new neighbors," Venus offered.

"Mars is—"

"Mars Maxwell Huntington-Smyth. My boyfriend, I guess. Significant other. Protector. Lover." Venus smiled at Maggie over her glass. "My all."

Maggie blinked. She hated the term "boyfriend" for anyone older than sixteen, but she had to admit that the English language didn't offer a lot of good alternatives. The word Maggie would have preferred to use in these circumstances was "husband," but she'd tried out that word once and hadn't had much luck with it. Perhaps Venus's "all" was the way to go—if one had an "all," which Maggie didn't.

"What does he do?" Maggie asked.

"Security," Venus said. "He goes off and fights the good fight and saves the world." She thought about that for a moment. "Or at least, he fights the good fight." She reached over and refilled Maggie's glass. "I travel a lot, too," she said. "I'm a personal facilitator."

"That must be interesting," Maggie said, wondering what a personal facilitator did.

"It is," Venus said. "I love it."

"What does a personal facilitator do?"

"Well, I just got here, so not much yet," Venus said. "But I guess you could say I help people overcome the obstacles they face in realizing their personal goals."

"Oh. Like a psychotherapist?"

"Sort of, only more hands-on." Venus's eyes were thoughtful and kind, so she'd probably be good at her job. "And you?"

"I work in a small law office," Maggie said. "Just two lawyers. My ex-husband used to work there, too, then there were three lawyers. I'm sort of a secretary, sort of a paralegal. I don't love it—it's pretty boring, really—but it pays the bills."

Venus nodded at the toys on the porch. "Raising kids alone is a big challenge. Do you want somebody in the picture? Maybe get married again?"

"I haven't thought about it too much." She'd been way too busy, not to mention completely frazzled at first. John had been gone since before Emily was born. They used to sit on the porch after work in the early months of their marriage and laugh about their daily annoyances. That had been fun. But after David arrived, John started coming home later and later. The laughter had died first and then, gradually, love.

But she missed the talking and laughing, the sharing, and the companionship. *Cuddling with someone warm in the winter*, she thought, *and sex,* the longing so sharp it caught in her throat.

"Yes," Maggie said, "yes, I would like to get married again. To the right person, anyway. But I can't picture it. I live in a small town, and three kids puts a damper on the dating scene. If there were a dating scene."

"It's hard," Venus said. "But I can see you with a wonderful guy. A guy who'll love you, love your kids, love your house." She tilted her bubble green glass in Maggie's direction. "It'll happen for you."

Just then a metallic rendering of the William Tell Overture trilled.

"Oops." Venus reached into her pocket for her cell phone. "My boss. Gotta go. Thanks for the company!" She jumped to her feet, smiling that radiant smile again, making Maggie feel a little dizzy as she watched Venus head back to her own yard. Her new neighbor was shaking her head and holding her hand over one ear, obviously having a bad connection.

"What?" Venus said as she vaulted over the fence that separated their yards. "I can't hear you. Are you *serious*? He's rotten to the core? That can't be right. She's much too nice a person for that. Say that again. *What?*"

And then Maggie couldn't hear any more as Venus climbed her back-porch steps, disappeared into her kitchen, and let the screen slam behind her. She was gone, leaving behind a faint aura of glamour and the empty wine bottle.

Well, Maggie thought looking at it wistfully, *I hope we can do that again.* Then she picked up her crossword puzzle and, frowning at the first clue, tried to think of a five-letter word for "reluctant."

Chapter 2

Before Maggie went to bed that Friday night, she made a to-do list and stuck it on the bulletin board so that she'd remember to take it with her when she left the house the next day. The list of Saturday errands was extensive, but the most important task was to go to the hardware store to pick up enough Super Glue to repair the kitchen floor tile and, while there, get a birthday present for her mother, Doris Perl.

Doris ran the Elite Gift Shoppe downtown and always threw herself a big birthday bash at the Starlight Supper Club for friends, family, and business associates. Her mother pretty much had all the material goods she could want, but Maggie didn't want to come without a gift. She'd put off shopping until the last minute, and now she was stuck for ideas and up against the clock. The party was tomorrow.

As a last-minute gift to herself, Maggie finished her to-do list with "sit on porch with coffee" and "do crossword," activities she had time for only on the weekends when the kids were with their father. Right after the divorce, when Maggie had spent all her time being either furious or depressed, she'd also added "get up" and "get dressed" to her list so she could feel accomplished at the end of the day. But that had been long ago and she was way over that.

Now that the divorce was behind her, Maggie thought she'd done the right thing, but at the time, she'd wondered. John's departure was devastating for the boys, but she'd felt crushed in the marriage. The ink was barely dry on the license when John had his first affair. She'd found out and he apologized and swore he'd never do it again. But he did, year after year, until Maggie felt numb and abused. One night she lay awake, long past rage, knowing that she couldn't go on. He'd come in at four and, when he got up at nine, she told him she wanted a divorce.

When everything was settled, she got three kids and an old house that every day fell into greater disrepair. John got the kids on alternate weekends and a new, twenty-five-year-old wife—the local television reporter he'd met when she interviewed him for a business segment. Mostly the arrangement worked fairly well. Better than their marriage had, Maggie thought without bitterness.

So now on this Saturday morning when the kids were visiting their father, Maggie made herself some toast and coffee and, on her way out to the back porch, crossed off "sit on porch, drink coffee" from her to-do list. She sank onto the porch swing with her full cup and, after testing the newly glued porch rail gently with her foot, pushed herself off into a shallow swing, the chains squeaking in rhythm.

It was another beautiful fall morning, with summer lingering, but, Maggie knew, not for long. She was warm enough out here today in just her jeans and a T-shirt under her pink flannel shirt, but that wouldn't last.

She sipped her coffee—strong and black, absolutely perfect—and looked over into her new neighbors' yard. Venus must have been hard at work again, although Maggie didn't know when she could have found time since yesterday. All the beds had been turned over, and paths of grass, neatly trimmed, bisected irregular squares of loamy earth. She thought she saw spears of fresh green poking out from some of the beds. Bulbs? It seemed early to plant bulbs, but September in Iowa was no time to be transplanting flowers.

Her coffee and toast gone, Maggie took her dishes into the kitchen and dumped them into the sink to wash later. Then she grabbed her to-do list and car keys and headed out to the driveway and her beat-up Civic. *The day is coming when I'll be able to sit on the porch swing as long as I want*, she thought as she pulled out into the street, glancing back at her shabby house. Maybe in another fifteen or twenty years, when the kids are grown and everything is finally and forever Super Glued.

ED MEDINA FINISHED sweeping the sidewalk in front of his store and leaned back on his broom handle to see what he'd accomplished. The leaves, twigs, dust, sand, grit, and paper scraps of the day had been swept up. His windows sparkled, his door was open, and all up and down the quiet main street of Cedarburg, the other businesses looked the same, everyone getting ready for a busy Saturday. The dirt vanquished for another day, he was open, his neighbors were open, and it was a fine morning, not that he had anything to do with that. And then Tom Strodthoff came down the walk and said, "Hey, Ed, howzit?" and Ed said, "Pretty good, Tom, you?" and Tom said, "I need a fan belt for my generator," and Ed said, "Let's go in and see what we've got," and then he and Tom walked into Medina Garden and Hardware and his workday began.

By nine his dad and all the clerks had arrived and the shop was busy. Even the garden part of the shop was still busy, selling rakes and bulbs and mulch and other stuff gardeners needed in the fall. In another month or two when winter descended and snow flew, the garden section of the store would more or less hibernate until spring, but the hardware store stayed busy year-round. There were always things to build and fix.

Ed watched his dad talk to some customers about tulips, his hand cradling the bulbs as though they were precious jewels, his face as brown and creased as the warm Guatemalan earth he'd grown up on. He thanked again the lucky star he'd been born under. When his parents had arrived in Cedarburg from Guatemala thirty-three years ago, speaking only a few words of English, he'd been only five, shy and terrified. His parents had been, too, of course, he'd realized as an adult. When he'd asked them later why they'd stopped when they got to Cedarburg, they just shrugged and said that the green hills reminded them of home. But Ed thought the lucky star had told them to stop.

Ed was at the cash register ringing up Tom's sale when Maggie Jorgenson walked into the store. Ed wondered what her ex had been thinking when he left Maggie for that young TV reporter. John Jorgenson had achieved everything Ed wanted for himself—that big, sprawling house that always needed something done to it, three kids, and most of all, Maggie. She was nice, funny and kind, and very attractive but not fussy about it. Like today—she wasn't dressed up, but she looked good, with her dark hair loose and glinting reddish under the store lights, and her pink shirt making her clear skin glow. She waved at him and he smiled and said, "Hi, Maggie."

"Hey, Ed," she said, beaming at him. "How's your stock of Super Glue holding up?"

"Running low. You should buy stock in the company." He watched her walk to the back of the store, all warmth and color and movement, and then he shook his head and returned to his customer.

When she came up to the cash register a few minutes later, she dropped a package of Super Glue and a bag of two hundred tulip bulbs on the counter and said, "Ed, what size ladder do I need to clean my gutters?"

"How far off the ground are they?" It was too bad she didn't have someone to help her with yard work. Her oldest could help some, but he was still a kid.

"How far? I don't know. Two stories?"

Ed laughed. "Maybe a twenty-foot extension," he said judiciously. "That would be tall enough to get onto your roof if you ever needed to get up there."

"Never in my lifetime, I hope," Maggie said. They talked about options, and in the end, he said he'd order a twenty-foot extension ladder because he didn't have one in stock. He could deliver it Monday after it came in on the truck, and he might as well bring gutter screens then.

"So, Maggie, let me ask," he said finally. "I've always wondered. What do you do with all that Super Glue?"

"I'll show you." She motioned for him to follow her out to the curb where her car was parked. "I'm surprised that you can sell such a superior product effectively when you don't know all its uses." She smiled at him, ripping open the package.

"I can tell I'm going to learn one more today," Ed said. "You're my best customer for Super Glue. You go through a lot."

"It's the secret to home and automotive repair." Maggie nipped off the top of the tube of glue and handed it to Ed to hold while she rummaged in the back of her car for a rag.

"This'll do," she said, inspecting it. "What we're going to do, Ed, is glue down this metal trim on the car." She pointed to a long strip of metal whose raw edge was curling up away from the body of the car. "That could poke out an eye."

Ed examined the wicked-looking piece of loose metal. "Doesn't do much for the aerodynamic properties of the automobile, either," he said.

Maggie laughed, gazing at the dented, rusted, shabby Civic. "Yes, after we glue down this metal trim, my twelve-year old Civic turns into a Porsche. Like Cinderella and the pumpkin."

"All because of Super Glue. It's a miracle."

"Absolutely," Maggie said. "Okay, first we wipe down the surface." She swiped at the car's door and fender with the rag. "And now we glue." She pointed to the tube Ed was holding. "I know that you know this, but once the glue is spread, you have to act quickly. That stuff dries like concrete in no time, something I've learned the hard way."

Ed squeezed out a thin line of glue on the metal strip and pressed it against the car door. The loose piece was too long for him to make good contact on the whole length of it, so Maggie stepped in next to him, pressing down one edge of the strip. She was so close that her arm brushed his, and he could smell the lemony scent of her shampoo. He closed his eyes, enjoying the contact, feeling guilty that he did.

"You can fix anything with this stuff." Maggie turned her head, her eyes incredibly large and blue and *way* too close. She was so close that if he moved one inch, he could kiss her. And that would be so not right. She wasn't just any woman. She was a *customer*. She had *children*.

"Metal, wood, plastic—you wouldn't believe," Maggie said now. "Plants that have been damaged. Even skin. If you've got a cut and no Band-Aid, Super Glue closes it right up."

"I'll remember that," Ed managed.

"That should do it for this side." She leaned back and gazed critically at the glued trim. "Can you give me a hand with the other side, too? I appreciate this, Ed."

He gazed at her, vibrant and warm. He needed to walk away, to resist her appeal. Someone like Maggie Jorgenson was all wrong for him. She didn't know tortillas from toast, and his parents still preferred speaking Spanish at home. Moreover, they were very, very Catholic. They wouldn't approve of her divorce, and she had three children who loved their father. A stepfather would not be good for them. This situation was not what he needed or wanted.

Whoa! he thought. He wasn't going to marry the woman. He wasn't even going to *date* her. He was simply helping her glue her car together. She was a *customer*.

"No problem, Maggie," Ed said, following her around to the other side of the automobile and another piece of loose metal trim. "I'm happy to help."

THREE HOURS LATER, Maggie was back home. She'd completed her errands, including finding a birthday present for her mother, a woman who claimed to want nothing but happiness for her only child. However, for some time now Maggie's happiness hadn't been anything she could box up and tie with a bow for her mother. Instead, Maggie had purchased two hundred mixed tulip bulbs at Medina's and would print up a gift certificate offering to plant them for her.

Maggie fixed herself a peanut butter sandwich and glass of milk for lunch, and then she wrapped her mother's gift and sat down at the computer and fussed over making a fancy border for the gift certificate. When she was satisfied with it, she printed it out and folded it into an envelope and taped it to the present.

That job finished, she still had almost an hour before she needed to get ready for Edith Nennig's funeral and wake. The timing of the funeral was unfortunate, coming as it did right before her mother's birthday party, but that couldn't be helped. Edith Nennig had been her first-grade teacher, and she had to pay her final respects. Probably a lot of people would be there, since the woman had taught almost everyone in town how to read. Until then, though, the porch swing beckoned.

Maggie picked up the paper and her crossword dictionary and headed out to the back porch. She jiggled the porch rail to see if it was still holding, which it was, so she pulled off the twine that had held it while the glue dried and then plumped down on the swing and got comfortable. Crossing her legs under her and folding her paper to show only the crossword, she glanced over to Venus's yard before she settled in.

The woman was an amazing gardener. Since this morning, she'd installed a fountain in the shape of some bacchanalian-type imp, whose little head was encircled by leaves and whose mouth was blowing into a pipe, from which water gushed in a gentle stream. Around the fountain, ivy clung and flourished in a rock garden, and blue chicory, coneflowers, and something white that Maggie couldn't identify bloomed with abandon. The grass pathways must have been given a fast-action fertilizer, because they weren't brown and dry and weedy anymore—they were a brilliant emerald green, a thick and luxuriant pelt. And the lush green spears that Maggie had seen this morning looked bigger. *Much* bigger. Maggie peered more closely. How could they have grown so fast?

Maggie shrugged and went back to her crossword. She loved living in Cedarburg; her mom was here, she had friends and a job that supported her kids even if she didn't like it much, and they had a secure, if shabby, house that someday would see better times. There wasn't excitement. There wasn't drama. That wasn't what Iowa was about. Iowa was about stability and calm and routine. Just about all the excitement you could find in Cedarburg, Iowa, was sitting around and watching the grass grow. It was safe, but maybe a little boring. That was okay, though. Maggie would take boring if she could get all the rest of it.

She checked out Venus's yard again, the lush, thrusting spears jutting from the dark earth, the vigorous green ivy with its brash, succulent leaves curling around the fountain, the bright blue flowers tumbling over the rocks, and the knowing, winking Pan smiling on all that fecundity. How did Venus do it? It was September in Iowa. Yards weren't supposed to look that good at this time of year.

Suddenly, watching the grass grow didn't seem quite so boring anymore.

Chapter 3

Ian Strachan, Mickey Adair, and Ray Corkin sat squished together in the back row of the small, crammed commuter airplane and, separately and together, considered their options, of which dying in a plane crash so far seemed the most preferable if not the most likely. The plane had bucked and pitched ever since it left Chicago's O'Hare field—and then the storm hit. An air pocket had caused Ian to toss his drink onto Ray's lap and Ray to toss his cookies onto Mickey's. Now, pale, damp, and desperate, they peered out into the storm and prayed for deliverance.

"This was a daft idea," said Ray. "We'll never find him." He clutched his stomach as the plane dropped five hundred feet and lightning flashed outside the window. He'd already used up his airsickness bag, but he'd lost all his lunch, so perhaps he wouldn't need another.

That's what Mickey, still grossed out from the first encounter with Ray's upset stomach, hoped, anyway. "Assuming we even get there," he agreed. "Assuming we don't die first."

"We're not goin' ta die," Ian said with more confidence than he felt. The truth was, none of them was much used to traveling, especially by air, but he was the leader, and he planned to show the boss that he was worthy of the trust that had been placed in him. "We're goin' ta get there, we're goin' ta find this Donald Nennig, we're goin' ta finish our business, and then we're goin' home. And our pockets will be a lot fatter for it."

"And we'll never travel again," Ray said, trying not to moan as the plane pitched in the darkness.

Amen to that, Mickey thought, taking another hit from his flask. He'd been crazy to go along with Ian's plan and take this flight to who knows where, but if he was daft—and now covered in puke—he might as well be drunk, too.

"Only by train," Ian said. "But if I'd a' known you were such a band of stinkin' sissies, I'd never a' brought you." And with that, he clamped the headset over his ears and tried to find something to listen to other than the classical music channel or the air traffic control commands. Just what he needed tonight in this sardine tin they called an airplane was hearing the controllers talk about bad weather and colliding aircraft. *Not bloody likely*, he thought.

Stuck in the middle seat, Ray closed his eyes against the apocalyptic visions going on in the heavens. He thought about trying to make a deal with God—like if God let him live, then Ray would do something for him. But Ray couldn't think of anything God might want from him, plus Ray was reluctant to make promises on which—down the road and through no fault of his own—he might not be able to deliver. So he closed his eyes and hoped the plane stayed up in the air until it was time for it to come down.

By the time they got to Dubuque, the rain had stopped but the skies were still threatening, with enormous pale gray clouds tinged with charcoal and black piled up against the horizon. A strong wind blew sodden leaves across the road and pierced their light jackets.

"Nice place," said Ray with what in his weakened state could pass for sarcasm, as they got into the bright red compact rental car at the airport. He opened the back door and fell across the seat, thinking for the first time that he might, after all, survive the afternoon.

"Aye," said Mickey, surveying the neat buildings and all the smiling people with blond hair and perfect teeth. He buckled himself into the driver's seat, lit a cigarette, and inhaled it deeply as he pulled out the ashtray with the little sticker that thanked him for not smoking in the car. "Daft buggers drive on the wrong side of the road. We'll be lucky if we get out of this job in one piece."

"We'll do that," Ian nodded, "and when we're done, you ungrateful louts will thank me for it all the way to the bank." He frowned at Mickey smoking in the car and took a small bottle of pills from his jacket pocket, from which he shook out a small handful and tossed them back without water.

"That's why we're here, mate," Mickey said, as he cautiously headed out of the rental lot and toward the open road. At the first left turn he got into the wrong lane by accident, but the oncoming car braked without honking until Mickey had righted himself, then the driver waved at him as he drove on.

"What's the plan, then?" he asked Ian.

"At five o'clock we go to his mum's funeral," Ian said. "We meet Nennig there. Mind, we don't want to stand out. We're to sit in the back, show proper respect, and act professional."

"I don't see why we couldn't have waited for him to get back to New York," Ray complained.

"Because we didn't know when he was coming back," Ian said, his patience wearing thin. "Our instructions were to find Donald Nennig, turn over the merchandise, pick up the payment, and skedaddle back to Glasgow. And do it quick-like. Sitting on our arses in New York waiting for him does not do that."

"This town is too small," Ray said, pushing it. "We might be spotted."

"And maybe we won't," Ian snapped. "Not if you sods do your jobs properly."

Ray fell silent, staring gloomily out the window, sulking

probably. Mickey couldn't much blame him. They'd come, hadn't they? Despite that buggering plane. But Mickey was older than Ray by four years and had been a partner of Ian's for all that time. The experience hadn't been wasted on him.

"We might be *spotted*," he said to Ray. "Doesn't mean we'd be *suspected*."

The country they passed through was brilliantly green and hilly, with big old oak and maples trees just starting to turn color, their leaves adding red and amber tones to the landscape. The towns with their neat clapboard houses and trim lawns, churches with white spires, and small farms with red barns and black-and-white cows, were pretty.

"It's nice here," Ray said. "Serene, like. Like a picture on a calendar."

"Not quite real?" Mickey asked.

"I guess," Ray said. "Yeah."

A few minutes later Mickey saw the small green sign on the side of the road: Cedarburg, pop. 2,016. *Jay-sus*, he thought. What had Ian gotten them into?

"We're here," he announced.

They drove through the town, looking for a hotel, motel, inn, B&B, or rooms to rent. Nothing. Other than that, though, the town had a diner with lots of customers and a couple of pubs and stores. Not the kind of town anybody would want to settle in, Mickey thought, but they wouldn't starve while they were here and they wouldn't lack for a pint, either.

"Keep driving," Ian said, when they had driven the length of the main street and found no lodgings of any kind. "Maybe there's something on the road going away."

And so it proved to be. Right at the edge of town where houses again gave way to pasture, perched between the ribbon of road and the edge of a tawny cornfield, a neat one-story motel beckoned. A square, black patch of asphalt served for a parking lot, and two pots of bright geraniums flanked the glass door under the hand-written sign that proclaimed OFFICE. Mickey turned into the drive under the neon LAY-Z STAY MOTEL, VACANCY sign and pulled up.

"Well, lads," Ian said with a grin, "we're home."

Mickey unbuckled his seat belt and got out of the car. He felt tired and stiff from the terrifying flight and long drive. But the fresh air was brisk and invigorating, clean and crisp, and he could smell the loamy earth and wet grass. Then the clouds broke apart and a beam of warm, watery sunshine broke through, lighting the field beyond and casting a rainbow from one end of the green expanse to the horizon. *You never know*, he thought. *Maybe things will turn out okay after all*, and went in to talk to the proprietor.

A short time later, though, he wasn't so hopeful. They'd checked in at the Lay-Z-Stay and then headed for the funeral, where, supposedly, they were to meet their fence for the diamonds. Now they were jammed together in the back of the hot, crowded funeral home, listening to a shaky soprano waver through her solo. The place was crowded with people and flower arrangements, and he couldn't pick out Donald Nennig in the crowd. All he could see from where he stood were the backs of what must be hundreds of people. The old dame must have had quite the following.

The soprano finished the hymn and sat down. The minister blathered for a while, everybody prayed, sang a song, and then it was over. The crowd stood up as one and shuffled forward, so Mickey fell in behind Ian, letting Ray bring up the rear.

"You think there's going to be a funeral lunch?" Ray asked, nudging him. "I could go for a Wimpy, if not."

Mickey shrugged, although he'd wondered the same thing. The crowd was bigger than a birthday bash for the Queen Mum, bless her departed, imperialist soul. Maybe this one liked a spot of gin, too, and she and the Queen Mum could forge a friendship over a few shots in a heavenly pub. He wouldn't say no to a spot of something right now himself.

And then the crowd moved and shifted and he saw Donald Nennig, their quarry, standing by his mother's casket, accepting condolences. He'd have to talk to them now.

"Sorry about yer mum an' all," Ian said to their fence

when they were face to face. "We hate to bother you at this sad time, but we missed you in New York. We're hopin' we can wind up our transactions out here."

"*Transactions*," Ray whispered, digging Mickey in the ribs. "Didja hear that? Ian's talkin' like a Wall St. banker. Rich, that's what that is."

"Of course," said Donald Nennig, nodding. "I appreciate your taking the time to come all this way. Let's plan for tomorrow. Come up to the house now for something to eat. We'll make arrangements."

Mickey felt happy at the promise of refreshments, and Ray poked him in the back, so presumable he was happy about it, too.

"Appreciate it," Ian said, "we'll do that." They shook hands and Ray and Mickey followed him out of the room, stepping around flowers and other mourners who seemed to be busy catching up on town news and gossip.

Once outside, Mickey lit another cigarette. He was relieved to be away from the reminders of the hereafter.

"Where's the house, then?" he asked his companions as they got back into the car.

Ian glanced around. "Dunno," he said. "Can't be that hard to find. Place is as small as a boil on a flea's bottom."

He rolled down the window and stuck out his head as two women walked by, one short and dark with a reddish glint to her hair, and one tall and blonde—and smashing. The blonde was absolutely smashing.

"Hey," he said. They stopped, the brunette looking inquiring and the stunning blonde speculative. "Can you tell us where the Nennig house is?"

The dark one stepped up to the car window. "You're headed to the wake? Straight down this street about three blocks and a right on Elm. It's a big, white house with a wraparound porch. Number seventeen. You can't miss it."

"Thanks," Ian said. He stared over the brunette's shoulder at the blonde standing at the curb. *Smashing,* he thought, taking in the blonde's incredible face, her streaky, silvery, wavy hair, and long legs. She smiled at him, a radiant, heart-stopping smile, holding his gaze for what seemed like an eternity, and his mouth went dry and his brain seemed to cease functioning, except that he heard a light buzz. Like a hum. And then she looked at her friend.

Dazzled, Ian followed the goddess's eyes and gazed at the brunette. The calm buzz filled his brain. *The brunette. She's even more gorgeous,* he realized, as he gazed at her. *Better than the blonde. Better than anyone.* She floated in a golden haze. Her eyes were kind and gentle, her dark hair with its beautiful reddish glow so soft that it drifted on the breeze. Her milky skin, her perfect figure—she was unbelievable. Unimaginable. Like an angel.

The brunette, who was still leaning through Ian's passenger side window, seemed concerned.

"Are you all right?" she asked, and he blinked. The golden haze that had surrounded her was gone, but she was so close to him that he could almost feel her breath on his cheek, a miracle by itself. Her skin was flawless, pale and translucent, like an opalescent pearl, with a faint flush on her cheekbones and a sprinkling of reddish freckles across her nose. Her eyes were a deep blue, the color of sapphires or the Firth of Clyde on a sunny day, with fine, arched brows above them, and now they locked onto his. She was clean and wholesome and friendly and worried. Why hadn't he noticed before how attractive she was? Much more attractive than the blonde. The brunette was *fantastic*.

"Oh, aye," he managed, clearing his throat. "Lovely. I mean, I'm lovely. I mean, fine, thank you very much." The brunette appeared unconvinced as Ian continued to gaze into her eyes.

Mickey cleared his throat. "Ian, you got the address? You ready to go?"

She stepped back from the window, saying, "Straight ahead, right on Elm. You can't miss it," and Mickey put the small car into gear and pulled away from the curb. Ian took a deep breath and shook his head. Then he adjusted his side view mirror so he could watch the brunette angel until they turned the corner onto Elm.

MAGGIE AND VENUS resumed their walk, heading down the street on their way to Edith Nennig's wake.

"Did you hear that?" Maggie said. "That accent! I think they're from Scotland."

"The one doing the talking seemed very taken with you," Venus observed.

"You think so? I was so startled that a man asked for directions, I didn't notice."

"I think he was dazzled by your beauty and charm," Venus said.

Maggie laughed. "Not to mention my wisdom and grace. I wonder what they're doing in Cedarburg? People don't usually come here to sight-see. They wouldn't come here just for Edith's wake, would they?"

"Maybe they know the family," Venus said. "And now maybe that dark one will get to know you, too."

"Because I dazzled him with my beauty and charm."

"Not to mention your wisdom and grace."

Maggie grinned. "Well, I'd never say no to a lovely accent."

Chapter 4

When Maggie got to Edith's wake, she offered her condolences to the Nennig family, breezed past the delicious-looking spread they'd provided, and introduced Venus to a few people. She didn't see the Scotsmen arrive—could they possibly have gotten lost in the four blocks to the house? But she couldn't linger. Her mother would expect her.

By the time she arrived at the Starlight Supper Club for the birthday celebration, the party was in full swing. People stood three-deep at the bar, laughing and greeting each other like long-lost explorers, and the buffet was mobbed. Many party-goers were dressed somberly in black, so they probably had come straight from Edith's funeral.

Nothing like a glimpse of mortality to put some life into the crowd.

She checked her coat and went to congratulate her mother, the birthday girl, who was surrounded by friends and neighbors. Everybody was talking about Edith's wake.

"So much food," moaned Eva Piepenburg, who with her husband, Fritz, owned the local bakery. "The Nennigs can't possibly eat it all."

"They have a pretty big freezer," said Todd Zorn, who owned Cedarburg's appliance store and knew to the cubic inch just how big the Nennig freezer was.

"How are the Nennigs doing?" Doris asked. She had gone to the funeral but skipped the wake so she could see to her own event.

"They seem to be doing all right," said Eva, whom Maggie had seen deliver a dozen loaves of bread to feed the multitudes. "They're eating okay."

Everyone nodded at this barometer of mental health.

"Great weather we're having, isn't it?" Maggie said. "My new next-door neighbor is planting her fall garden, and she's making incredible progress."

"I wonder when we'll get the first snow," said Todd, a snowmobile enthusiast. His staff, in addition to selling appliances, would order a snowmobile for customers who wanted one.

"I don't care when it snows," Doris said. "I'm treating myself to a Caribbean cruise."

"What?" Maggie asked, wondering if she'd heard right. "Really? When? For how long?"

"I was going to tell you, dear." Doris patted Maggie's hand. "In a few weeks. I'll be gone fifteen days. A vacation, but I'll be buying things for the store for Christmas, too."

"You have to be careful with viruses on those trips, especially on those cruise ships." Todd said. "Drink boiled water *only*."

"I'll have a great time," Doris said. "I'm thinking about baskets this year, and maybe some carved wooden animals and, of course, tree ornaments. And who knows what else I'll find?"

Maggie had always loved her mother's store. She had happy childhood memories of playing there after school. The best times had been in the months right before Christmas, when huge shipments came in and she helped her mother unpack—big vases and decorative bowls and cute ceramic planters swathed in shredded newspaper, colorful costume jewelry and bright scarves, wooden plates and spice racks from exotic places, and Christmas ornaments and candles and artificial wreaths for the season. Every crate had contained a mystery, every box a possibility, and she'd always been excited when she'd reached in deep and pulled out something wonderful.

Maggie tried not to feel depressed about her mother's taking a cruise to shop in the Caribbean when she herself was going nowhere. *I'm divorced and I've got three kids, a boring job, and a house held together by Super Glue,* she thought. *How did that happen?*

"I'm going to get some food," she said. "Does anybody need anything? Mom?" and when everyone said no, Maggie got up to see what she could find.

The Starlight was Cedarburg's largest entertainment venue. Over in one corner a band was setting up. *Dancing,* Maggie thought. It had been a long time since she'd gone dancing. The beautiful bar, hand-carved out of teak and rescued from a demolished luxury hotel in Chicago, extended the full length of the room and was hung with tiny pink and white lights. The place was festive.

The buffet—a salad bar and a big table of warming trays—was set up against the opposite wall. At the end on a carving table sat a huge prime rib roast. Lenny Weber, the Starlight's owner, wrestled with the oversized piece of meat, carving off manageable slices for the diners. *Mom's store must be doing well,* Maggie thought, *to pay for all this.*

The kid who was tending bar didn't look old enough to be serving liquor, but he poured her a glass of wine and she took it to the buffet, where she filled a plate. Then she returned to her mother's table, where the group had resumed talking about Edith Nennig's funeral.

Maggie sliced into her prime rib. "Who are those guys with the Scottish accents?" she asked, tasting her piece of roast and sighing in appreciation. Lenny's prime rib was to die for.

"I didn't catch their names," Todd said, "but somebody said they were business associates of Donald's."

"They're in the jewelry business?" Maggie spooned

sour cream into her baked potato. "In New York? I wonder why they're here, then. Food's delicious, Mom."

"Thanks, dear," Doris said. "Lenny always does a nice job."

"Did you try the chicken?" Eva asked. "Scrumptious. And the mashed potatoes are perfect."

Maggie nodded, sampling the three-bean salad. "I was just surprised that all those guys with accents were here in Cedarburg."

"Maybe they're wholesalers, too, on the European side," Fritz Piepenburg said. "Donald's a wholesaler, right? He travels a lot. He must deal with a lot of people."

"Hey, it's not so weird that Donald Nennig's European business partners would come to Cedarburg," Todd objected. "We're not stuck in the wilderness, you know. We've got attractions."

What attractions? The biggest attraction Cedarburg had that Maggie could think of was this prime rib. She picked up her plate and glass. "I'm going back for seconds," she said. "Is everybody all set here?" Fritz gazed longingly at the buffet, but Eva put her hand on his arm and he shook his head. Maggie handed her plate to a passing waiter and headed to the bar for a second glass of wine.

"Make it a double this time," she said to the underage bartender. He seemed confused about a wine double, but he poured her a glass without mishap while she perched on the stool, watching her mom get up to work the room. Doris made the rounds, talking to each person. Very civic-minded, she'd held every office of the Cedarburg Merchants Association over the past thirty years and knew everyone in town.

"Hey, Maggie," someone said next to her, and she turned and saw Ed Medina pointing to a bottle on the shelf behind the teenaged bartender. "That's it," he said to the kid, who reached for the Jim Beam.

"Hey, Ed." Ed looked different than he had at the store this morning. He was more dressed up, wearing dark slacks and a pale, cream-colored shirt with creases in the sleeves that were rolled up at the cuffs. He looked nice. Handsome. The pale shirt contrasted against his dark hair and eyes and the warm tones of his skin.

Ed took the glass the teenager handed him and turned on his stool to face the same direction as Maggie. His knees bumped Maggie's as he turned, and she felt a little shock, a little slide of heat, as they touched. *What?* she thought. *What's that about?*

They sat for a moment, their backs to the bar, watching the crowd. Ed's heat seemed to radiate from his body, like a direct electric current passing from her thigh to his. *Edison could have done his connectivity experiments here*, Maggie thought, flustered at sitting so close to Ed. And then, *I have to lay off the booze.*

"Nice party," Ed said finally.

"Nice of you to come," Maggie said.

"I always enjoy myself at Doris's birthday bash. Besides, I can't turn down your mother. She'd put me on the next committee to investigate something really complicated." He took a sip of his bourbon and watched the band tune up on the stage. They rocked into a decent version of "That's Life," a good song for a woman who turned seventy that week.

Maggie laughed. "Did Mom tell you she's going on a Caribbean cruise to shop for her store?"

Ed shook his head. "No. She'll have fun with that. You ever been?"

"I haven't traveled much at all." *Divorced, three kids, a boring job, a Super Glued house, going nowhere.* "Family camping trips, that's it."

"There'll be time when the kids are older." Ed smiled at her. "Or maybe some year you can go for a week and help Doris when she's on a buying trip."

"Maybe," Maggie said without conviction. "You must have done a lot of traveling."

"I haven't been on a Caribbean cruise," he said, "but we—my folks and brothers and sisters—we go back to

Guatemala every year to visit relatives."

Maggie took a sip of wine. "Sounds nice," she said. "Do you miss it? Guatemala, I mean."

Ed shrugged. "Nah," he said. "I was five when we came north. This is the only place I remember. It's home for me. My parents miss the old country, and they still favor the old ways, but they love it here, too. This town has been good to us."

"Do you remember the trip up here?" Maggie asked, suddenly curious. "If that's not too personal."

"Not too personal. I just don't remember much. The first thing I remember—we were hitchhiking in a pickup truck, and the driver dropped us at the old Scholz farm, I'm not sure why. Why there, I mean. We were hungry and tired, and my folks were going to ask the farmer—that would have been Herman Scholz—for something to eat in exchange for a day's work, and probably a place to sleep in the barn, too, I suppose. I remember that, because they told me to be good and not say anything."

"That must have been scary. A new country, a language you didn't speak well."

"I didn't speak any English at all. I think my folks had a few words—please, thank you, like that. I was scared out of my mind, and my folks probably were too, but they didn't let me see it. We walked up the driveway—I remember the shade of those big old oaks. You know the place."

Maggie nodded. "It's a beautiful farm. You lived out there a long time."

"We did. More than twenty years. But the day we got there, we walked up that long driveway to the farmhouse, and Herman was trying to pull up a tree stump with his tractor. And it wasn't coming out. So my dad went over to help."

"How did they communicate?"

"Who knows? Spanish met English, but they were both farmers and they figured it out, because after a while, the tree stump came out and they got the hole filled in."

"So you stayed."

"We did. After they got the stump out, Herman took us up to the house, and Betty Scholz fed us, and then mom helped with the dishes, and we never left after that. Well, they didn't have any kids, and they needed help with the farm."

"That's an incredible story," Maggie said.

"Thirty-three years ago," Ed said. "Long time." He grinned, a sudden glint in his eye.

"You know, there's a lot of great crafts in Guatemala. I could introduce Doris to my uncle Esteban. I think they'd hit it off. You could go, too."

Maggie saw the flash in his dark eyes and wondered what it would be like to go on a cruise, someplace where it was always warm and she didn't have to lift a finger. *I'd wear fabulous clothes, and a handsome Latin man, a man sort of like Ed, would ask me to dance and he'd make love to me under a starry sky.*

Whoa! Maggie's foot slipped off the bar stool. A handsome man who looked like *Ed?* What was she thinking? She wasn't going on any cruise, there was no man, no one would make love to her under starry skies because her clothes weren't fabulous. Ed? Where did *that* come from?

Ed nodded at the band, which was now introducing their next song. Maggie recognized "Chapel of Love," an old fifties pop tune updated by a group called—she squinted at the banner draped behind the musicians—the Freaky Wizards.

"I like this band," Ed said. "They play a lot of older tunes. Want to dance?"

Her dream come true. She'd known Ed since forever, of course, they'd gone to school together, but he was three years older than she, and that made a difference when they'd been kids. But now she wasn't just a customer who bought Super Glue and he wasn't just somebody who ran the hardware store. They were grownups at a party. He'd asked her to dance.

He tapped his foot to the music, smiling at her. He was so handsome with those warm brown eyes and dark, dark hair. He was solid, too, and strong, with wide shoulders and a broad chest and all those lovely angles and planes in his face. *Why didn't I ever notice how attractive Ed is?*

"I'd love to dance," she said, hopping off the stool.

"Great," Ed said. They stepped onto the polished wooden surface, his hand warm in the small of her back. Then his arms were around her and he was leading her down the floor in a brisk foxtrot.

Maggie smiled, but she felt tongue-tied, not that she had anything to be nervous about with Ed. But she rarely had the occasion to have a man stand this close to her, and nobody male except her sons had touched her in quite some time. The last time she'd gone dancing, she'd been with a bunch of girl-friends to hear a rock and roll band. It had been a long time since she'd danced like this with a guy. She thought she'd forgotten how.

Then Ed smiled back at her and, holding her tighter, spun her around in a circle, and breathless and laughing, Maggie came back without missing a step. Ed was a great dancer. *Who knew?*

After that Maggie concentrated on the music and fol-lowing Ed. The music ended, and they were both flushed and laughing after Ed had spun her out and she'd come back too fast and bumped a bit ungracefully into Ed's chest right at the end. They stood there looking at each other, surprised and pleased with each other.

"I haven't done that in ages," Maggie said, winded. "I'm seriously out of practice. Plus, you pack a mean spin."

"My sister taught me," Ed said. "She would have hu-miliated me if I didn't get it right."

The band started another song, a slow one this time. Maggie wanted to dance again. She wondered if he would ask and then decided she wouldn't wait to see. So she said, "Again?" and Ed seemed surprised, but he smiled and said, "Sounds good," and she went into his arms for the ballad.

The slow dancing was a lot different. Ed held her close enough so that if he wanted to do a tricky dance move, she'd stick with him, but not so close that she'd feel like he was making a pass at her. She wondered what she'd do if he *did* make a pass at her. Then she scolded herself for being silly, even as the idea of Ed making a pass made her skin flush.

He smelled good—clean and fresh. His shirt beneath her hand was soft and pressed, well used and well taken care of, and she could feel the warmth of his body through the cloth and the flowing of his muscles across his shoulder as he moved across the floor. He was taller than she, but not by much, since she was wearing heels, and she could gaze almost directly into his eyes, which she liked. She'd never been able to look at John without tilting her head back, so she never felt that she could really see him.

"You're a great dancer," Ed said. "You don't seem out of practice to me."

She felt a steady heat coming off him, and she realized that some of the heat was coming from her, generated every time his thighs brushed hers as they swayed across the floor. She closed her eyes, enjoying the rush of pheromones. Dancing like this was probably dangerous, because everything seemed magical. She felt her head tilt toward his shoulder almost against her will, tempting fate.

Then the ballad was over. Ed stopped moving against her, stopping all that friction that was the best thing she'd felt in months. The band struck up another tune, another fast one, and she smiled at him and Ed didn't even ask, he just swung her into it. He held her close and they did the two-step until they were both breathless and laughing again.

When the music stopped, Maggie reluctantly dropped her hands from Ed's shoulders and stepped away from the heat of his body. "This is the best time I've had in ages, Ed," she said. "Thanks."

Ed smiled. "I enjoyed it, too."

They walked back to the bar, right on time to hear the muted ring of a cell phone.

"Mine," said Maggie. "Sorry." She took it out of her purse, glanced at the display, and sighed.

"Boys, what's going on?" she asked. She watched Ed take a step back to give her more privacy, picking up the glass of Jim Beam he'd left half-finished on the bar. David and Kyle wanted permission for an outing John had promised them, but she cut them off after a minute or two.

"We don't have to decide right now," she said, "We'll talk about it when you get home. I have to go. Have fun. Be good." She disconnected.

Ed smiled in her direction and drained his glass, setting it on the bar.

"My kids," she said unnecessarily.

"I figured," Ed said.

Way to kill a hot date, she thought. *Have the kids call at the crucial moment. Or any moment. Not that it's a real date. Or even a real moment.*

"Guess I'll see what the birthday girl's up to," Maggie said, tucking the phone back in her purse. She smiled at him. "Thanks again for the dance."

"My pleasure." Ed smiled back. "Let's do it again sometime."

"I'd like that," Maggie said. "Time and weather permitting."

He laughed. "Time I've got, but I can't do anything about the weather."

How about tomorrow, then? Maggie thought. *Tomorrow works for me.*

Chapter 5

"Hola, Papi," Ed said, stepping into his parents' kitchen a couple of days later. Smaller even than the trailer they'd lived in at the back of the Scholz's property for so long, the house was neat and tidy and usually smelled of his mother's delicious cooking. Not today, however.

"¿Cómo estás?" Alberto had taken the day off from the store to take care of Isabel, who'd been ill with the flu for a couple of days, and Ed had decided to check up on them both. "¿Tienes hambre?" *How are you? Are you hungry?*

"Si," Ed always felt hungry in his mother's kitchen. "¿Cómo se siente mamá?" *How does mom feel?*

"Let's heat up some soup," Alberto continued in Spanish. "Your mother might enjoy that. She's feeling better—she got up today."

"I'll do it." Ed rummaged in the refrigerator for the soup pot while his father put bowls on the table.

"How was Doris's party?" Alberto asked. When he and Isabel had retired from farming, they'd taken over a dilapidated building downtown and turned it into a hardware store. They'd run Medina Hardware for ten years until they sold the business to Ed, so they knew Doris Perl well and would have gone to her party if Isabel had been up to it.

"A big crowd, like always," Ed said as he put the soup

on the stove to heat. "It was fun. I danced with Maggie Jorgenson." No sooner were the words out of his mouth than he regretted them. Papi would be all over that.

"You are interested in that one?" Alberto asked, pursing his lips.

"We danced a couple of times, that's all," Ed said.

"Who did you dance with?" Isabel walked slowly out of the bedroom, still wearing her bathrobe, but she seemed stronger than when Ed had seen her yesterday.

"Maggie Jorgenson," Alberto said.

Isabel shook her head. "Eduardo, *hijo,* that will never work," she said. "And here your brother has been trying to get you to meet his wife's cousin Luz. Such a nice girl, he says. And he says she is an excellent cook and only twenty-three, so she'll want children."

"I know, Mama, but I'm not going out with Luz. She's too young for me, and I don't need a cook when I have you." Ed went over to kiss his mother's cheek. "I'm not going out with Maggie Jorgenson, either. She's Doris Perl's daughter, and I danced with her a couple times, that's all. Can you eat some soup?"

"I want you to be happy," Isabel said, holding onto Ed's hand as she lowered herself gingerly onto a kitchen chair. "You should be married. To a nice girl. Someone who understands you."

She means someone Catholic, someone who speaks Spanish, Ed thought. *Someone from the old country.* In other words, someone like them.

"Mama, I'm too old to think of marriage," he said, dishing up the soup.

"It is never too late," Isabel said. "You will meet the right woman. I know it."

"I know you won't disgrace us," Alberto said.

"How could I disgrace you?" Ed asked, startled. "You mean, if I married someone like Maggie Jorgenson, that would be a disgrace?"

"Of course not." Isabel seemed pained. "She is a nice

person. A good daughter to her mother. A hard worker. But she is *divorced*, Eduardo. She has children, and they are not always well-behaved. The ex-husband doesn't care, but that doesn't mean he would want you to step into his shoes. There are too many differences there, too many problems. *Of course*, she is a nice person. And a good customer. But she is not for you."

"Well, I happen to agree with you," Ed said, not liking himself for saying it. He remembered dancing with Maggie, what it felt like to have her twirl out and bump into him, laughing. He remembered her warmth. Her vitality. The heat he'd felt sitting next to her on those stools. Even gluing down the metal strips on her car.

His father thought he would bring *disgrace* to the family if he married Maggie. Not that he had given a moment's thought to even to going out with her—far from it. He'd enjoyed dancing with her, that's all. But his parents' opinion made him both furious and depressed.

He picked up his spoon, but now the soup didn't appeal to him. For the first time in his life, he didn't feel hungry for his mother's food.

ON MONDAY PRECISELY AT NOON in the legal offices of Wusterbarth and Hedrich, Maggie surveyed the top of the three-foot-by-five-foot desk that constituted her professional domain and found it good. Her papers were filed. Her plant was watered. The answering machine was on. The lawyers were out. All was well in her world.

She exchanged her low-heeled navy pumps for her white athletic cross-trainers and slipped on her tailored navy blazer over her navy rayon dress. Then she picked up her purse and walked out of the red brick building that housed the law firm, locking the door behind her. If she hurried, she'd have time to run her errand at Nennig's Jewelers and still eat lunch.

Nennig's had only one customer when she got there, a man whose back was to her as she entered the store. Just then

Joe Nennig, Donald Nennig's brother, came out from the back room.

"I'm sorry, Mr. Strachan," he said to the customer, "but Donald isn't answering his phone." And then seeing Maggie, he said, "Oh, hi, Maggie, be right with you."

"Do you have any idea where I can find him?" Mr. Strachan said, and Maggie realized with a start of recognition that Joe Nennig's customer was the same fellow who'd asked for directions to Edith Nennig's wake on Saturday. "I had an 11:30 appointment to meet him here." Then he turned and saw Maggie, and his face lit up.

"Hello," he said, smiling at her. "Thanks again for the directions to the wake."

"You found the house okay?"

"Aye, right," Ian said. "Your directions were pure dead brilliant. And to whom do I have the honor of speaking?" He stuck out a big hand.

Maggie smiled, stepping forward and shaking hands. "Maggie Jorgenson."

"Ian Strachan." He held her hand for a second too long, and Maggie had the chance to look at his face close up again. Ian's wasn't a handsome face, but it was strong and square, with a sharp chin and a dark shadow that wasn't quite a stubble, the kind of face that the bad guy in a *noir* movie would have.

Behind them, Joe Nennig cleared his throat. "I wish I could tell you where my brother is, Mr. Strachan," he said. "But it's hard to keep tabs on him. What with our mother passing so recently, he's probably taking care of some unexpected business. Paperwork. You know."

"I'll wait a few more minutes," Ian said. "You can take care of Mrs. Jorgenson here."

He'd used "Mrs." Was he trying to find out her marital status? Maggie was flattered, but she wasn't willing to give out that kind of information yet—and in front of Joe Nennig, too. It would be all over town in minutes if Joe thought she was flirting with this Scottish guy.

"How can I help you, Maggie?" Joe asked, and Maggie pulled her stalled watch out of her purse and showed it to him.

"Probably the battery," Joe said. "Give me a minute and I'll put in a new one."

He disappeared into the back, and silence reigned in the showroom.

IAN FELT ALL FIZZY just observing at the bonnie lass.

"So, are you enjoying your stay here in Cedarburg?" she asked. Her musical voice was pitched low, like a harp on a misty morning. Was she married? She hadn't risen to the bait when he'd called her Mrs. Jorgenson. He hoped that she was, in fact, married. She was something else, hot and bothersome and virginal looking, all creamy, but he didn't need any serious entanglements. A married woman was the way to go.

"It's been bloody marvelous," he said, and she laughed. It was the most melodic sound he'd ever heard.

"Marvelous?" she said. "*Cedarburg?*"

"You laugh," he said, hoping she'd laugh again. "We were nearly killed in an airplane smash coming in. Our only entertainment has been goin' to a funeral. And our business partner here in the States—that's Donald Nennig—manages to hide himself in a town so small it could get lost in a flea circus."

Maggie did laugh again, and Ian basked in the idea that he could make this incredible creature laugh. Then Joe came out with her watch and Maggie paid him. *Now or never*, Ian decided, so he told Joe that he wouldn't wait any longer for Donald and he and Maggie walked out of the shop together.

"Can I buy you lunch?" he asked. She paused for a second. He found himself hoping—more than he'd ever hoped for anything—that she'd say yes. She hesitated for a second, but then she smiled.

"Sure, that sounds great," she said. "I can't take a lot of time because I have to get back to work, but lunch sounds good."

"Name the place," Ian Strachan said recklessly. "Sky's the limit."

MAGGIE WAS SURPRISED that Ian asked her for lunch and wasn't sure they should go, gossips being what they were, but then decided, why not? She clearly was on a roll with men, first dancing with Ed and now Ian asking her to lunch. At least she'd get a good meal out of it, because the only place to eat in town was the Wee Bite, and you never went wrong there.

The diner was crowded, as usual, but they came in as Chuck Winkel was leaving a booth with the Leitners, people that Chuck erroneously thought were potential clients for his financial advisor business. But Maggie had drawn up the elderly couple's will, and she knew how little they had to invest. At least they'd gotten a free lunch today.

She snagged the booth and handed Ian a menu.

"The Wee Bite," Ian said. "Is the place run by a Scot, then?"

"Peg runs it," Maggie said. "She has aspirations."

Ian studied the laminated card. "What do you like here?"

"I like everything here," Maggie said, "but today I'm getting the turkey club sandwich."

Ian nodded. "Turkey," he said. "Something only a Yank could eat." He pondered the menu some more. Maggie saw Peg watching them from behind the counter, waiting for a signal that she should come over for their orders.

"Chili?" Maggie suggested. The chili was maybe her second-favorite thing on the menu.

"Allergic to tomatoes," Ian said.

"Pork loin special?" Maggie tried again. She'd had that once, and it was delicious.

"Heartburn."

"Chef salad?" That should give the health nuts some reassurance.

"Cucumbers give me gas."

Too much information.

"I don't know then," Maggie said, giving up. If she'd known Ian was such a picky eater, she might not have agreed to have lunch with him. She had three smaller picky eaters at home, and she didn't really enjoy persuading people to eat something.

Ian shook his head and put down the menu. "I don't eat a lot of beef, but maybe I could try the meatloaf."

Finally. Maggie motioned for Peg to come over.

"Hi, Maggie," she said, eying Ian with curiosity. "What'll it be today?"

"Turkey club sandwich for me, thanks," Maggie said. Then, bowing to the inevitable, she made the introductions.

"Welcome to Cedarburg." Peg smiled at Ian. "What would you like?"

"I have a few questions," Ian said.

"Sure," Peg said.

"The meatloaf," said Ian. "Do you drain all the fat off as it's cooking?"

Maggie felt her heart sink, but Peg seemed to take Ian's question in stride. "Yes," she said.

"Do you add anything to the meat—spice, bread crumbs, hardboiled egg?"

"Salt, pepper, nutmeg," Peg said. "Nothing else."

"No green pepper?" Ian asked.

"No," Peg said, shifting her feet.

"Are the mashed tatties real, or are they from powder?"

"Real potatoes," Peg said, looking affronted. "Real gravy. Real mixed vegetables. Fat drained. Nothing added."

Maggie didn't blame her for taking offense. She felt offended on Peg's behalf.

Ian sighed. "I think I should have a big salad," he said. "Can I get it without cucumbers? And tomatoes? I'm allergic to tomatoes. And cucumbers give me gas."

"No cucumbers, no tomatoes," Peg repeated, making a note on her pad.

"And could you sprinkle on a little Parmesan cheese? About a quarter cup. Garlic dressing on the side. With a slice of lemon if you have it."

"Will that be all?" Peg asked, glaring at Ian.

"A glass of water," Ian said. "No ice."

"Coming up." Peg snapped her order book closed.

"Thanks, Peg," Maggie said. It wasn't enough that she'd brought her rambunctious kids in here, now she'd brought Ian in here, too. Would Peg ever let her return?

Peg stalked off to drop the order in the kitchen, and Maggie fiddled with her silverware, remembering how she'd thought Ian resembled a film *noir* villain, one of those characters with a dark, lean appearance who blended with the shadows. Whipsaw thin, those guys could flatten against a dark wall without anybody knowing they were there. Because, like Ian, they were all picky eaters.

Maggie checked out her own rounded lap. No *noir* there.

"So, Ian, I understand you're in the jewelry business," Maggie said. "Been partners with the Nennigs long?"

"Before this trip, I'd met Donald just the one time when he was in Edinburgh on business, but my, ah, company has been working with him for quite a while now." He reached into one jacket pocket and took out a handful of pill bottles, lining them up on the table. "We've been a wee bizzo in Europe, really, but we're expanding, working on a big deal now. This is my first visit to America."

"So, new responsibilities for you? A promotion?"

Ian reached into the other pocket and took out more pill containers, lining them next to the others until the entire edge of the table was lined with plastic pill bottles. Was the man sick? Cancer? Something worse? He hadn't said anything. And he didn't *look* sick. Maggie wondered if she should say something. It was an awful lot of pill bottles. Although they didn't seem to be prescription drugs.

"It's a bit of an experiment. We're testing the waters over here."

Peg brought over a basket of bread, spotted the pill bottles lined up in her booth, slammed the basket down between them, and flounced off. Ian pulled the breadbasket closer and examined a roll.

"If we do well, then we'll be coming back more often."

"And what does your company do, exactly?" Maggie hoped he didn't touch every roll while he searched for the perfect one.

Ian frowned at the small, foil-wrapped butter packets heaped in a bowl on the table.

"Do you suppose we could get some olive oil?" he asked. "Butter's loaded with cholesterol. Killer on the arteries." And then he remembered Maggie's question. "Diamond wholesalers," he said. "Primarily."

"I don't think Peg has olive oil," Maggie said firmly. "So you're expanding. Do you have to know a lot about diamonds? Or do you make deals, or what? I'm not quite sure what you actually *do*."

Ian bit into his unbuttered, unoiled roll and placed the remainder carefully on the table. "My group is involved in trading," he said. "I don't, ah, acquire the stones. Somebody else does that. I just do wholesale. Like Donald Nennig here. I used to wholesale to jewelers; now we're trying whole-saling to smaller wholesalers. You know, moving higher on the diamond trading food chain." He opened the first pill bottle, shook a few tablets into his palm, tossed them into his mouth, and chased them with a big swallow of water.

"Saw palmetto," he said, by way of explanation. "Prostate."

Way, way too much information.

"But enough about me." Ian glanced at his lunch companion. He wasn't sure why Maggie appealed to him so much. She wasn't beautiful in a conventional way; her legs were shapely under that dark dress but not especially long, and the rest of her was curvy but not really buxom. But she was luscious and wholesome and soft, sort of like an ice cream cone that you could spend all day licking, and he wouldn't mind finding out what flavor she was. "What about you?"

"Not too much to tell," Maggie said, settling back. "I've lived in Cedarburg all my life. Always meant to travel but never did because the kids came so early."

Ian almost choked. He'd never thought that someone as innocent-looking as she was would have children. She didn't give the impression that she'd even know how to go about it.

"Kids?" he asked.

"Three," she said, and he paled. "Two boys and a girl."

"Married?"

"Divorced." His heart sank. She'd better not be on the hunt for a boyfriend, husband, caretaker, or meal ticket. He was a crook, for god's sake; he was a *criminal*. He didn't have time to get mixed up with gorgeous divorcees who had more brats hanging off them than lights on a Christmas tree.

"Job?" he asked. "I think you said you had to get back to work."

Maggie nodded. "I'm a paralegal-slash-legal secretary for the local attorneys."

Ian heard a rushing in his ears. "Really?" he asked, feeling faint. What cruel joke was this? How could he get out of this mess? The last—the absolute last—thing he needed was a bunch of legal beagles sniffing around this gig. Only thing that'd be worse would be if she'd said she was a polis.

"That must be interesting," he said finally.

"It supports me and the kids, but it's not that interesting. We handle routine things, wills, estates, divorces. Stuff like that. Small-time criminal cases sometimes."

"I've always thought solicitors were evil," Ian said, just as Peg brought over the salad and turkey club. Peg frowned at him with disapproval.

"Not ours," Maggie said firmly.

"One turkey club and one salad, no tomatoes, no cucumbers, one-quarter cup Parmesan cheese sprinkled, garlic dressing on the side," Peg said as she put down the food. Ian examined the bowl.

"What about the lemon?" he asked.

"We're out," Peg said, her mouth a thin line.

"Salt and pepper?" Ian asked.

"On the table," Peg said.

"More water?" Ian asked.

"Coming right up," Peg said, moving off again.

"I need to take my supplements," Ian said.

"Are you sick?" Maggie picked up her turkey club and took a big bite from the corner, licking her lower lip to catch the mustard that squished out the side. Ian watched her tongue flick out and felt nothing.

"No," Ian said, "I don't want to *get* sick. I take only what's necessary." He began to pry the lids off the pill boxes on the table.

MAGGIE SIGHED AND glanced at her watch. She still had a half-hour before she could go back to work. She hoped she wouldn't die of boredom before then. Her social life was pathetic if she'd rather go back to work than be taken out for lunch by a wealthy gem wholesaler from Scotland.

Well, she might as well eat. She was hungry, Ian was paying, and nothing was wrong with Peg's food. She took another bite of her sandwich.

"So you might find this interesting," she said, wondering if they had anything to talk about besides Ian's dietary restrictions. "We got this case the other day. Some guys got caught stealing farm equipment. You know, like those giant pickers? Well—"

Ian seemed to choke on his salad. It would serve him right for bringing all those pills into Peg's diner.

IT WAS LATE AFTERNOON when Venus pulled off her leather garden gloves and went inside. She was expecting Mars, who had been gone for three days on a job somewhere, and she wanted to be ready for him.

An hour later, showered and shampooed, she peered into her closet with a sigh. Her favorite black knit miniskirt, but what to wear with it? The black cashmere sweater—history. The cobalt blue cowlneck—at the dry cleaners. She settled on the pink angora. *I'll look good no matter what I wear*, she thought with unselfconscious satisfaction.

She checked herself in the mirror one last time and went

downstairs, pouring herself a glass of wine just as Mars breezed through the front door.

"Babe," he said, dropping his duffel bag.

"Mars," she said, wrapping her arms around him. Their kiss was a convergence of long-time intimacy, of deep knowledge of each other. When Mars broke away, he buried his face in Venus's neck.

"I missed you," he said, nipping her ear. "Nice sweater."

"I missed you, too," she said, running her hands down his arms, feeling his muscles flex beneath her fingers. "And you ought to like it. You picked it out."

"Pink's a good color on you," he said raising his head to smile at her. "But now I'd prefer to get it off you."

"That can be arranged," Venus said.

"I'd hoped so," Mars said. "It's good to be home."

Sometime later, their clothes discarded, Venus and Mars lay on the large sofa in the darkening room, their arms and legs entwined. Then the phone rang.

"That's your cell, babe," he said, not moving.

"Damn," Venus said, also not moving. "It's the boss."

"You have to answer it."

"I know." She sighed. The phone trilled again. "Okay, I'm getting up." Still, she didn't move. The phone persisted.

"Babe."

"*Okay.*" With great effort and regret, Venus disentangled herself from Mars. Once she was up, though, the cold floor got her moving, and she grabbed the phone and the afghan lying across the sofa in one smooth gesture.

"Yes," she said into the phone. And then, "What? I can't hear you." She walked into the kitchen, trying to find a better connection.

"I got it wrong? *What?* I can't hear. You said, 'headed for the slammer,' that's why I set her up with him," Venus said. "Ian's definitely headed for the slammer. And you said 'rotten to the core.' I don't see how *I* made a mistake. That's *your* mistake."

The connection was terrible. She wrapped the afghan

around her like a toga and stepped outside.

"Okay," Venus said. "*Not* the guy who's headed for the slammer. *Now* you tell me. Maggie was *supposed* to get the financial planner. Okay. He's a terrible bore? Why do you want her to have a terrible bore? She's a very nice person. She deserves the best." When the connection broke, she dropped the phone, annoyed with her boss and her task.

"A slight miscommunication," Venus said when she got back to the living room.

Mars cocked one eyebrow. "No harm done, I trust."

"None." She sat down and stroked his arm. "Are you hungry?"

He nodded. "Maybe we could go out and get something and then catch a movie."

Venus smiled at him. "That would be fun."

Mars smiled back at her in her afghan toga. "We could have dessert after."

"Count on it," Venus said.

Chapter 6

When the supplier's delivery truck came in on Monday, Ed headed out back with one of the clerks to help the driver unload. Everything went first onto the loading dock, and from there it was sorted either for the store's inventory or for immediate local delivery.

Maggie Jorgenson's extension ladder had come in. Ed remembered how pretty Maggie had looked at her mother's party, how much fun she'd been to dance with.

I'll make the deliveries today, he decided, waving Jason back into the store, much to the clerk's surprise. Even as he made the decision, Ed knew that he wouldn't pursue a divorced woman with three kids. The kids would never take to him, and his parents would give him nothing but grief. Not that he needed his parents' approval for anyone he dated. Far from it. But he didn't want to bring unnecessary trouble down on his head, either—not when he worked with Papi every day in the store.

He went through the back and into the garden department. "Papi, I'm heading out to make the deliveries," he said.

His father regarded him shrewdly. "Why not Jason?" he asked. "That's his job."

Ed shrugged. "Today I'll do it."

Alberto continued with the gimlet eye. "Maggie Jorgenson's

ladder came in," he said in Spanish so the other clerks wouldn't understand him.

Ed shrugged again. "*Si*," he said. "And?"

"Don't give me that," Alberto said. "You know what I'm saying."

Ed felt a surge of annoyance. "I *don't* know. What are you saying?"

Alberto shook his head. "I'm saying, be careful with what you're doing."

"I'm just making the deliveries, Papi."

Alberto shook his head again, but Ed snagged the keys to the delivery truck from behind the counter and headed for the back door.

He'd be careful, all right. He knew what his father meant. Knew in the back of his mind that Maggie was a woman with a complicated life. Knew that those complications could spell trouble for him, not to mention any relationship they might try to have.

But he was simply delivering a ladder. What harm could that do? None. No harm, no foul. That was his motto.

MAGGIE GLANCED UP from dinner preparations as Kyle stomped into the kitchen. Her younger son let the screen door slam behind him and thumped his book bag and baseball glove on the cluttered kitchen table. The noise scared Emily, who was sitting in her high chair tossing Cheerios onto the floor, and she started to whimper. Kyle's face was flushed and hot, his eyes hurt and angry, his shirt dirty and pulled out of the waistband of his pants, his shoes scuffed.

"What happened, sweetie?" She slid the chicken into the oven and straightened up.

"Nothing," Kyle said, his voice tight. He turned to the refrigerator and caught the toe of his shoe on a piece of buckled linoleum tile. "Stupid," he muttered, kicking the tile. The piece broke off and sailed across the floor into the corner. Maggie sighed. More Super Glue coming up.

"Kyle," she said to his back. He had the refrigerator

door open and was leaning into it, but as far as Maggie could see, he was using it to hide or cool his face, since he didn't seem to be taking anything out. Emily started to cry, and Maggie picked her up to soothe her, getting drooly cereal mush on her shoulder as Emily clutched her.

"Kyle," she said again. "Close the refrigerator door and tell me what happened."

"Nothing happened," he said again, taking out the milk. "Are there any cookies?"

"You may have some fruit or a peanut butter sandwich," she said. "Was it something at school?"

"No," Kyle said, rummaging around for bread and opening the cupboard door for the peanut butter. Maggie wiped Emily's face and hands and made cooing noises to get her to stop crying, and Emily did stop, her eyes bright with tears, gazing from her brother to her mom to make sure the big noises were over.

"Well, what then?" Maggie persisted.

Kyle whirled to face her. "It was baseball practice, all right?" he said. "I hate baseball, it's a stupid game, and I'm never playing it again." He slammed the milk down on the counter and stormed from the kitchen. Emily started to cry again, and Maggie put her back in her high chair.

"Shh, Emmy," she said, handing her more Cheerios to demolish. "If you're going to be a sports star groupie, you've got to get used to drama."

Emily gave up crying to gum her snack, and Maggie put the milk back in the refrigerator, thinking. Then she opened her junk drawer, took out the Super Glue, found the corner piece of the linoleum tile that Kyle had kicked off, and re-glued the linoleum piece to the floor.

Then she went upstairs. She thought about asking David to talk to Kyle with her, but through his open bedroom door she saw that he had his headphones on and was playing air guitar. He wouldn't appreciate the interruption, and she didn't know how much help he'd be, anyway. She knocked on Kyle's door and went in.

"About baseball," she began.

Kyle had been lying on his bed. He sat up, his face angry. "Mom, I told you. I hate it, I'm not playing it anymore." Maggie sat on the edge of his bed.

"Well, I'm sorry, but you wanted to be in the after-school sports program, so for a few weeks, you've got to play baseball," she said. "Baseball's not so bad; lots of guys earn millions of dollars playing it. They can't all be wrong."

Kyle kicked the side of the bed.

"Here's what we'll do. We'll get you a new bat and ball so you can get some extra practice in. I used to play baseball. David and I will play with you and we'll ask your dad to take some practice swings with you the next time you go."

"You don't know anything about baseball," Kyle said belligerently. "And you don't know anything about Dad. He never likes doing stuff like that."

"I know a lot about baseball, and your dad will play with you if you ask him," Maggie said, not sure if John would or not. Kyle looked unconvinced.

"Practice helps everything," Maggie said. "And think of this: it's only for a few more weeks. Then you switch to football. You like football."

"We get baseball again in the spring," Kyle said, unrelenting.

"But then you'll be older and taller and heavier, and you'll have had a lot more practice," said Maggie.

Kyle said nothing, but kicked his heel rhythmically against the side of the bed.

"Did the other kids make fun of you?" Maggie asked, wishing she could bear the pain for all her children. Kyle didn't answer, his eyes hot again.

"Well, not for long," Maggie said. "I think you need a new bat; David's is probably too heavy for you. We'll get you one tomorrow, and we can get some practice in before you go to your dad's. You'll see. Pretty soon you'll be the first kid picked."

Kyle snorted. "You don't know how to play baseball,"

he said.

Maggie cuffed him on his shoulder. "Do so," she said. "Hold on a second." She went into her room and opened her closet door, reaching to the highest shelf in the back. She returned to Kyle's room carrying a dusty volume, wiping it off with her shirttail as she went.

"Okay, wise guy," she said. "Check this out." She opened her high school year book and flipped through it until she found what she was searching for. "There," she said, pointing. "The outfits could be better, but check out that hot shortstop."

Kyle squinted at the dated picture of young women holding up a trophy.

"Stupid girls in dorky uniforms. What kind of team is that?"

"That's my high school baseball team. I'm the shortstop. My name is different, but trust me. We won three league championships."

Kyle stared at her for a moment in disbelief, and then his face closed up again. "Yeah, but you were girls," he said, peering at the hairdos and the uniforms.

Maggie stood and ruffled his hair. "Yeah, but we girls could beat the pants off you guys without even half trying," she said, grinning at him, "and tomorrow you'll see."

She'd barely gotten downstairs and checked on Emmy before the doorbell rang.

"It's not only sports stars giving us high drama, Emmy," she said, wiping her hands on a dishtowel. "You also get high drama if you're a single mom with three kids. The excitement never stops around here. Who do you think that could be?"

When she flung open the front door, it turned out to be Ed, who stood leaning on her doorframe, secure and solid, grinning at her.

See? This is exciting, Maggie thought, remembering the dancing and feeling her blood kick higher in her veins.

"Hi, Ed," she said, smiling at him. "What's up?"

"I've got your gutter screens here." He straightened up and jerked his thumb back to his truck parked in her driveway. "And your ladder. Where should I put them? The garage?"

Of course, gutter screens. *Be still my heart.* But she should be grateful. Ed was standing here on her porch, looking good, with the equipment for her home improvement projects.

"Oh, thanks for bringing them by." Maggie saw Ed squint at her blouse and remembered that she was covered in cereal gunk. *Excitement tends to get drowned in a toddler's drool,* she thought, wondering if she'd have time to put the gutter screens on at least one side of the house before supper. "I guess, just lean them up against the side of the house. Maybe I can do a little outdoor maintenance in a few minutes."

"You're going to clean the gutters out *now?*"

Maggie checked her watch. "Yeah, I think so. I've got about an hour before supper."

"It'll be dark soon."

Maggie grinned. "Ed, it'll be *Christmas* soon. I have to do it sometime. Might as well get a start on it now."

"Tell you what," Ed said. "This is my last delivery today. I've got time. I'll do it."

"Oh, I can't let you do that." Maggie felt surprised and touched, but she felt an edge, too. She didn't want Ed—or anybody—feeling sorry for her. "You have to get back to the store. Thank you for offering, but I can do it."

"No problem, Maggie." Ed had already moved off the porch. "Got an outdoor vac or a whisk broom—something to brush out the leaves?"

She shook her head, exasperated, watching him walk to his truck. *Men,* she thought. *Always trying to fix your life.* But she had to admit, she appreciated the help.

He turned to see her still watching him. "Get something to sweep out the leaves," he said again. "And get a move on. It'll be dark soon, not to mention Christmas." He grinned at her, opening the tail of the pickup to take out the ladder.

She sighed, but she went into the garage and found a ratty old broom with a handle that was much too long to clean gutters. She stamped on the handle, trying to break it, but even as old as the broom was, it didn't crack under her weight.

She carried it around to the side of the house. "I found this old broom," she said. "Will that work? I thought maybe you could break off the handle."

Ed finished setting up the ladder, and Maggie enjoyed watching him work, the careful way he set the ladder and tested it for his weight, his arm muscles flexing as he jimmied the ladder closer into the house, his shirt straining across the muscles of his back. He glanced at the broom and sighed.

"I'm sorry," she said, feeling both defensive and apologetic. Ed was totally right about that broom. "It's the best I can do. Unless you'd rather have a rag?"

"You don't have a saw? So I can get a smooth edge? So no one gets splinters?"

"I have a hedge clipper, if that helps."

Ed laughed. "This will work." He took the broom from her, put the stick end on the sidewalk, and brought his foot down sharply against the handle, snapping it just short of the brush.

"And just like that, I have a whisk broom," Maggie said. Maybe she should start buying more tools and less Super Glue. Make repairs more permanent.

"Let's see how it works," he said, going up the ladder to sweep out her gutters and put in her new gutter screens.

Maggie watched his backside for a minute, enjoying the view. Despite her intentions to be annoyed, she felt grateful about having kind neighbors, so she said, "Ed, you're a mensch," and Ed said, "Maggie, you're *chistoso*."

"What?" Maggie said. She didn't remember the word from her high school Spanish, so she went in to look it up. Emily had mashed cereal goo all over her high chair, so Maggie wiped her off again, set her on the floor, and gave her some toys to play with while she googled a language translator. *Chistoso.* Funny. Ed had called her funny.

She could hear Ed outside, cleaning the gutters. When he had worked his way around to the back of the house, and she had mashed the potatoes and tossed the salad, she stuck her head out the back door.

"Would you like some coffee?" She asked. "Beer? Water? Want to stay for supper?" Where did *that* come from, she thought, in a sudden panic. *Please say no.*

"Thanks, but I'll have to take a rain check." Ed scrutinized his work one last time before he climbed down the ladder and folded it up. "I've got to get back and close the store."

Maggie felt relieved and strangely disappointed. What had she been thinking, to invite him? How weird would that be, with Emily, in a constant damp mess, and Kyle in a rage about playing baseball, and herself, still covered with Cheerio drool. Not exactly hot dinner date material.

"I appreciate this, Ed," she said, as he handed her the broken old broom, her new whisk broom. "Let me know if there's something I can do for you."

"Nothing to it, Maggie. These go in the garage now?" Ed shouldered the ladder and leftover gutter screens. Maggie nodded and walked with him to the garage, clearing a space next to the recycling bin for him to stash the ladder. He leaned the extra gutter screens against the wall and settled the ladder over them, and she felt better about his thoughtfulness. Ed was being neighborly, making sure his customers were happy. He didn't feel sorry for her.

He hadn't made any moves on her either, not that she'd expected him to. Still, after dancing, she'd kind of wondered what it would be like if…. *no.* She wasn't going there. This was a small town, there'd be gossip, and she had three kids to protect.

And maybe he'd already forgotten about their dancing. So all was well, everything was on an even keel, and now one big chore was out of the way. That was terrific, and she beamed at him, feeling happy and relieved that she wouldn't have to spend the next weekend cleaning out the gutters.

Putting up gutter screens didn't have much headline appeal, but today Ed had done for her what she'd needed doing, and today he was her knight in shining armor, even if his prancing steed was a pickup truck with a logo on the door and the armor took the form of a broken-handle broom. How many times did a person need to be in the headlines, after all? But cleaning the gutters—that needed doing every year, and you didn't get a lot of press attention for doing it, either.

Ed smiled down at her, his dark eyes even darker in the fading light, his body solid and sure. Maggie could feel the warmth radiating from his broad chest and the smile in his eyes, and she wanted to lean into him and absorb all that heat and feel all that strength pour into her. *I'm tired*, she thought, *and I don't know what to do about Kyle, and I'm happy I don't have to clean the gutters*.

"There is something you can do for me," Ed said. In the dark closeness of the garage, his voice was soft and intimate, like velvet stroking her skin. He reached out to touch her on the back of her hand, and his fingers were so light and gentle that a shiver started at the base of her skull and went all the way down her spine.

"What's that?" Maggie asked, suddenly breathless.

"You can dance with me again," Ed said, and Maggie felt flushed with the knowledge of what dancing with Ed again would be like, and wanting it.

"That wouldn't be a favor," she said. "You have to think of something I might not want to do."

They smiled at each other, and Maggie felt herself leaning into him, and she thought he was leaning into her, too. Then she thought, *what am I doing? I have three kids and I'm covered with cereal goo; nobody likes people who have this much mess in their lives*. She blinked and pulled away, Ed took a step back, and the moment was over.

"Come in for a minute," Maggie said. "I'll write you a check for the ladder and gutter screens."

They went silently into the house, and Ed inhaled

deeply when he stepped into the kitchen.

"Smells good," he said, as Maggie dug through her purse for her checkbook.

"Thanks," she said. "Just your basic roast chicken and mashed potatoes." She uncapped her pen and held it poised over the blank check. "What do I owe you?"

He handed her the invoice for the ladder and screens. Watching him, Maggie saw the kitchen through his eyes—a messy room, with a knapsack on the table and children's drawings, tests, and book reports dangling from magnets on the refrigerator door. Clutter obscured the counter and baby toys littered the floor. She was glad a second time that he'd refused her invitation to supper. He didn't look like he wanted to stay. In fact, he looked like he wanted to flee.

"Sorry for the mess," she said, filling out the check.

"You've got kids. Comes with the territory."

"Well, thanks again." She handed him the check. "I guess that'll do me until my next tube of Super Glue."

Ed grinned, tucking the check into his shirt pocket. "Or until we go dancing."

Like that would ever happen.

But she smiled back. "I'll hold you to that."

Maggie walked him out the back door to his truck, and for the first time since he'd come over, she glanced into Venus's back yard.

"Wow," she said to Ed, "Look at that." Venus had made serious headway with her garden. Two apple trees had been planted at the far end of the yard, their overhanging boughs, laden with ripe, red fruit, almost touching. A small wrought-iron bench had been tucked under the trees. The beds around the fountain and rock garden had been planted, and the foliage was thick and lush, although in the almost total darkness, Maggie wasn't sure what the plants were. The spears in the near beds had obvious buds on them that seemed like they'd open soon. In a matter of days, Venus had turned a weed pit into something that was green and lush and nurtured.

Ed nodded. "Nice yard."

"My new neighbor," Maggie said. "She's taken dande-lions and crab grass and she's turned it into fruit and flowers. It's a miracle."

Ed turned back to her. "Miracles happen."

"Not in *my* yard." Maggie tried not to feel even the tini-est bit envious about Venus's gorgeous garden.

Ed smiled as he stepped off the porch. "Yards aren't the only place where miracles happen."

Chapter 7

Ian Strachan sat on the orange Naugahyde chair in the motel room and considered their situation. Outside the window, past the Lay-Z Stay's parking lot, corn rustled in a gentle fall breeze. Inside, an empty, grease-stained pizza box, soda cans, and a plastic salad container littered the room.

But when he shifted his gaze and looked into the belligerent eyes of his colleagues, Ian saw trouble. He hadn't unloaded the diamonds because he hadn't met with Donald Nennig, who was proving to be more elusive than the Loch Ness monster at a fog-bound photoshoot. Ray and Mickey were out of sorts, out of patience, and out of cash. They wanted results—or they wanted out of Cedarburg.

"Donnie Boy will turn up," Ian said. "He can't hide forever."

He watched the bright little goldfish swim around the small glass bowl that he'd bought at the hardware store for next to nothing. Pretty pebbles lined the bottom, and a tiny, green plastic castle tilted sideways in the middle. Every doctor on earth said that tropical fish were restful additions for a stressful environment. Watching the fish swim around took his mind off how he couldn't find Donald Nennig and sell the diamonds.

Ray scowled. "What makes you think Nennig's gonna turn up? He's doing a good job hiding so far. We've been here for four bloody days, and we haven't seen hide nor hair of him since the funeral on Saturday."

"Did you check the diner?" Mickey asked. "The store? His mum's? Maybe he's packing up his mum's stuff."

Ian nodded. "I've been there. He's not there. I've called numbers he isn't at. I've made appointments he hasn't kept. I've stalked places he hasn't been. I always just seem to miss him." He reached into his shirt pocket and took out a little bottle, shaking out a couple of pills and downing them without water. Vitamin B complex. For stress.

"We better find him soon, because I'm down to my last twenty and the return ticket," said Mickey, who'd never earned enough legitimate income to qualify for a credit card and who thought bank accounts were invitations for the tax man to come calling. "And I'm not selling the ticket. The thought of staying here gives me the willies."

"Me too," said Ray. "Maybe we should go back to New York and wait for him there."

"We don't know when he plans to go back," Ian said. "And we'll run out of money faster there than here."

"Maybe we should go back to Glasgow," Mickey said. "Make the wanker come to us." Ian and Ray scowled at him. Going back to Glasgow without selling the diamonds was not an option. They—literally—might not survive it.

They sat, silent.

"He better turn up soon, is all I can say," Mickey said, kicking the edge of the bed in frustration. "Or I won't be responsible for the consequences."

MAGGIE FROWNED AT the huge pile of work on her desk and then glanced at her watch. She'd be lucky if she got out of the office on time, much less early. She wouldn't be able to go to the hardware store with Kyle to get his new bat.

She sighed and called her mother.

"Elite Gift Shoppe," her mother said.

Maggie explained her problem. "So tell Kyle to go to the hardware store by himself, or with David," she said. On the days the boys didn't have after-school programs or go to a friend's house, they were supposed to go to her mother's shop and help out or do homework until Maggie got off work. "I'll call Ed and tell him I'll come by later to pay him for the bat."

She hung up and scanned her phone directory until she found the number for the hardware store. But once she found it, she didn't press the button. The thought of calling Ed, even for business, made her a little breathless.

Get a grip, she scolded herself. *He doesn't think of you like that. You've got three kids, and no guy asks for that much trouble. Knock it off.*

She pressed the button.

"Medina Garden and Hardware," Ed said.

"Hi Ed, it's Maggie," Maggie said, her heart pounding in spite of herself.

"Hey, Maggie," Ed said. "Are you calling me to go dancing?"

Maggie felt a stab of longing, remembering how much fun it had been and how good it had felt to have his arms around her. She yanked her mind back to the present. *He's being polite.*

"I wish," Maggie said with real regret, gazing at the folders on her desk. "No, it's something else. Kyle needs a new baseball bat. I think David's are too heavy for him, and we need to get in some serious practice. I told him we'd get him one today after school, but I won't be able to leave work early enough. Can you help him? And I'll be by after work to pay you." She considered the folders again. "Well, I might not make it today. But tomorrow for sure."

"No problem, Maggie," Ed said. "You're in luck. The baseball stuff is on sale. End of the summer. I think we've got something that'll work for Kyle. And don't worry about payment. Come in when you can."

"I'm running late today," Maggie said. "It seems like

everybody has to update their papers right this minute."

"Don't you just hate that?" Ed asked, and Maggie laughed and then Ed got a customer and had to go.

"Who was that?" Alberto Medina asked when Ed had hung up.

"Maggie Jorgenson," Ed told his father. "Kyle is coming in after school to pick out a new bat."

"You should stay away from her."

"It's her son who's coming in to buy something," Ed said, holding on to his patience. "She's a *customer*."

"You don't look at her like she's a customer."

"I don't see her often enough to 'look' at her in any way at all."

Alberto eased onto one of the tall stools they kept behind the register. "I agree with you that she's a nice woman. She's got a good, steady job and pays her bills on time. But her husband left her. There has to be a reason for that."

"He's an idiot," Ed said. "That's the reason."

"And now she has three children to raise. That's just problems for the next guy."

"I'm not planning to raise her kids, Papi."

"And—"

Alberto stopped. Ed knew what he wanted—but was reluctant—to say. The big problem with Maggie Jorgenson wasn't that she was divorced with three kids, although that was a problem. The big problem was that she wasn't from the old country, she was white, she didn't speak Spanish. She was *different*.

And Alberto didn't want to say anything like that because he loved his adopted country and the citizens of Cedarburg, many of whom had been open and welcoming when he arrived as a frightened, undocumented immigrant. And those who had not been welcoming then had mostly come around in time.

So Alberto wanted to return the hospitality and say that he'd be happy to have his eldest son, his first-born, choose and wed a woman of the town. But making that overture about a divorced woman with three children was not possible for him, because Alberto was old-school, and he believed the old ways were best.

Ed was second generation. He liked American food, music, and customs. And while he respected his parents and admired everything they'd accomplished, he didn't feel compelled to follow their advice—especially their advice about whom he should date. But if he ever did marry, one thing he knew for sure—his marriage and his entire life would be a lot smoother if his parents approved of his choice.

MICKEY WALKED DOWN Elm St., away from Edith Nennig's house. Mickey had rung the doorbell and then peered through the windows in case Donald was hiding from them in there. But nobody had answered the door or seemed to be inside. He could tell that people had been there. Furniture seemed to be missing, and boxes were piled up. But no one was there now.

He didn't much like small towns—he felt too exposed in places where everyone knew everyone else, and the quiet streets made him nervous. Today was no different. It was too early for kiddies to be home from school. Everybody else must be at work, or else the stay-at-home housewives were busy watching the telly or eating bonbons or having it on with the mailman or each other, because he saw no one. The wide, empty street, lined with neatly maintained houses, was silent except for the chattering of birds and the occasional, distant roar of a lawn mower. Cedarburg was about as far removed from the tough Glasgow tenement he'd grown up in as the moon.

He'd been a criminal since the age of ten, nothing serious, a robbery here, a stolen car there, first something to test himself against the other boys and then just enough to augment the meager wages he'd earned between layoffs at one factory or another where he'd worked since he was sixteen. He'd been with Ian for four years, mostly as an occasional courier for items it didn't pay to examine too closely.

This jewel gig was the biggest job he'd been on with anyone, and it was headed for disaster. Ian was losing his grip, and he feared that he'd take them all down with him in this puny town with its freshly painted white houses, big yards, and picket fences that defined every city boy's vision of hell.

After a few blocks the street dead-ended in a cul-de-sac by the river, beyond which green-and-gold fields stretched to the horizon and oceans of amber met an unblemished blue sky. He'd never in his entire life felt so trapped, not even the night he spent in a Glasgow jail, and that was an experience he didn't care to repeat.

This was the same but different. He was stuck in this small town with a boss who couldn't get the job done, and he couldn't go anywhere or do anything because he didn't have any money. He didn't have any money because Ian couldn't find Donald Nennig, who'd buy the diamonds Ian was carrying. And until they sold the diamonds, they'd be stuck here.

Of course, he had options. He might be broke, but he still had all the skills that had gotten him through life so far. Here he was, on a quiet street in a quiet town, with nobody at home to peer out the windows. It was the perfect opportunity to nick a car.

Ian would go off his trolley, pissed off that somebody else had taken the initiative, and it wouldn't be the most lucrative venture he'd ever undertaken. He'd have to drive the car someplace else—maybe as far as Chicago—to flog it, and without a proper fence, he wouldn't get much for it. Then, from wherever the sale went down, he'd have to find his own way back to Cedarburg.

None of that would be easy. But it would be something to do, and he could put some money in his pocket while they waited for their share of the diamond deal to go down.

He glanced up and down the street again, differently this time, assessing. It looked exactly the same. Quiet. Nobody home. Cars parked at the curb. The edge of town right there.

Perfect. He'd search for an unlocked car. He bet there'd be a lot of those.

He strolled down the cul-de-sac, sizing up the parked cars with a new eye. The first vehicle was unsuitable, at least ten years old, with one fender blue and the rest of it gray. Nothing but a rust bucket. The next few were locked, and Mickey almost snarled in exasperation. In a town like this, why lock the car doors? What could possibly happen?

What he needed was an oldish car in good condition or a newish car with the keys inside, because old cars could be hotwired, but modern cars with their computer components and key fobs had made hotwiring a skill of the past. Very annoying for up-and-coming car thieves.

And then he saw it—a newish sedan that opened when he tried the handle. With luck, someone so careless would have left the keys somewhere, too. He checked on top of the tires but found nothing. He slid into the car and reached underneath the seat. Nothing. But he struck gold behind the driver-side visor.

He stuck the key in the ignition and then the door opened and a hand the size of a dinner plate with a grip of steel grabbed him by the upper arm and yanked him from the vehicle. Mickey hit his head on the doorframe as he was dragged out and shoved to the pavement.

So far, he wasn't hurt, but he knew from vast experience that that could change at any time. The bruiser who was manhandling him was at least six and a half feet tall, well developed, with a thick crop of wavy dark hair, narrowed gray eyes, and a scowl so ferocious that even Mickey felt fear. *With neighbors like this, no wonder they don't bother to lock their cars.*

"*What the hell?*" he yelled, deciding to brazen it out. "Who are you? What do you want?" What he really wanted to know was where this guy had come from. The street had been empty, Mickey would have sworn. His attacker wasn't wearing a uniform, so he couldn't be a cop. He was incredibly strong, though. Unbelievably strong. The man had tossed him out of the car as though he weighed nothing.

"Name's Mars," Mars said. "Remember it. Planning to go somewhere in that car?"

"To the store. For the wife," Mickey lied. "What's wrong?"

Mars put his hands around Mickey's neck and picked him up off the ground, nearly cutting off his air, and shoved him up against the car, his hands still on Mickey's throat. Mickey clawed at the hot bands of steel around his neck, trying to draw a breath and hoping that this guy didn't plan to kill him. He croaked and clawed against the hands that were suffocating him.

"Your stealing the car is what's wrong," Mars said, loosening his grip just enough so Mickey could talk.

"This isn't my rental?" Mickey gasped, all innocence. "All these sedans look alike to me."

Mars inspected him, his mouth a thin, grim line. Then he slowly and deliberately tightened his hands on Mickey's neck once again. Mickey grabbed at Mars's fingers, trying to pry them away, feeling a pounding in his ears. His vision had a red halo around it. He tried to poke the brute's eyes with his fingers, but Mars leaned back and kept squeezing. Mickey's struggles grew fainter. His hands fluttered around his neck, but he couldn't find any purchase on his attacker's body. He couldn't breathe. And he knew he was going to die.

"You were trying to steal that car," Mars said, bending close to Mickey so he could hear him and understand the threat Mars was making. "Don't ever do that again. I will see you. I will come after you. I know who you are, who you're with, and what you want here. Next time I will not be so lenient. Do not forget." And with that, he shook Mickey by the neck with one hand as though he were a rag doll and dropped him to the ground. Then he opened the car's door and tossed the keys inside.

Mickey opened his eyes a few minutes later, after he got his breath back. His neck was tender and bruised and his tongue swollen, but his vision and breathing were back to normal. Best of all, his tormentor was gone.

So. Stealing cars was off the table. What could he do now for extra cash?

WHEN KYLE GOT TO the hardware store, Mr. Medina was busy with a customer. His grandmother had told him that Mr. Medina was expecting Kyle and David to come in after school to get a bat, but David wanted to hang out with his cool friends so he wouldn't come. Grandma sent Kyle to the hardware store anyway, but he wasn't sure that this was a good idea. If David was too busy to help him buy a bat, he wouldn't want to play baseball, either. And no matter how many championships his mother might have won in high school, his mom would play like a girl, and now she was old, too.

The customer left, and Ed glanced up and saw him in the doorway, shifting from one foot to the other.

"Hey, Kyle," he said, coming out from behind the counter. "Your mom said you need a new bat."

"I hate baseball," he said. "It sucks."

Ed frowned. "You can't play right without the right equipment. Let's see if we've got something that will fit you."

"How can it not fit you?" he asked, following Ed to the back of the store. "It's just a bat."

"But there are all sizes and kinds of bats, you know." Ed stopped in front of a couple of bins full of bats. "Okay, first we'll measure you." He backed Kyle up to a shelf support that had a tape measure fixed to it. "Stand up straight." He leveled his pencil over his head to the measure. "You're fifty-five inches tall." He did a quick calculation. "Four feet seven. How much do you weigh?" he asked. "Do you know?"

"About seventy-five," Kyle said, by now curious.

"And you're nine years old?" Ed asked. He nodded.

Ed picked up two charts that were hanging from the shelf and showed them to him. "See these guidelines? You don't want to use a bat that's too heavy or too long for your size, because that puts too much pressure on your wrist and arm. So besides not hitting well, you can hurt yourself."

"Really? I thought all bats were the same. I mean, yeah, some are heavier. I thought you could hit longer with those."

"That's right, you can. But the player has to have the weight and the height behind those bats, or you won't get the distance, either. These charts are only a guideline. Everybody's different. So let's take a couple of swings with a few bats and see which is the most comfortable. Do you like wood or metal?"

Kyle tried not to roll his eyes. "I don't know," he said.

"Okay, so we'll try a couple of each." Ed reached into the bin and pulled out some bats. "Let's go into the alley and take a few practice swings."

"How come you know so much about baseball?" Kyle asked when they were out behind the store. He'd picked up an aluminum bat and was swinging it wildly.

"I like the game. I used to play a little. Now I sell bats. Have to know something." He came up behind Kyle and showed him how to stand. "Here. You hold the bat like this. Choke up a little." He curled Kyle's fingers around the bat. "Place your feet like this." He nudged Kyle's feet into place. "And step into the swing like this." He stepped back and showed Kyle the swing in slow motion. "Now you try."

Kyle swung.

"That's pretty good," Ed said. "Let me show you again. Watch my shoulders."

Kyle watched and then swung again.

"That's better," Ed said, digging a ball out of his pocket. "Now we're going to swing at the ball. If you practice real hard, you might get to be as good as the Latin players."

"What do you mean?" Kyle asked, trying to concentrate on his stance. "Who? What about Babe Ruth?"

"Well, Babe Ruth," Ed conceded. "He played a long time ago. They didn't let Latin guys play back then, so we can't make a fair comparison. How about Sammy Sosa? You heard of him? Now, watch this pitch." He pitched the ball to Kyle, who swung and missed.

He *hated* this game.

"You took your eye off the ball," Ed said. "Choke up on the bat some more. Otherwise, it looked pretty good."

If his swing looked so great, how come he couldn't hit the ball? But the bat felt pretty good—better than the one he'd been using at home, anyway. He moved his hands up the bat the way Ed said and repositioned his feet. "I've heard of Sammy Sosa," he said. "He was good. Who else?"

Ed pitched the ball again and Kyle nicked it, sending it skittering toward the trash can on the other side of the alley.

"Good one," Ed said. "A sacrifice bunt on the third base line advances the runner on first."

Kyle laughed. "I'd rather hit home runs, like Sammy Sosa."

"Well, sure," Ed said, "but it's a team sport. Sometimes you have to play in a way that's best for the team. Okay, now, who else? Couple of years ago, Alex Rodriguez was the highest paid player in baseball. Now Miguel Cabrera makes thirty million or more a year. You ever hear of Roberto Clemente? Plus Juan Marichal, Orlando Cepeda, all in the Hall of Fame. Now try this wood bat."

"I want to get a good hit on this one first," Kyle said.

"Then watch the ball," Ed said. And he pitched to him again.

THE KID SHOULD BE good at this, Ed thought, watching Kyle's form. *His mom could really play.*

The pitch was perfect, right over what would have been the plate. Kyle stepped into his swing and brought his shoulders around, keeping his eye on the ball. The bat connected with the ball with a solid metallic ping, and Kyle and Ed both watched as the ball launched into the air in an ascending arc, straight down the center of the alley, high and soaring.

"Home run!" Ed jogged over and high-fived the youngster. "Way to go!"

Kyle pumped his fist in the air and did a victory dance.

"Sammy Sosa," he shouted, "you are *toast!*"

Chapter 8

Venus waited to call Maggie until she knew that she'd finished filing a divorce decree.

"Wusterbarth and Hedrich," Maggie said.

"Maggie?" said Venus, although she knew it was Maggie. "It's Venus."

"Don't tell me you want to divorce Mars. I can't handle another divorce today."

Venus had to laugh. "I'll never divorce Mars. The man is a god. No, I was wondering if you'd want to have lunch at Peg's today. Maybe at noon? I want to ask her for her vegetable scraps for my compost pile."

"Sounds like fun, although I can't imagine how compost could improve your yard," Maggie said. "Your timing is great, because I brought a two-day-old cheese sandwich for lunch. *Compost* would taste better than that."

Venus disconnected the call, her mission accomplished, and turned to Mars, still stretched out on the bed. The mussed and tumbled sheets only partly covered him. His hand played with a loose strand of her blonde hair. She lay back down next to him, twining her legs around his and putting an arm around his waist.

"Maggie and I are on for lunch," she told him. "Today it's the financial planner. I do *not* understand why Dr. J

thinks that colossal bore is right for her. I mean, I *like* her.
She's *cool*."

"It doesn't do to question the boss."

"Don't I know it. Well, she deserves her heart's desire,
so if it works out, I guess I'm okay with it. And if it *does*
work, we'll be just about done here."

"I'm in no rush," Mars said, shifting and pulling her
closer so he could kiss her. "I like this job. I'm doing fine in
Cedarburg." He nipped her bottom lip and then licked it, and
she closed her eyes and he felt her breath escape in a soft
sigh.

"Me, too," Venus said. "Everything's good in Cedarburg." And then she lost herself in Mars, knowing she had
hours yet before she had to think about what she should wear
to meet Maggie.

WHEN LUNCHTIME ARRIVED, Maggie left her office to
walk to the diner and saw Venus approaching from the other
direction. The woman looked amazing. Today she wore a
flowing red skirt and a tight red-and-white striped top, with
black flats and a large, black straw bag, which somehow
made her seem both elegant and wanton, a cross between
Audrey Hepburn and Mae West. Maggie glanced down at
her own navy suit and sighed. She should be so lucky to have
Venus's looks and clothes like that. If she wasn't covered in
dark gabardine, she was covered in baby-food mush.

"Your garden's already fabulous, Venus," Maggie said
as they went into the diner. "But I'm sure Peg will give you
all the scraps you want." She checked around for seats. All
the booths were taken, but two counter seats were available
near the end. "Are you okay with the counter?"

"Absolutely." Venus slid in next to Chuck Winkel, the
financial planner, who was chatting up Todd Zorn, the appliance king, on the other side. Chuck nodded at them when
they sat down.

"Hi, Maggie," he said.

"Hey, Chuck," Maggie said. She watched as Venus

smiled her breathtakingly radiant smile at him. She sure did know how to charm people. Chuck seemed mesmerized, gazing back at her as if starstruck. Then, still smiling, Venus glanced at Maggie. Chuck blinked and turned his gaze to Maggie.

"This is Venus," Maggie said. "Venus, this is Chuck."

"Hi," said Chuck. But he was still staring at Maggie.

"Hello, Chuck," said Venus. A faint smile played on her face as she watched the financial planner, whose gaze remained on Maggie.

"Hi," said Chuck again, more vaguely this time. Venus turned down the wattage and picked up a menu. Maggie looked around for Peg, a little uncomfortable under Chuck's unblinking scrutiny. What was up with that?

"Um, Maggie," Chuck said, wiping his fingers on a paper napkin before digging out his wallet to pay his bill. "I was wondering if, you know, you'd like to get together some time. Tonight, maybe."

Maggie glanced at him in surprise. "Sorry, Chuck," she said. "I can't make any commitments to investment programs other than what I've got right now. Things are just too tight."

"I don't mean that," Chuck said. He swallowed. Twice. "I mean it would be fun if we did something socially. Went out. If you want to. Have time." He struggled to a close.

Maggie stopped wondering where Peg was and gaped at Chuck Winkel. He wanted to go out? With *her*? And should she? Did she want to go out with Chuck Winkel? The financial planner who couldn't plan his own career?

She thought of her lunch with Ian Strachan, Donald Nennig's Scots business associate. What a failure that had been. Then there was dancing with Ed Medina, who was much nicer than Ian and lots more fun, not to mention many degrees hotter, but who hadn't asked her out. Still, a girl had her memories, and she seemed to be on a roll. Why not go out with Chuck? He was nice enough. Maybe he had unplumbed depths.

"All right," she decided. "If I can get a sitter."

Chuck's face lit up. "That's great," he said. "I'll give you a call later this afternoon. If not tonight, how about tomorrow? Whenever you're free."

"I'll see what I can set up," Maggie promised, touched by his enthusiasm. Had Chuck been carrying a torch for her? You never knew with people.

He dropped some money on the bill and stood up to go. "I'll talk to you later, then," he said, his eyes lingering on Maggie's face before he left.

"Nice to meet you," Venus said.

"Oh, right—same here," Chuck said, not seeing her, and Peg waved goodbye to him as she came over to clear his plate and ring up his bill.

"Hi, Peg," Maggie said. "Have you met Venus Tane? She'd like to talk to you about composting."

Venus gazed at Peg full in the eyes and smiled a radiant smile. "I bet you have a lot of scraps you throw away," she said.

"Sure, take whatever you want," Peg said, dazed.

WHEN MAGGIE GOT HOME from work, Venus was out in her backyard, building a compost heap.

"That was quick," Maggie said, pointing to the pile.

"Everyone here is so nice," Venus said. She stabbed her pitchfork into the ground and walked over to Maggie's sagging fence, stripping off her gloves as she went. Maggie knew it was wrong to envy someone her appearance and clothes, but she couldn't help it. Venus was gorgeous in her gardening gear, all her curves displayed and never a hair out of place. Today she was wearing pink corduroy overalls—pink! Corduroy!—and except for a few grains of earth clinging to the soles of her handsome leather boots, she was absolutely clean. While Maggie wore a navy suit that—at best and even in dim light—could be described only as "wrinkled." Plus, Venus had Mars. But then, Maggie thought, *I have a date.*

"You're going out with Chuck Winkel tonight?" Venus asked now, and Maggie nodded.

"My mother usually babysits," she said. "The kids like to go over there. David's getting too old to want to stay at Mom's, but not quite. She spoils them shamelessly. Lets them stay up too late, eat too much junk food. I figure every so often it's good for them."

Venus laughed. "What are you doing with Chuck?" she asked. "And what are you wearing?"

"Good question," Maggie said. "He suggested a concert in Dubuque. Of classical music. That sounds, ah, nice." *It sounds like I'll fall asleep in the middle.*

"Dubuque. That's a drive. It sounds like he wants to do something special."

"I guess," Maggie said. "I'm not sure what to wear. I have a few things left over from when John and I were married and we went to functions for the firm. They're pretty dated by now. These days all I wear is tailored navy to work and jeans at home."

"If you don't have anything you like, I'm sure I have something that will work for you."

Maggie hoped she didn't seem too interested. If Venus had anything that was at all close to her size, she was going to jump on it. The woman had fabulous clothes.

"I could never wear your things," Maggie said. "We're not the same size."

"You'd be surprised." Venus vaulted over the fence. "Come on, let's see what you've got. Tonight's a special night. I can feel it." And dropping her gardening gloves on Maggie's porch, she led Maggie into the house to rummage through her closet.

Two hours later, the kids were at her mom's and Maggie was nervous but ready to go. She gazed into the mirror one last time, smoothing Venus's dress over her hips and touching her hair. If she did say so herself, the dress did terrific things for her. Venus had examined all of Maggie's outfits, rejected everything, and then dragged her over to her own house to make her try on her things. Maggie hadn't wanted to borrow this beautiful turquoise dress, it was too wonderful, but Venus had acted like this date was the biggest night of her life, and Maggie did love the dress. It fit like a glove, and it brought out the red highlights of her dark hair and made her skin glow.

Maggie twirled in front of the mirror. She looked *great* in this dress. She could go dancing in this dress. And then she thought of Ed, and how much fun it would be to dance with him in this flirty turquoise dress, and she wondered if he would like her in it, and she thought he probably would. And then she thought of going to the classical concert in Dubuque with Chuck and tried to regain her enthusiasm.

Just then she heard an asthmatic car chug into the driveway and wheeze to a halt. That was Chuck now. A couple seconds later the car horn tooted a couple of times. *So much for romance.*

The outing hadn't gotten off to an auspicious start, and they hadn't even left yet. Chuck had originally suggested dinner first, but then his mother had felt some pain and wanted to go to the clinic. That didn't leave them enough time for a meal beforehand, so he changed the plan to dinner after the concert. Maggie hoped she could last that long. First no dinner, now a summons with the car horn. She sighed, picked up her coat, locked the door behind her, and joined Chuck in the car.

The drive to Dubuque took almost an hour and was very pleasant with the sun setting as they drove. It was strange to be talking with someone you saw fairly often but had never had more than ten minutes of conversation with. Home-town gossip saw them through small breaches and minor silences, and Maggie found Chuck agreeable and pleasant. So far, so good.

They found the auditorium without difficulty, but when they arrived, they learned that the concert was sold out. Chuck had failed to reserve tickets.

"Who thought a classical music concert would sell out

in Dubuque?" he asked Maggie by way of apology.

"Our concerts are popular and very well attended," the woman behind the desk at the entry way told him severely. "The sell-out was announced on our tape-recorded phone message, had you called to inquire."

"I'm sorry about the concert, Maggie," he said as he unlocked the passenger door for her. "I know you're disappointed."

"It's all right, Chuck," Maggie said, although she *was* disappointed. Here she was, all dressed up and no place to go, the story of her life, but it was a shame about the turquoise dress. How could she show it off now? Maggie felt like she'd let it down.

And then she realized she was a lot more disappointed about not showing off the dress than going to the concert or spending time with Chuck.

What had she been thinking? Chuck was a nice guy, a guy that *somebody* beside his mother could love, but that somebody wasn't her.

"Maybe we could stop for dinner or a hamburger or something on the way home," she said. "I'm starving."

"That's a great idea." He smiled at her, looking relieved. He turned the key in the ignition, grinding the engine until it roared into life.

As they drove out of town, Chuck told her of a great roadhouse he knew on the way back to Cedarburg that served fantastic steaks and burgers, she'd love it there. The thought of food cheered her up. She didn't get to go out often, and as much as she liked Peg's diner, going someplace new, someplace festive, sounded like fun.

Conversation didn't go as well on the way back, partly, Maggie thought, because they'd already updated each other on all the acquaintances they had in common, and now they didn't have the concert to talk about. Then Chuck spotted the restaurant he'd been thinking of, and Maggie saw with a sinking sensation—distinct from the rumbling of her stomach, which had a different feeling altogether—that the parking lot was way too empty and the building way too dark.

"I think it's closed," she said.

"It can't be closed." Chuck pulled into the driveway and cut the engine. "It's Friday night."

The restaurant was closed—permanently, the sign said—and apparently for some time. Maggie sighed. Her evening was complete.

"We'll just go back to Cedarburg," Chuck said, decisive for the first time that evening. "Something will be open there. Peg's. Or maybe the bowling alley."

I'll be wearing this turquoise dress to the bowling alley, Maggie thought. "Sounds like a plan," she said brightly.

The car took longer to start this time. The grinding went on and on before the engine caught, and Maggie held her breath, hoping that they could get home and she could get this date over with. Was it too late to claim she wasn't hungry? She thought it probably was. Well, she could eat a hamburger, and then the date would be over and never again would she have to go out with Chuck Winkel.

They were silent now. Maggie was busy listening to the car, which seemed to struggle up every hill. If it weren't for the downward momentum they gained on the other side, she wasn't sure the car could make it up the next one. *Just a few more miles*, she thought, *and we'll all be home where we belong*.

And then the car rolled down a hill, gave a huge hiccup, and died.

Maggie didn't look at Chuck.

Chuck didn't look at Maggie.

"I wonder what that could be," he said.

"I don't know," she said.

He turned the key in the ignition, and although the engine turned over, it didn't catch. Chuck popped the hood and got out to peer at the engine, but it was dark, he didn't have a flashlight, and Maggie thought it was likely that he didn't know how internal combustion engines worked, anyway.

Maggie checked her cell phone—no signal—and then got out to inspect it, too.

"Do you know anything about cars?" he asked.

"Not really," she said. "I can check the oil." They checked the oil, Maggie being very careful not to get any on the turquoise dress. That wasn't it. The car had oil.

"Well," Chuck said.

"I don't have cell service out here. Do you?"

"Forgot my phone." Chuck sounded gloomy.

"Okay. Well, there was a pay phone outside at that closed restaurant," Maggie said. "I think you'll have to walk back there and call Denny at home and ask him to come out to tow you." Denny owned the service station in town.

"Tow me."

"Yes. Or jump you, if it's the battery. Thank heaven it's not too late. He'll still be up." It *would* have been too late if they'd gone to the concert. So there was a god.

"Towing is so expensive, but I suppose that's the only solution."

"I think so. How else could we get back? I guess if you don't want to walk back to that restaurant you could wake up one of the farmers around here and ask if they'll let you make a call. That's an option."

Chuck frowned at her, and Maggie felt a spurt of rage. He thought that *she* would make that hike? Or a magic fairy would appear and wave a wand and Denny would simply appear?

"It has to be you," Maggie explained carefully, "because I can't walk that far in these high heels, and I didn't bring any other shoes." They both gazed for a second at Maggie's very high turquoise heels, also a loan from Venus.

"It's miles back to the restaurant," Chuck said.

Maggie curbed her exasperation. How could one person be so helpless? She remembered for a fleeting, wistful second Ed's volunteering to put up her gutter screens. He would have walked back without question. But of course, his truck wouldn't have broken down in the first place.

"You could walk the other way, toward Cedarburg," she said. "It's longer, but maybe someone will drive by and pick you up."

"I suppose that's an option."

"I'll just wait here, then." Maggie was really annoyed now. Her *kids* would be more helpful than this. "I won't be too cold, don't worry about it."

"I wasn't worried," Chuck said, and then seemed to realize that wasn't the right thing to say. "That's good," he added. "Well, I guess I better start."

"I guess you better," Maggie said. "Of course, if you see anybody on the road, you could flag them down. That would go faster."

Chuck nodded. "I'll go as fast as I can."

"Yes, well, just *go*," Maggie said, unable to curb her impatience any longer.

"See you." Chuck trudged off in the direction from which they'd come, back toward the roadhouse.

"Good luck." Maggie pulled her coat more tightly around her and got back into the car to wait.

What on earth else could happen tonight?

Chapter 9

Time passed. Crickets chirped. The corn rustled in the slight evening breeze. The occasional small animal tiptoed across the road, intent on its nocturnal forage. Maggie didn't want to turn on the radio for fear she'd run down the car's battery, but it was a beautiful night, not too cold, with clear skies and millions of tiny, brilliant stars sweeping across the heavens. She opened the window and leaned her head against the doorframe to get a better look. And then she saw a shooting star.

As a sign of good luck, it wasn't much. Here she was, on a date with a guy who couldn't buy tickets in advance, didn't check to see if the restaurant would be open, didn't take care of his transportation, and then complained when he had to walk to make a phone call. *I've already got three kids*, she thought, *I don't need another one*. And then in the rear-view mirror, she saw the flash of headlights over a hill. A vehicle was coming.

She jumped out of the car and stood by the side of the road, ready to wave it down. And then a large, old pickup truck lumbered into view, and Maggie recognized that it belonged to Tom Strodthoff. She waved like mad and the truck eased to a stop, the engine still running. Maggie went over to the driver-side window.

"Hey, Maggie," Tom said. His wife, Louella, sat next to him in the cab. "Having car trouble?"

"Yes," Maggie said, "But it's Chuck Winkel's car. We're on our way back from Dubuque. You didn't pass him on the road, did you? He's supposed to be heading back to that roadhouse to call Denny."

"Didn't see him," Tom said. "Although it's dark. That dress you got on there sort of acts like a stop sign. That's why we saw you." He eyed the dress until Louella cleared her throat and Maggie pulled her coat closed.

"You want a lift?" Tom asked. "We got room."

"I don't want to leave Chuck out here alone without his knowing where I've gone," Maggie said.

"We can go get him, too," Louella said. "He can't be that far back."

"Thanks, then," Maggie said. "I'd love a lift." She went around to Louella's side of the truck, Louella scooted over, and Maggie got in. Tom did a careful U-turn in the road and they went back to find Chuck.

When they found him, he was sitting on a big, flat rock, just out of the ditch, almost out of sight. No wonder the Strodthoffs hadn't seen him on the road. *She'd* barely seen him, and she was watching for him. The truck rolled to a halt.

"Chuck?" Maggie asked from the passenger window. "What are you doing?"

"My feet hurt," Chuck said. "I think I have a blister."

She sighed. "The Strodthoffs offered us a ride into town," she said. "You can call Denny from there."

Chuck got up and limped to the truck's passenger door. "You have to move over," he said to Maggie.

"You have to sit in the back," Louella said from the middle. "There isn't room to move over."

"Sit in the back?" Chuck examined the empty truck bed, which was clean for a working farm truck, but that wasn't saying much.

"If you want a lift, climb in," Louella said. "We've got to get to the high school to watch our Elsbeth play in the game." The Strodthoffs had six daughters, and all of them had been powerhouses on the girls' high school basketball team. Katrina, three years older than Elsbeth, had a scholarship to play on her college squad.

Chuck went to the back and climbed in.

"It's been a long night," Maggie said into the silent cab.

"It would be," Louella said.

When they got to town, the Strodthoffs let them off at the bowling alley on their way to the high school.

"You want us to drop you at home?" Louella asked. "Them shoes ain't meant for walking."

"Chuck and I are supposed to get a burger," Maggie said. "And I'm hungry, so I'm taking him up on it."

"Up to you," Louella said. "Enjoy the rest of your evening." She waved at them as the truck eased back into the street.

Maggie turned to Chuck, his face a sickly blue from bowling alley's giant neon sign. Maggie supposed her skin looked blue, too, but the neon sure did wonders for the turquoise dress.

"Are you still hungry?" Chuck asked, although why she wouldn't be was a mystery to Maggie. But she just said, "Yes," and they went in, Chuck limping on his blistered foot and now also smelling faintly of manure.

The place was full—way too full, Maggie realized after a second, even for a Friday night. The bar was lined three deep, all the booths were jammed, and a few adventuresome couples danced to the jukebox. Through the door on the left, Maggie could see that the bowling alley was filled with raucous players.

"It's league night," she said, turning to Chuck and shouting so she could be heard. "We won't get served."

"Wait a minute," Chuck said. "I have to make a phone call."

Maggie watched him go, hoping he was calling Denny. She watched him thread his way through the crowd to the back of the bar, down the long hallway that led to the amenities. Maybe he needed the restroom and was too bashful to say so, she thought, and decided to wait for him outside.

The night was still warm. Maggie leaned against the building, enjoying the mild evening air. She said hello to the people she knew, people who'd come out to cool off from dancing or enjoy a little quiet. She hoped Chuck wouldn't take long. She wanted to get home. She could make a peanut butter sandwich and have a quiet bath. She wouldn't have to pick up the kids from her mother's until tomorrow morning. She closed her eyes, thinking of the bath and the calm house.

"Hey, Maggie, what are you doing here? You're pretty dressed up for the league bowling crowd." She opened her eyes to see Ed smiling next to her, his velvety brown eyes warm in the semi-darkness. Chuck came out and joined them.

"Hi, Ed," he said, sounding harassed. He turned to Maggie. "Mother is upset about something. I'm sorry, Maggie, but I've got to hurry home."

"That's okay, Chuck, you should go. I'm only a couple blocks away. I'll walk." She'd take off her shoes and go barefoot. It wouldn't be a sacrifice.

"Are you sure?"

"Absolutely," said Maggie.

"Okay, well, be seeing you." He shuffled down the street, nursing the blister on his heel. Maggie and Ed watched him go.

"I can give you a lift." Ed pointed to the vehicle at the curb. "My truck's right here. I was on my way home from my folks' place when I saw you. I gotta ask you something, though." He walked her around to the passenger side of the truck and opened the door.

Maggie nodded. "Sure. What?"

"None of my business, but were you on a date with Chuck Winkel?"

"Sort of," she said. "But it didn't work out. I thought I was on a roll, but I overshot."

"Oh," Ed said, sounding confused. "I wondered. Because

you guys really got your signals crossed if you thought you were going somewhere nice in that dress and he took you to the bowling alley."

Maggie sighed. "No kidding."

"You look great, by the way."

"Thanks." Maggie beamed at him, pleased that he'd noticed, glad that somebody besides her appreciated the turquoise dress.

By the time they were half-way to her house, she had told him the story of her evening. Ed laughed, and even Maggie could see the humor in it.

"I feel guilty laughing," she said. "Chuck's a nice enough guy. Maybe if he moved out away from his mother, he wouldn't be quite so, I don't know. Hapless. But I should have known. I *did* know, but I overruled my better judgment."

"No concert, no restaurant, no car—don't tell me you still haven't eaten?"

"I'm saving myself for a peanut butter sandwich," Maggie said. "They're utterly reliable. At the House of Jiffy, it's never league night."

"If you like," he said, sounding tentative, "I have some stew at home. It's pretty good, even if I did make it. It might be better than a peanut butter sandwich right now."

Maggie turned to see him better. His large hands lay loosely on the steering wheel, his nose, thin and aquiline with a slight bump to give it distinction, his dark hair thick and straight and shaggy, lying over the top of his collar. He wore a leather jacket over a white T-shirt and jeans, and she could see the strength in the muscles that lay across his chest, that flexed in his thighs as he shifted the gears, and the strength in his hands and voice. He was everything that was solid and, well, *sexy*, and her mouth watered. The stew would be good, too.

"Stew sounds wonderful," she said.

Ed lived above the hardware store. He parked in the alley and led her up the enclosed stairway, taking her hand and turning on the lights so she wouldn't trip in her spindly heels.

And then they were inside, where everything was cozy and neat.

"This is a great place, Ed." Maggie took off her coat and tossed it over a chair. "I didn't realize how big it was up here. And you have some wonderful stuff." His shelves were filled mainly with books, but open spaces were jammed with beaded bowls and elaborate pottery candelabra, hand-painted vases filled with bright paper flowers, and goofy wooden animals with outrageous teeth and tongues—things he must have brought back from vacations or visits to relatives, she realized. It was organized, colorful chaos. When he didn't answer, she turned to see what he was doing and was startled by the expression on his face.

"What?" she asked.

ED KNEW THAT HE was being rude, that he was staring at her, but he couldn't help it. *My god*, he thought. She was— amazing.

He had to say something.

"You look" —he swallowed— "wonderful."

"You like the dress?" She seemed self-conscious, smoothing her hands over her hips. "I borrowed it for the evening."

"The dress is great," Ed said, swallowing again. "But you—you do something for it." He let the vision of her fill his head. He'd never seen anyone so vivid, so alive, and now she was standing there in his living room, making his place brighter with her presence. She seemed to radiate sparks, with her dark hair glinting red, her skin so silky and pale, and her blue eyes darkening as she observed him. And that turquoise dress, making everything shimmer.

"Well," he said, turning to go into the kitchen. "Let me put that stew on." *Before I make a fool of myself here.*

He rummaged around in the refrigerator for the stew pot and then pulled out a bowl for the microwave.

"Can I help?" Maggie asked, leaning against the door. Every inviting curve called out to him through the magic of that dress, and suddenly there wasn't enough air in that kitchen for both of them. He thought about pulling her close, pulling her next to him, hip to hip, shoulder to shoulder, pulling her into a dance where two became one, and kissing her, breathing into her, feeling her breathe into him, sharing the same air because there wasn't enough to go around. And then he thought, *get her out of here before I do something stupid.*

"Would you like some wine?" he asked. "There's a bottle out there in the cupboard. You could open it."

"Wine would be great," she said and disappeared to find it. He heard a cupboard door open and close and then she was back, her vampy shoes clicking on the floor tiles. He handed her the corkscrew before she could say anything.

As the microwave timer ticked down, Maggie twisted in the corkscrew and then the cork came out with a soft pop. "Got glasses?"

He handed her two and followed her out to the dining room with plates and bowls.

"It's nothing fancy," he said, "and there's not much else. But it should fill you up." He sat down at the table, setting a full bowl of stew down for Maggie and a modest portion for himself.

"It smells great," Maggie said, sniffing the air. "This is nice of you, Ed. Much better than peanut butter." She poured the wine into the glasses and handed him one.

"Cheers," she said, raising her glass.

"Cheers." What was he doing? Whatever it was, he was in way over his head. He knew that for sure.

The stew was made with crumbly chunks of lamb in a rich broth, full of tomatoes and white beans, carrots and potatoes, and Maggie ate two bowls, wiping hers clean with a piece of the crusty bread that Ed had put out on a thick blue plate.

"You made this?" she asked, leaning back in her chair. "It's fantastic. I have to say, Ed, you've completely turned around my evening. Thank you."

"I'm glad I could help," Ed said. "I made the stew, my mom made the bread."

"Did your mom teach you to cook?" She toyed with her empty wine glass, and he poured her a little more.

"She and Betty Scholz did," he said. "Betty taught mom how to make American food, but at home we still ate mostly Guatemalan dishes. So I learned to cook both American and traditional food." He grinned. "Later on, when I was on my own, I was glad that I'd learned how to make Betty Scholz's blueberry pie. I wouldn't want to live without that."

"You'd make someone a good husband. Cooking and all."

"I almost did," Ed said, stacking the bowls. "I got engaged to someone for a while when I was in the service. Out on the coast. A long time ago."

"Why'd you break up?"

Maggie was getting awfully personal. It was probably the wine talking. Not that he objected when wine talked, exactly, as long as it didn't take over the conversation.

"Lots of reasons. We were both way too young, for starters. After that, culture clash mostly. I mean, this is the only country I know. But she missed Mexico. She was sixteen when she came, so she had good memories of home. In the end, we had almost nothing in common except that we both spoke Spanish."

"Did your parents want you to marry a Guatemalan girl?" Maggie asked.

"They still do. They think I'll forget my heritage otherwise. And they don't say this, but I know they think that if I marry anyone but a Guatemalan that I disrespect them somehow." He flashed her a grin. "Although they *say* that all they want is for me to be happy."

Maggie laughed. "My mom says the same thing. I guess all parents tell their kids that."

"I suppose."

"You'd be a fine catch for somebody. You can cook *and* put up gutter screens. Do you want to get married some day?"

Ed shrugged as he carried the bowls back into the kitchen. "I'm thirty-eight," he said over his shoulder. "I think it's too late for me. I have a brother and two sisters; they all married young and all of them have kids. I'm probably better off as an uncle."

"Maybe. But you read all the time about celebrities who have kids into their seventies. Or even later."

He washed his hands and dried them on the kitchen towel.

"Celebrities," he grinned. "Yeah, well, celebrities live in a different world. My folks raised us kids to think of marriage and family as something you did basically right after high school. They saw family as a solid foundation for building a good life."

"It can be that, if you pick the right partner."

"My folks don't believe in divorce. They were lucky themselves, and I think my siblings are mostly happy, but—"

"Sometimes divorce is inevitable," Maggie said.

Ed nodded. "I think of relationships as something like parachuting or bungee jumping. I leaped—got engaged, that is. I smashed. Lesson learned."

"In my case, marriage was more like car crashing or train wrecking than parachuting or bungee jumping," Maggie said. "First, your life passes before your eyes. Then come the mangled body parts and blood and gore everywhere."

Ed laughed, but he remembered what he'd heard about John Jorgenson, the unfaithful husband. He tossed the towel onto the counter and poured them a little more wine.

"Is that why you didn't remarry?" he asked. "No need for more train wrecks and car crashes?"

"Safety first," Maggie said. "That's me." She took a sip of her wine. Ed waited.

"I don't see getting married again," she said finally. "My first one wasn't so great, so I know I'm not that good at it. And now I've got kids, so lots of issues there. And besides—who wants a woman with three kids?"

Not me, Ed thought, feeling like a jerk. "You just need to find somebody who likes kids."

"Or at least prefers me to his mother."

Ed snorted. "If anyone saw you in that dress and would still rather spend time with his mother, there's no hope for the human race."

"Well, thank you, Ed," Maggie said. "And thank you for the stew. It was delicious. You're a lifesaver." She sat back and beamed at him, and Ed smiled back, and suddenly, the air seemed thick and pulsating.

"You must get back to visit Guatemala fairly often," Maggie said, jumping up to inspect a shelf and breaking the mood. "All these great objects. I love this kind of craft work."

Ed watched Maggie leave the table, taking all the light and energy with her. He got up and put on some catchy music, then stood next to her and pointed out a few things that she might find interesting. She was standing too close again, and … *Take her home,* his warning voice said. *You fed her, you're done. Get her out of here.*

"Would you like to dance?" he asked, and Maggie said, "That'd be fun."

So he kicked the rug aside and spun her around and then back to him, and she threw back her head and laughed. They danced until the music came to an end, and when it did, Maggie collapsed on the sofa.

"That was a lot of fun," she said. "But I have to stop. Any more in these shoes and I'll never walk again. Although I love the shoes."

"They look great," Ed said, trying not to stare at her legs.

"That's all that matters," Maggie said, and they both laughed.

"Need some water?" Ed asked. "I'm kind of thirsty now." Mainly he wanted to stop staring at Maggie's legs. He got up to pour it, and Maggie kicked off her shoes and followed him into the kitchen. So when he turned around with two glasses of ice water, she was standing much too close, all light and texture and color and brighter than anything he'd thought possible.

"Here," he said, handing her a glass, and she tilted her head back and poured the water down her throat. Ed watched the graceful lines of her neck as she swallowed the water, and when she set the glass down and turned back to him, a bead of moisture clung to her lower lip.

He had to. He couldn't resist her for another second.

"Maggie," he said, stepping closer. Her luminous eyes held his, and then he tipped her head back with one hand as he slid an arm around her waist and bent to kiss her.

He meant just to taste that little drop of water with his tongue, to lick it off her lower lip and let her go. But when his mouth covered hers, he already knew he'd gone further than he meant to, and then he felt her respond, her body relaxed and soft in his arms, her lips opening against the pressure of his own, and all that color and energy that was Maggie exploded behind his eyes and he was lost.

He slid his hand from her chin down past the slope of her breast, over her waist to her back, molding her body to his. Her softness made him dizzy, with her thighs and hips and breasts and arms all pressing against him. He tangled her soft hair in his hand while he leaned into her, lost in the moment and her glorious heat and color. She was like liquid sunshine, the sweetest fruit nectar. He couldn't get enough of her.

WHEN THE KISS ENDED, light years and billions of sparkles later, Maggie pulled away with deep regret. "I should go," she said.

Ed kissed her again, briefly, his lips warm against her skin. "Why? You could stay here."

"I don't think so. I mean—" Maggie hesitated. "It's late. I need to get home. I have to pick up the kids from my mom's early tomorrow."

She thought Ed looked disappointed, but she wasn't sure. She hoped so, a little bit, anyway.

Ed got his jacket and Maggie put on her coat, but she winced when she tried to put the high heels back on.

"Leave them off for now," Ed said. He looped the straps of her shoes around his finger, and then they walked down the stairs to the door. When they got there, Ed swept her into his arms and carried her outside.

"Ed, don't be silly! Put me down!"

"When we're in the truck." He carried her without even seeming to breathe hard, and when they got to his truck, she opened the doors for him and he sat her gently on the seat. "Dancing should not be a blood sport," he said, as he buckled himself in.

"It was worth it," Maggie said.

By the time they came to a stop in front of her house, Maggie had regained her senses. Ed helped her out of the truck, but she didn't want him coming into her messy house. Wondering if she should ask him to stay. If he would ask.

"I can manage from here," she said.

"Sleep well, Maggie," he said, kissing her on the cheek. "Thanks for the dance."

"You're welcome." Maggie wished things could be different—that they could both be younger versions of themselves, with more options and fewer obligations. "Thanks for the ride. And the stew."

And the date, because it seemed like the date that she'd gone out on several hours ago hadn't started until she'd walked into Ed's apartment over the hardware store.

Ed stood at the curb, his face hidden by darkness. "Anytime," he said. "Come over anytime."

And then he got into his truck and drove off.

She watched him go, swamped by longing. Still, it was better that he left. They shouldn't even get started, because she didn't really want to have a short-term affair. And they didn't have a future together.

Just for starters, she had three kids, and he'd all but said he was happy being uncle to his nieces and nephews. And even if he liked her kids, they might not accept him. His parents would object, too, and while he obviously didn't live his life to please his parents, they obviously were a close-knit family.

And the big problem with having an affair was, she

didn't think she could handle it. If she went to bed with Ed, she'd fall hard for him. She knew she would. Ed was a lot of things that John had never been, and even if she wanted, needed—even *craved*—those things, she couldn't afford to get involved, because she'd fall in love and Ed wouldn't.

And that would be worse than not getting involved at all.

Chapter 10

Saturday morning was always a busy time in all the stores. Nobody would notice him. This would be easy. That's what Ben had said, and Ben knew.

Stifling his nervousness, David Jorgenson entered the hardware store, walking with what he hoped was the right mixture of nonchalance and determination. Ben was already thirteen, and he said this was how it was done. Ben seemed to know everything. And if Ben could do it, he could do it.

Mr. Medina—Ed—was busy with a customer at the checkout. David didn't see any clerks nearby, or Alberto Medina, who was probably in the garden center. Now was the time.

David walked past the checkout and headed toward the back, where the Super Glue was kept. He picked up a tube, holding it in a hand gone damp. Then he went over to the paint aisle. There at the end was what he was really here for: the wide-tipped magic writers, the colorful pens that all graffiti artists loved. He'd already decided what colors he wanted, so he didn't hesitate. Red, blue, gold, and black all disappeared into the deep pockets of the baggy jacket he'd worn specifically for that purpose. And in ten seconds, he was out of the aisle, headed toward the checkout.

"More Super Glue, David?" Mr. Medina asked, smiling

when it was his turn, and David felt his mouth go dry. He couldn't meet Mr. Medina's eyes.

"Yeah," he said, and Mr. Medina took his change, rang up the glue, and dropped it into a bag with the receipt.

"Is your mom doing a lot of fixing up around the house?" he asked, holding the bag.

"Yeah," he agreed. Could he just grab the paper sack with the glue and go? If he did that, would Mr. Medina suspect something? He didn't know what else to say. Ben had never talked about this, what you did once the deed was done, how you got out of the place with no one suspecting.

"I suppose she has a lot of fall projects," Mr. Medina said.

"I guess."

Mr. Medina looked at him for a long moment, and then held out the bag with the glue.

"Take care," he said, and David took the sack and escaped from the store.

MICKEY ADAIR CAME OUT of the Wee Bite—and what a shite name for a diner that was!—a toothpick wedged in the side of his mouth, a scowl on his face. Here he was, another day stuck in this lousy town, another day when Donald Nennig, that nutter, had skipped a meeting, another day when Ian let them down. Another day with the diamonds not unloaded. He'd had to empty out his pockets just now to pay his pathetic bill. It was his rotten luck that they were traveling with a fortune in diamonds and didn't have a tenner for a pint.

He walked down the street in a black cloud, acknowledging the nods of recognition and cheery hellos from some of the people on the street. This was the worst. They'd been in this damn town for so long that people knew them. Pretty soon they might as well advertise: jewel thieves seek fence. And in this town, the fence would be made of wood, painted white, and surrounding a big clapboard house.

His route took him past Denny's service station. He'd

thought about pinching some of the cars Denny had parked in his lot and around the streets, cars that had been repaired and were waiting for pickup. But after his encounter with the enforcer on that dead-end street, he'd given up all thoughts of doing anything illegal while he was here.

He squinted into the station now. Two cars were cranked up on hydraulic lifts, but no one was working on them. Another car was parked inside, two more were outside. Denny seemed to have plenty of business, but none of it was getting done. He saw Denny up front behind the counter, talking on the phone. He went in.

Immediately he regretted it. Denny was on the phone, but the big guy with wavy dark hair—the guy that Mickey had been calling the enforcer ever since he'd met him on that quiet cul-de-sac—was waiting at the counter. *Shite on an eff-ing stick.*

But the enforcer merely nodded, and Mickey nodded back, fisting his palms and thrusting them into his pockets. He didn't have to worry. He hadn't actually stolen the car, and the bruiser wasn't a cop, so he couldn't do anything to him. *Except beat the crap out of him.* But he didn't intend to give the enforcer another excuse to get that close.

Denny hung up the phone and turned to the big guy. "We can get that part for you by Monday," he said. "I can try to get you fixed up by Wednesday. But I'm short-handed right now. The guy who usually helps me, his wife's cousin died over in Illinois, and they won't be back for a week."

Mars nodded, smiling. "That'll be fine. We're in no rush."

Mickey cleared his throat. Denny turned to him with a frown, and Mickey said, almost without realizing it, "I could help out. I'm pretty good with cars, and I'm looking for short-term work."

Denny blinked and Mickey wondered where that had come from; in fact, he wondered why he'd gone into the service station at all, when he didn't want a job. He wanted out of this town, his share of the diamond sale tucked inside his overcoat. But the words were out now, and Denny was already watching him, Mickey thought, like a cat watched a cornered mouse.

"What's your experience?" Denny asked.

"I can do anything with cars," Mickey replied truthfully.

"Can you put in an afternoon right now?" Denny asked, "and we'll see how it works out."

Mickey saw his worst nightmare—steady, honest employment—come to life. "That would be grand," he lied, and Mars smiled.

"I see my car will be in good hands," he said.

"Yours and Chuck Winkel's both," Denny said, and took Mickey out to the garage to find a pair of coveralls that would fit him.

"CAN YOU HEAR ME NOW?" Venus yelled into her cell phone, slamming out her back door and standing in the middle of her garden. It was lush and green in the glorious fall afternoon, the fountain splashing amidst the white and purple flowers of her rock garden, the golden sun warming her plants, her Puck, and her bench, which she sank into.

"The reception is terrible here," she said into the phone, trying not to let her exasperation show. "Not enough towers, too many hills. What? Say that again." She listened for a minute.

"I *know* the financial planner's a terrible bore," she said. "I *told* you. She doesn't deserve that. *Nobody* does. What? Well, of course I'm relieved, but—what? Who? Are you *sure*? That guy? You say, he'll come to the door? Well, of course the postal carrier comes to the door! What? All right, then. If you're sure. I don't like it, though."

She listened intently for a minute, a frown on her face. "You know you could *text* me. That's easy enough. Or send me an email. Even a fax. Then there wouldn't be these mixups. *Okay*, I *heard* you. I *said* I'll take care of it."

Irritated, Venus disconnected the call. Why did Dr. J insist on calling her when they had such bad connections? It was inexplicable. There were lots more ways to communicate clearly and effectively. He could even write a letter and put a stamp on it.

She didn't trust this most recent communication, either. *He'll come to the door?* That didn't sound right. Just like the financial planner, who'd been a terrible bore, and the jewel thief, who'd been rotten to the core, hadn't sounded right. Why would Dr. J think that the postal carrier was a good choice for Maggie's life mate? It didn't make sense.

But there was no arguing with the ruler of the pantheon. He said, deliver. So deliver she would.

DAVID ENTERED THE back door of his house, shrugged out of his jacket, and flung it over one of the hooks. Then he charged upstairs. He'd been over at Ben's since late morning, right after he'd stolen the pens from the hardware store. He and Ben had marked up their books; they were hoping that they could get out after dark and tag something—some garbage cans, or maybe even a building. He'd go over to Ben's for supper and they could go out after dark; Ben's mom wouldn't notice. Ben's mom hardly noticed anything.

He powered up the computer that everybody shared and started his Playstation2. The computer was set up in the alcove in the upstairs hallway where everyone could get to it, but at the moment he was home alone, so he was safe.

He was well into Grand Theft Auto when his mom came upstairs. He hadn't heard her come in, and he tried to switch screens before she saw what he was doing, because this game was for adults and his mom would throw a fit if she saw it. Ben's older brother Kevin had gotten him this copy, and it was a cool game—violent with a lot of creepy characters. But his mother wouldn't understand, and he and Ben and Kevin had agreed this would be their secret.

"David, we have to talk," his mom said and then stopped and stared at the screen. "What are you playing?"

"Nothing."

"Show me."

"It's just a game."

But her eyes were riveted on ferocious characters in black pummeling cartoon girls popping out of really tight costumes. "Where did you get that?"

David knew he was in trouble. His allowance wasn't big enough to pay for video games.

"Dad bought it for me," he lied.

"No, he didn't. Try again."

David kicked the drawer of the computer desk, trying to think of something.

"David?" His mom never gave up. "The truth, please."

David banged his foot against his desk. "Kevin gave it to me."

"Ben's brother?"

David nodded.

"You're not old enough to play this game. Give me the controller."

That was so unfair! His mom didn't understand *anything*. "Mom! I just got it! I haven't seen it!"

"*Give it to me now.*"

She always ruined all his fun. What was so bad about a video game? But he didn't see what else he could do. He threw it at her.

"*Do not throw things at people unless you're playing baseball,*" she said. "What has gotten into you?"

Sometimes he just hated his family.

His mom squatted next to him, but he wasn't going to look at her. He turned his head away.

"David, Ben's brother should know better than to give you a game like this," she said. "He's showing poor judgment by giving you something this expensive and this violent. Before you go over there again, I need to talk to Ben's mom."

David's heart sank. His mom had called Ben's mom before he went over there the first time to see if it was okay, but if his mom and Ben's mom ever had a heart-to-heart, he'd never be allowed to go over there again, because Ben's mom never seemed to know what was going on. And that was most of the fun—that they could do pretty much anything they wanted over there, whereas his own mom always wanted to know what he was doing and where he was going and with whom.

"Can I go now?"

"*May* you go, and no, you may not. This video game is not even what I came up here about. David, where did you get these?" She held out his giant pens, which he hadn't even noticed that she had until now. He stared at them, not knowing what to say.

"Ben gave them to me," he said.

"I don't think you're telling the truth. Ben's parents don't have the money to be giving you games and big pens like this. And I don't want you having pens like this, anyway. Now where did you get them?"

David gazed out the window.

"Your allowance isn't big enough to pay for something like this," she said. "I haven't given you any extra money. Your grandma hasn't given you any money. You haven't earned any. So where did you get them?"

David felt like crying or throwing up or shouting, he wasn't sure which.

"Did you steal them?"

He banged his foot against the desk again.

"If you didn't steal them, where did you get the money?"

He still didn't look at her. "It's no big deal," he said.

"Stealing is *no—big—deal*? Wrong. Stealing is a *very* big deal. Where did you steal them from?"

David sighed. It was all out now, anyway.

"The hardware store."

"Come on." His mom finally stood up. "Right now. We're going to the hardware store."

David swallowed. His mom would ground him for life. And what would Mr. Medina do?

MAGGIE WAS SHOCKED. David was *stealing*? David was playing violent, raunchy videogames aimed at *adults*? Where had her innocent eleven-year-old son gone to, and how could she get him back?

And how was she going to explain this to Ed?

All the way to the hardware store she asked David questions, trying to figure out what he'd been thinking. She didn't get it. Of course, the divorce had been hard for him, and his father had never been all that involved with his sons. Still, that seemed like a lame excuse. David just said "all the kids did it," and even though Maggie talked about responsibility, pride, and honesty, she didn't think she'd gotten through to him. By the time they got to the hardware store, she felt dizzy and sick.

Ed was working the checkout. She came in, one hand on David's shoulder, for his support and hers. Ed saw them in the doorway and smiled. It was a different smile than he'd given her before, one that encompassed David as well as herself, and it was thoughtful, not spontaneous. *He knows*, Maggie thought, and felt something shrivel inside.

"Hi Ed," she said. "Can we talk to you?"

"Hey, Maggie, David," he said, and called to Alberto to take over the checkout. He waved for them to follow him, and they walked to the back of the store, through a door marked "employees only" and into a small, crammed, dusty office hacked out of a giant storeroom filled to the ceiling with shelves full of hardware and other stuff. He pulled out the creaky, broken desk chair for Maggie, pointed to an overturned crate for David, and leaned against the side of the desk. The office was not built for three.

"What can I do for you?" he asked, looking from one to the other.

Maggie glanced at David, who was closely observing the floor. "David has something to tell you."

David continued to gaze at the floor.

"What's up, David?" Ed asked.

David glanced up, but said nothing.

"David," Maggie said, prodding him. It was bad enough her kid had stolen; he needed to own up to it.

David swallowed. "It's about when I was in earlier."

"This morning?"

David nodded. "I—I took something. When I bought the glue. I took some giant marking pens. Without paying for them," he added.

"I see," said Ed.

"And I'm sorry and I won't do it again," David said in a rush. Maggie realized she'd been holding her breath while she watched David, hoping he understood the gravity of what he'd done, and now she exhaled with relief. At least he'd come clean.

"So how are you going to pay for the pens?" Ed asked, and Maggie instantly reached for her wallet.

"No, not you, Maggie," Ed said. "I asked David how *he* was going to pay for them."

"I don't know," David faltered. "I don't have any money. I get an allowance, but—"

They all knew what the *but* meant. The allowance wasn't a lot. And right now, it was all spent.

For a long minute nobody said anything. David fidgeted, shifting his glance from his mother to Ed. Maggie watched Ed. Ed watched David.

"We have a problem then," Ed said.

ED WATCHED DAVID because he didn't want to see the pain on Maggie's face. This was what happened when you got mixed up with divorced women with kids. You got problems. You got trouble. And then their trouble became your trouble.

Although in fairness, David's stealing had nothing to do with getting involved with Maggie. But with anybody else, he might not feel quite so bad about it.

His parents were right. He didn't need these aggravations.

"Tell you what," he said finally. "I could use more help in the store. If you come in after school for two hours a couple of times a week, I'll give you minimum wage and we'll deduct the pens from your check until they're paid off."

I must be crazy to be doing this, he thought.

"What?" The kid seemed not to have heard him.

"But you have to get here on the days we agree and do your work, whatever someone tells you to do," Ed said. "You don't, and I'm calling the school and the cops about this theft." He'd never do that, he'd talk to Maggie about it, but it couldn't hurt to scare the kid a little.

And David did look a little scared. *Good.*

The boy glanced at his mom. "Is that okay?" he asked Maggie. "A real job?"

Maggie turned to Ed, her eyes surprised and thankful. "That would be fine," she said. "It's very generous of Mr. Medina—Ed—to let you do that. You better thank him."

"Thank you," David said. "Will I learn how to fix stuff? Lawnmowers and faucets and stuff?"

"If you want," Ed said. "Come in Monday and we'll get started."

"Okay!" David said.

Maggie stood up to go, steering David with her, and Ed turned to her. "David, why don't you go into the store and ask Alberto if there's a store T-shirt that would fit you. If you're going to be an employee, you've got to have the uniform. I need your mom to fill out some paperwork for you."

"Sure!" David said, and bounded out of the storeroom.

"That was wonderful of you, Ed," Maggie said after the door swung shut after him. "I don't know how to thank you."

Ed shrugged, wondering why he'd offered the troublesome kid the job in the first place. It wasn't as though he needed more help in the store, and an eleven-year-old couldn't do much.

On the other hand, he couldn't let a kid in his town turn into a juvenile delinquent if he could help it. He didn't want the kid ripping off all the stores on Main Street. Or doing something worse.

"I imagine the worst punishment will be what he gets when he gets home."

"He'll get punished," Maggie agreed. "But to give him a job. That's fantastic."

"There's something else," Ed said. "He might not just be stealing. He might be sniffing, too. He bought Super Glue this morning, and you were in here last Saturday buying some. No matter how many repairs you're making, you can't use up that much Super Glue in a week. I wondered if I should call you."

"You can call," Maggie said, "if you think the kids are doing something they shouldn't. I want to know." She took a breath. "*Sniffing*. I sure hope not. I'll watch him like a hawk. If he even *peeks* at the Super Glue, I'll ground him until he's twenty-five."

She glanced away, then added, haltingly, "After school, when they're not in a program, they're supposed to go to my mom's store until I get home from work. But sometimes they go to friends' houses. They're allowed, but I don't think David's friend Ben is a good influence on him."

Ed nodded. Raising kids wasn't easy, especially when there was only one parent.

"I'll keep an eye on him over here," he said. "I can find stuff for him to do, and a hardware store is probably a more interesting place for a boy than a shop like your mom's. If you want, I can get him tired pretty quickly. There's a lot of heavy lifting goes on around here. Just give me the word." He smiled at her.

"Thank you again," she said.

He led her out of the office, back into the brightness of the store. "Don't worry about it," he said.

After they left, Alberto came over to where he stood near the front counter. "So you're giving the juvenile delinquent a job now?"

Ed would have bet his store that, had they been outside, Alberto would spit on the street. He shrugged, tamping down his annoyance, but honestly curious.

"What should I have done? The kid stole from us. We'll get some cheap labor from him. Maybe he'll learn a lesson. Anyway, somebody has to intervene before he goes too far down the wrong road."

Alberto shook his head, disgusted. "We won't get no decent work from a kid that young."

"Probably not. But I don't want him stealing from us anymore. Not him, and not any of his friends, either. This way, maybe he'll feel like he has a stake in the store. I'm hoping, anyway."

"You're only doing it because you got an itch for that kid's mama."

Ed turned on his father, feeling some anger.

"Please speak more respectfully of her," he said. "She is a hard-working person doing the best she can, and yes, I do like her. And if she and I decide to do anything about that, it won't be any of your business."

"Pah," Alberto said with contempt. "You know I got nothing against Maggie Jorgenson, except for who she is, what you want with her, and who her kids are."

And wasn't that just about everything. Exasperated, Ed watched his father stomp to the back of the store. What did his father expect? He was a grown man, old enough to know his own mind—*way* old enough—and owner of the biggest business in Cedarburg. He wouldn't let his parents dictate who his friends were—or who he dated.

Still, if he ever did ask Maggie for a real date, his parents wouldn't like it. And they'd let Maggie—and her kids—know about it.

Chapter 11

Over at the Elite Gift Shoppe, Doris Perl rang up Millie Rathke's purchase, a bronze bust of Scheherazade that Millie wanted to give her granddaughter, who had a new job teaching English at the high school. Doris would miss old Scheherazade. The pensive statue of the storyteller from *1001 Arabian Nights* had been gracing her store shelves for almost ten years, and in her more frivolous moments had displayed strands of rhinestones, festive scarves, and once, a Santa cap. But now Millie had bought her and wanted her gift wrapped.

"I'll just go downstairs for a box," Doris said.

She opened the basement door and went down into the soft mustiness. The basement was huge and dry, and Doris rummaged around until she found a box that would be big enough. Then she grabbed a bag of shredded newspaper she kept for these occasions. Both her back and her arm twinged as she muscled the big box and the bulky bag back up the stairs. She wasn't as young as she used to be. Tonight she'd need a long, hot soak in the tub.

She buried Scheherazade in the shredded paper inside the box, and then sealed and wrapped the package with festive gold paper and hand-tied a red bow. As she curled the ribbon, she felt the twinge in her arm again. It was going to be a long day if this pain kept up.

After Millie left, Doris rearranged the shelf to fill the hole that Scheherazade had left, moving over the fanciful glass flower vase and lifting up the potted philodendron from where it had been on the floor. On Monday she could do more to rearrange the shelves and maybe the windows, too. On Saturday there were too many customers to do much other than space things out when something sold.

She backed up to study her handiwork and decided it would do for now, and then turned to see that her doormat had bunched up when Millie left. *Somebody could trip over that,* she thought, and bent down to straighten it out. Out of nowhere a blinding pain shot down her arm and through her chest. She could feel sweat break out on her forehead and into her scalp, and suddenly she couldn't breathe. *A hot bath isn't going to fix this*, she thought before she collapsed onto the cool, polished wood floor of the shop.

DAMN DONALD NENNIG, the bloody wanker, and the horse he rode in on, Ian thought, as he walked down Main Street, cursing the entire Nennig family from Donald to his brother, Joe; their recently and dearly departed mother, Edith; and any other Nennig family members he had yet to meet. Donald had stood him up at the jewelry shop for about the fifteenth time since they'd arrived. At this rate he'd die of old age and be buried next to Edith before he got the bloody diamonds sold.

Ian glowered at the downtown shoppers, the shop fronts, the sidewalks, and the bright blue sky, hating the town, their situation, and his powerlessness to improve it. And then he realized that something was wrong with the shop he'd just passed.

He went back to look. There, lying in the empty shop, was a woman, an old-ish sort of woman, crumpled up on the floor and passed out there in a heap.

Ian gazed up and down the street, wondering what he should do. He saw kids and shoppers across the road. Cars driving by. He was closest, and the old lady was lying there, not moving. He decided to go in.

Her leg was pushing against the door, and Ian had to nudge her aside a bit to enter, but as soon as he was in the shop he could see that she was very ill, not passed out as he'd thought. Her face was grayish and her breath labored; a pale sheen of sweat glistened on her face.

Ian knelt down. "I'm going to call an ambulance," he said, not knowing if she could hear him, but her eyes flickered open.

"Yes," she said softly on an exhale.

Ian went behind the counter where he found the phone. He stalled, not sure what emergency number you called here in Iowa, but then he saw "911" on the speed dial. He called, and the dispatcher said they'd send an ambulance right away. He took that with a grain of salt, though. "Right away" could mean a long time in some places.

There was a tiny sink behind the counter, which was lined with items used for potting plants. Ian saw a drinking glass there, and he filled it with water, taking a small bottle out of his pocket and shaking out a pill. Then he knelt again beside the woman and lifted her head and shoulders.

"I want you to take this pill," he said. "It will help you."

The woman opened her mouth and Ian dropped the aspirin on her tongue, then handed her the water. Some of it spilled out the sides of her mouth when she swallowed.

"Did it go down?" Ian asked.

The woman grimaced and nodded.

"It's an aspirin," Ian said. "I think you're having a heart attack."

The woman's eyes flickered. "I think so, too," she said.

Now what? Ian hated illness. And the woman, still gray, still breathing heavily, lying on that hard wooden floor, appeared to be both very ill and very uncomfortable. He took off his jacket, folded it several times, and put it under her knees. Then he took off his sweater, folded it several times, and put it under her head.

"Now we'll wait for the ambulance," he said.

It seemed like an hour, but of course it wasn't, by the time the paramedics arrived. They bustled in with the gurney, lifted the woman, attached an IV, stuck an oxygen tube in her nose, and prepared to roll her out to the ambulance.

"You a relative?" one of them asked.

"No," said Ian.

"If you find a relative, we're going to Mercy Hospital," the paramedic said. "Have them bring insurance information."

"I gave her an aspirin," Ian said. "Three hundred fifty milligrams."

The old woman opened her eyes then.

"Call Maggie, please," she said. "And thank you."

The paramedics rolled the gurney into the ambulance and jumped in after it. The ambulance took off, lights and siren flashing, leaving Ian alone in the Elite Gift Shoppe, holding his sweater and jacket.

Call Maggie? he thought. Was everybody in this town related to everybody else?

He sighed. What kind of life was this for an honest jewel thief? Here he was, practically living, if you could call it that, in Smallville, Iowa. He couldn't find Donald Bloody Nennig if his life depended on it, and then when he turned around, he was keeping somebody company while they had a massive coronary.

He didn't have Maggie's number, but the old woman surely did, so he went back to the phone and looked around for a phone book or card file. And sure enough, there in the card file, he found Maggie Jorgenson, so he called.

She sounded like she'd run to the phone. Ian remembered her, all that vitality and warmth, and how she was ruining her health with all those fats and refined carbohydrates she liked eating. He bet she didn't take a single vitamin or supplement, either.

"Thank you so much for helping her," Maggie said fervently, when he'd finished explaining what had happened.

"I'm going to the hospital right now. Can you close the shop? There's a lock on the door, just a latch, really, you can close the door behind you and it should lock automatically. It'll be safe enough." Ian promised to lock up, and they disconnected. And then when he turned around, three customers smiled at him expectantly.

"I was wondering about those candlesticks in the window," the first woman said.

Ian thought about telling her the shop was closed, but he didn't have anything better to do, not until Donald Nennig decided to grace them with his presence. The afternoon stretched long before him.

He walked over to the display. "Gorgeous, aren't they? Let me show them to you."

MAGGIE BURST INTO the hospital, Emmy balanced on her hip and clinging to her neck, and Kyle and David following in her wake. The information desk directed them to the ward, and in minutes, she'd had a quick chat with the doctor and a short visit with Doris. The visit was not reassuring: Doris's color was poor and Maggie was scared to see all the tubes running into her nose and arms and under hospital gowns. The nurse explained what everything was for, but the machines, drips, pumps, and computers made everything seem like a set from a science fiction movie, not a comforting sight.

The drama of the ward passed to the drudgery of insurance claims and verifications. Kyle and David hung out in the waiting room, watching Emily and doing a pretty good job of entertaining her. David seemed more like the bright boy he used to be, bragging to Kyle that he had a job at the hardware store, rather than the surly teenager he'd been threatening to become.

Once the insurance was taken care of, Maggie got a list of things to bring Doris from home. With the kids getting restive, Maggie decided it was time for comfort food. She gathered the kids and headed for the Wee Bite.

BY FIVE O'CLOCK, Ian was ready to call it quits. The store had been busy all day, and he'd sold some big stuff. Who knew he'd have such a flair for retail? He was especially pleased that he'd been able to sell the overpriced hand-blown glass bowl to that pretentious twit in the ugly suit. The shite wouldn't know quality merchandise if it sat up and bit him on the arse.

He gazed around the shop, feeling satisfied. Some of the shelves looked a little empty of stock now. He should see if there was anything he could put in those spots. He'd been lucky that everything was so well marked. No questions about what he should charge. The only bad moment had been the jewelry. He'd felt silly displaying the jewelry, but he'd sold some despite his embarrassment.

He tidied the trays of earrings his last customer had looked at and then rearranged them to put all the pearl sets together, all the like gems together, all the plain gold together, until he was happy with the display. Then he wondered where the old woman kept her stock. He opened a door and found a closet, then found the door going into the basement.

A half-hour later he'd brought up a dozen or so more items. The prices weren't marked on these, but Ian had never been anything if not creative with pricing structures. He'd found two identical forged metal umbrella stands, so he put artificial flowers in one and the woman's umbrella in the other, side by side at the door. He arranged the English tea service on a tray and put it in the window, taking out the carved wooden elephant to do so and putting that front and center on the middle shelf. When he stepped back to inspect his efforts, he decided that everything looked inviting.

He wondered how much money he'd taken in. He'd been so busy, he hadn't been able to keep track. He opened the cash register, took out the crumpled bills that crowded the slots, and started to count. Fifteen minutes later he held almost eight hundred dollars in his hands. Of course, he didn't know what she'd started with, so say seven hundred dollars. Not bad for a day's work.

He straightened the piles of bills, counted out one hundred dollars, put that back in the cash register, and stuck the last seven hundred dollars into his wallet. That should take care of his paycheck. Then he turned out the lights and closed the door behind him on his way out.

MAGGIE PULLED INTO the driveway, the heavenly smell of Peg's meat loaf in their take-out containers driving her crazy. She was hungry, thirsty, and ready to collapse from fatigue and worry. The kids were hungry, thirsty, tired, and fussy. Soon, though, the hungry and thirsty part would be taken care of.

"David, Kyle," she said, as she turned off the ignition and popped the trunk, "take in the bags from Peg's, please, and whatever groceries you can carry. I'll get the rest."

"Okay," David said, getting out of the car.

Maggie lifted Emmy out of her car seat. Holding her keys and the fussing toddler, she grabbed the grocery bags from the trunk. But Emmy kicked and the keys slipped out of her fingers. Before she knew it, the key ring had dropped with an audible rattle into the dark recesses of her car.

She felt around. The keys weren't under the grocery bags or in the wheel well. So where *were* they?

David and Kyle got antsy, whining that they wanted to go into the house. Emily was cold and started to whimper. And still, no keys. And without the keys, they weren't getting in the house.

It wasn't her most stellar moment. She was frustrated. She was worried. She was hungry. She raised her foot and kicked the bumper of her car. Her faithful, reliable car, which had served her without complaint, through winter and summer, for almost fifteen years.

And she was rewarded with a slight clink.

A *clink?* From the *bumper?* Maggie kicked the bumper and heard it again. She reached down, felt the small gap between the bumper and the body of the car. Unbelievable. The keys had slipped *into* the bumper of her car.

How to get them out? She could whack the bumper off, if she never wanted to have the bumper again. But she had kids—she did want to have that little bit of protection. Maybe she could pull the keys out with something.

She strapped Emily back into her car seat and then went into the garage, where she found a piece of wire. She shaped it into a hook and then slid it into the bumper and fished around for ten minutes, and although she touched the keys, she couldn't hook the keys with the wire.

She was out of ideas. Her doors were locked, and although her house was held together with Super Glue, her doors and windows were secure. Safety first, after all.

"David," she said. "Take your bike and run over to the hardware store and tell Ed or Alberto or Jason—whoever's there—that we've locked ourselves out of the house. Ask him to bring over whatever he needs to get us back in. New lock, new keys, a hammer. Whatever."

Fifteen minutes later, David was back with Ed. She had huddled up on the porch with Kyle and Emily and opened the takeout containers to feed the kids, because who knew when they'd get inside? In the meantime, they were cold and tired, she was terrified about her mother. She knew the three of them looked like desperate homeless people. She didn't care. She just wanted to get inside where it was warm.

Ed and David piled out of Ed's truck, David's bike in the truck bed, and Ed lifted out his toolbox and climbed the stairs to the porch. He smiled cheerfully. *Way* too cheerfully, in her view.

"Trouble?" he asked.

Chapter 12

Maggie glared at him, broad and solid on her front porch, and felt a wave of annoyance flow through her. Some people were too damn competent for their own good. She rolled her eyes.

"My keys fell into the bumper of the car," she said. "We can't get in the house."

"I didn't know it was possible to lose keys in the bumper of a car," Ed said, setting down his toolbox. "How did you manage it?"

"One thing led to another. So now either we whack off the bumper, or we change or rekey the lock. Or break a window. Whatever. I'm not fussy."

"What about your car keys?" Ed asked. "How will you get those back?"

"I've got a spare set in the house," Maggie said, holding out a green bean for Emily. "If I ever get in the house again."

"If you're okay with your security setup, let's rekey the lock," Ed said. "That's cheapest. David, you can help. Here's the first thing you'll learn how to fix. We don't get a lot of calls to rekey locks, this being a law-abiding community, but every so often something dramatic and unexpected happens, like accidents with keys and car bumpers. It pays to be prepared."

David grinned, not quite daring to laugh.

"Just what I need," Maggie said, "my elder son and the hardware guy taking cheap shots at my expense."

"I wouldn't exactly call them *cheap* shots, house calls being what they are," Ed said. "We're wondering if you wouldn't rather use Super Glue as a closing mechanism for your doors rather than locks. Somehow locks seem so boring."

"Am I paying for this?" Maggie asked. "I don't think I'm paying for this."

"All part of the service," Ed said and then ruffled Kyle's hair and opened the toolbox.

"How's the swing?" he asked him, and set to work showing David what he was doing, poking and jabbing, taking out the existing cylinder, removing pins, installing new ones. David handed over tools like a surgeon's assistant and sometimes did some poking himself, Ed looking pleased when he got the hang of it.

"We'll have to make you an apprentice," he said when they were finished, and David grinned.

"There you go," Ed said, dusting off his hands and dropping a new set of keys into Maggie's hands. "Maybe you want to keep a set of keys outside so you won't lock yourself out. Like in the garage or underneath a flower pot or someplace else you can reach. Not like inside the bumper."

"Thanks," Maggie said. She'd never wanted to keep a set of house keys outside because she never wanted the possibility of John's finding them and letting himself in when she wasn't home. But now that she saw how cold and hungry her kids were—and Ed, who'd had to leave his store at closing time to rekey her door so she could get into her house—that didn't seem like the best idea anymore.

"Come in and have some meatloaf," she said to him. "We only need to warm it up a bit. Unless you have to lock up the store? And I'll write you a check."

"Okay," Ed said. "Store's locked up. David was lucky to catch me. I'd love some meatloaf, if there's enough to go around."

Maggie stared at him while he went down the porch steps and locked his toolbox away in the cab of his truck. *Tonight* he accepted a meal invitation? Tonight, when they were all tired, cold, and crabby? His timing sucked.

She stood up with Emily, stabbing the new key in the lock, and Kyle gathered up Peg's takeout boxes. Ed came back up the porch steps with a small black oblong box.

"I found something for Kyle the other day," he said. Kyle perked up, dropping the food boxes back on the bench.

"You did?" he asked, going to Ed to see. "What?"

Ed handed him a DVD. "I'm hoping you still have some old technology."

Of course they did.

"*Batting Skills for the Young Player*," read Kyle. "Wow. By Alex Rodriguez! Do you think it will help?"

"Can't hurt," Ed said.

"I'll check it out," Kyle said. "Thanks. Mom, let's go in so we can watch."

"Grab the food, then." Maggie turned the key in the lock and pushed the door open.

"It opens," she said. "A miracle. The car keeps its bumper another day." The boys darted inside and up the stairs, and Maggie carried in Emily. "Thank you for that, too," she said, turning to Ed. "The video, I mean."

"My pleasure," he said, smiling at her.

Maggie walked into the kitchen, putting Emmy on the floor and giving her some toys to play with. "Just let me re-heat the food a bit. Would you like some salad? That would be easy to add."

"Whatever you have in the boxes is fine," Ed said. "No need to fuss on my account."

Maggie put the food into bowls and stuck the first bowl in the microwave, then went to the refrigerator and opened the door.

"Beer?" she asked. "Something softer? Stronger?"

"Whatever you're having," Ed said. "Beer would be good."

He's not a picky eater, Maggie thought, grateful for small mercies. Of course, she'd interrupted his dinner hour. She took out two beers and uncapped them at the edge of the counter, handing one to Ed. She tilted her own back and took several deep swallows.

"My mom's in the hospital," she said when she put the beer down. "Heart attack." Her eyes filled with tears, which she brushed away impatiently, hating the sudden loneliness and fear that flooded her heart.

ED HAD WATCHED her drink her beer, thinking that nothing seemed to wear Maggie down, she always kept her sense of humor. *That's the great thing about her*, he thought, but when she told him that Doris was in the hospital, he could see how worried she was. No wonder she'd lost her keys. Sometimes events piled up on a person. Ed wished she had a dozen doors he could rekey for her, and then he put down his beer and went over to put his arms around her. She resisted for a second, and then with a sniff wrapped her arms around him. He cradled her head against his shoulder, stroking her hair, running his fingers through it, feeling its softness.

"Doris had a heart attack?" he asked, leaning his cheek against her hair. "I hadn't heard. How bad is it?"

"Maybe not too bad." Maggie sniffed against his chest, relaxing against him. "It happened this afternoon. Ian Strachan—I don't know if you know him, he's Donald Nennig's associate?—found her right away and called the ambulance. And gave her an aspirin, too. The doctor said that was quick thinking."

"That's good." Ed stroked her back, not knowing what else to say.

"We went to see her. She talked to us a little, but mostly she was sleeping."

"That has to be good, right? Resting must be good."

"I guess so." Maggie sniffed again. "They put in a stent."

"They know a lot about heart conditions these days," Ed said, still stroking her back and now her hair, too. "They'll be able to help her."

"I guess so," Maggie said again, rubbing her head against Ed's shoulder.

"She's probably working too hard. Needs to cut back more." Maggie hiccupped, which tore his heart, and then lifted her head. She still looked woebegone, with tear trails down her cheeks, but although her eyes were bright with tears, she seemed to have stopped crying.

"If you need anything, call me," he said.

"I will." Her mouth trembled.

"I mean it." He wanted to still the tremor, wanted her defiant and cranky again, like she'd been on the porch. "Doris is a friend of mine. I've known her a long time. Sat on all those damn committees with her. She's tough. She'll get through this. Whatever you need from me, just ask."

And then her mouth was on his as soft as a butterfly's wing, brushing against his lips, her breath a gentle whisper against his own.

WHEN SHE KISSED HIM, Maggie knew she was responding to the comfort he offered, and it worked, too. Warmth stole through her. She felt courage returning, hope returning, strength returning, and when he responded, she felt energized, taking all the strength he offered. She ran her hands over his back and wanted him closer. She wanted the fulfillment his mouth promised.

"Mom? Is dinner ready?" David yelled as she heard the thundering of feet on the stairs.

She jerked away, regretting the loss of the moment and the heat Ed had created. She saw that his shirt was wet with her tears, and she hoped that she hadn't left any mucous trails, too. Quickly she ran her hands through her hair.

"Food's hot," she said, opening the microwave door as the boys burst into the kitchen and Ed turned back for his beer. "Did you wash your hands? Grab some plates."

They heaped up their plates and carried them into the living room to eat. Kyle wanted to watch the baseball video, so he, David, and Ed sat on the sofa and she sat across the room on the recliner with Emily in her lap.

They watched the video, wolfing down meatloaf and mashed potatoes, the boys drinking milk and Ed drinking beer, Emily on Maggie's lap, sleeping, and Maggie feeling inclined to join her. She leaned her head back against the chair. She saw Ed pointing to something on the screen, Kyle nodding. Everybody seemed happy.

The next thing she knew, Ed was lifting a sleeping Emily out of her lap. At some point somebody had covered them with a blanket. The boys were gone, the TV was off, the plates and glasses were cleared away, the living room was clean.

"Did I wake up in somebody else's house?" she asked sleepily.

Ed laughed, gazing down at her. "You needed to rest," he said, swaying from side to side, rocking the sleeping Emily. "You've had a hard day. And I've got to get going."

Maggie felt disappointed. "This was great," she said, struggling to her feet. "The evening recovered, thanks to you."

"You're a brave woman, Maggie. Your kid gets into trouble, your mom winds up in the hospital, you lock yourself out of your house, but meatloaf and beer give you a whole new outlook on life."

"Don't forget the baseball video. That played an important role, too," Maggie said, walking him to the door. "Thank you for everything."

"That's what friends are for." Holding the sleeping Emily in one arm, he wrapped the other around Maggie's waist and pulled her closer. She leaned into him, enjoying the strength and heat of his chest, and smiled up at him. He kissed her, lightly and quickly.

"Here's your daughter," he said, handing over the sleeping toddler and opening the door. He paused. "Well—see you."

"Ed," Maggie said, keeping him, not knowing what she wanted to say, wishing he could stay and create that feeling

of warmth and strength with her again, wishing for something she couldn't even name.

"Maggie," Ed said, smiling at her. He stood in the doorway, comfortable and easy in his body, competent with just
about anything he handled, and Maggie felt a rush of desire.
Here he was, a man she'd known most of her life and wanted
now with the urgency of discovery and the familiarity of long
standing.

"Come again," she said, "when you can stay longer."

He leaned into her and kissed her again, hard this time.
"I will," he said, his breath fanning her cheek. He put his
hand there, caressing her skin, his thumb brushing her lower
lip. She turned her head, leaning into his hand to kiss his
palm.

"I will, Maggie," he said, his voice husky, his eyes holding promise she hoped that he'd keep. "I most certainly will."

Chapter 13

The noon rush was over at the diner, and Peg thought it hadn't ended a moment too soon. She had a headache. Her feet hurt, her back hurt, both her waitresses had called in sick, she'd run out of chili, she'd run out of change, and she'd run out of patience. Maybe it was time she considered a different career—an easier, simpler one—smashing rocks at the state prison, say, or digging ditches someplace where guys called each other Bubba. She'd have to give it more thought when she had the time and energy to think about it.

She'd cleared two tables and was working on the third when Venus Tane opened the door for a customer she'd never seen before.

"Hi, Peg," Venus said. "This fellow needed something to eat, and I told him you cook like an angel." She smiled at the stranger, a dazzling multi-megawatt smile, and then beamed at Peg. The stranger shifted his attention to Peg.

"Got to run," Venus said, heading toward the door.

Neither Peg nor the man noticed her departure. Peg felt dazzled as she gazed at the stranger, who reached out blindly for a counter stool. He was tall and rangy, dressed in a worn trench coat and a serviceable but not stylish suit. He had dark hair and eyes, but it was his face that was remarkable. His face was scarred and pockmarked and creased with folds and dimples and lines that made the Grand Canyon look as flat as the Kansas prairie in moonlight. His was a face that had seen trouble and pain, a face that had seen a lot of the world's darkness and was surprised by none of it.

Then he smiled. And, like a miracle, in that instant his face was transformed into a sculptured thing of beauty.

Peg was mesmerized by the beauty of his smile. And then she walked over to him, wiping her hands on her apron as she went.

"Hello," she said, holding out her hand. "My name is Margaret Sontag. People call me Peg."

The big man folded her outstretched hand into his massive one. She could feel the warmth of his skin, the bones underlying it, and the strength that its gentleness overlay.

"Margaret Sontag," he said, saying the name slowly as though he could taste it. "Peggy Sontag. A bonnie name." He smiled at her, and Peg felt a tingle start in her scalp and shiver through her until it reached her toes. "It suits you."

He had a Scots accent, and for a minute she wondered wildly if all of Scotland was emigrating to Cedarburg, Iowa. Her hand was still caught in his large one, and he seemed content to hold it, his thumb caressing her knuckle. His skin was slightly roughened, and she thought she would melt from his touch, drown in his eyes.

"My name is Grayson Mochrie, Peggy Sontag, and I hope you have time enough now that you can join me for lunch or a cup of coffee." His voice was deep and rumbling, although he spoke softly, only to her.

"We're out of chili," she said, breathless. "But everything else is available."

"That's fine, then," he said, squeezing her hand before releasing it. "I'll take whatever you're offering."

MAGGIE HAD JUST finished her cheese sandwich and apple at her desk when Isabel Medina walked into the legal offices of Wusterbarth and Hedrich. Her heart sank. This visit could not be about legal business. Alberto and Isabel's will was updated and on file, and unless the couple wanted a divorce—and there was no gossip that they did—this meeting could only be about her and Ed. Isabel must be on the warpath because she'd found out that Ed had stayed for supper the night before.

Maggie couldn't think of a single way to avoid the conversation. The office was empty except for her. Henry Wusterbarth was in municipal court, and Timmy Hedrich was at the municipal golf course. All the municipals were populated by the lawyers from Wusterbarth and Hedrich. She was holding down the office all by herself for the rest of the afternoon. Isabel had all time in the world to say her piece, whatever it was.

"Maggie," Isabel said.

"Mrs. Medina," Maggie said. "Isabel."

Isabel sat down in the chair next to Maggie's desk.

"You know why I am here," she said.

"You better tell me," Maggie said. She couldn't presume too much. What if, after all, Isabel needed some advice or wanted to have other legal work done? Maggie would never get over the embarrassment if she got this conversation off on the wrong foot.

"You have been dating my son Eduardo," Isabel said.

"I'm not sure I'd call it *dating*," Maggie said.

Isabel rolled her eyes, making a sound with her tongue that sounded a lot like "ptui." Maggie wouldn't have believed it if she hadn't been sitting right there.

"Let us not play games," Ed's mother clearly was not the submissive, eyes-cast-downward female that she gave the impression of being at the hardware store. This woman had a will of iron.

"You have been dating Eduardo," Isabel said again. "Nothing against you, but this must stop. You are not right for him."

"Evidently you *do* have something against me." Maggie felt her blood pressure go up. It was one thing to understand hypothetically that a guy's parents thought that you weren't good enough for their son, but it was another thing altogether to hear it said to your face.

"Maggie." Isabel softened her voice a tad. "You must see this yourself. Eduardo is still a young man. He wants to have children. His *own* children. Your children already have a father. Your oldest boy is almost grown. And now your mother is ill. She needs you. Your family is what it is. Complete. Finished. But Eduardo needs to start fresh."

She was thirty-five and Ed was thirty-eight. And Isabel thought she was finished but Ed needed to start fresh? Like she was a stale loaf of bread left to mold on the shelf, but Ed was yeast waiting to happen?

Isabel might be saying only what she'd thought herself about her relationship with Ed, but she was saying it really badly. After all, every mother wanted what was best for her children. But as much as Isabel might try to push Ed around, she had no right to try to push *her* around.

"Ed has to live his life the way he wants, and so do I," she said. "And whatever we decide to do—to see each other, or not—that is *our* decision to make, not yours."

Isabel snorted. "Pah! You of all people should know that when a person marries, they marry the whole family. You cannot be happy unless the whole family accepts."

"Perhaps," Maggie said. "And perhaps there is no pleasing all the people all the time. Perhaps the whole family should learn to accept that the next generation will make its own decisions."

"We will never agree to your marriage to Eduardo," Isabel said. "Such a thing is not in his best interest."

Maggie tried not to look shocked. Did Isabel and Alberto really have this power over Ed? She couldn't believe it.

"Ed and I are not talking about marriage, so that should please you," she said. "But if he does decide to marry—whoever that is—he doesn't need your approval. He's the best judge of what's good for him, don't you think?"

Isabel stood, one hand on the back of the chair. "I had

nothing against you until today, when I learned that stubbornness is one of your faults. Listen to what I say. Alberto and I—we will never accept the two of you together. You cannot be happy with Eduardo, and he cannot be happy with you. Give him up."

One thing for sure: she and Isabel would never see eye to eye on this.

"Thanks for coming in, Isabel," Maggie said. "I'm glad we had a chance to clear the air."

VENUS WAS PLEASED with her morning's work. She'd helped that nice Scottish policeman find the diner and possibly helped him and Peg find each other, Maggie would soon be going out with her potential future husband, the mail carrier, the *man who came to the door*, not that Venus thought *that* was a good idea, and here at home, her garden was coming along nicely. The lilies were spectacular. The apple and pear trees had taken root. The sweet alyssum, nasturtiums, Mexican sunflowers, and pincushion plants were flourishing. Everything was proceeding exactly as she'd planned, and better than she'd hoped.

Then her cell phone rang.

"Yes," she said optimistically. She heard a lot of static, a few words.

"Dr. J," she said, "say that again." She listened.

"You *told* me already. The one who carries the mail to the door. I *know* that's what you said. But I'm telling you, we can do a lot better than that for Maggie."

She listened again, with less patience this time.

"I *said*, we can do *better*," she shouted into the phone. "But you're the boss. The mail carrier it is. But when I get back, we have to talk."

Irritated, she disconnected just as Mars came out the back door and down the steps. He'd been upstairs, lifting weights in the spare bedroom. His T-shirt was sweat soaked in a V that started at his shoulders and tapered to his waist, and the muscles in his powerful legs flexed as he walked.

Venus felt her mouth go dry as she watched him approach, and he grinned knowingly as he handed her one of the two glasses of lemonade he carried and dropped onto the bench beside her.

"The boss?" He nodded at her phone. "What did he want?"

Venus rolled her eyes. "He's lost his mind," she said. "He called *again*. Told me *again* that I'm supposed to set Maggie up with the mail carrier. Which I *know*. And now he has another job lined up for us, so we're supposed to get the lead out, he says. What's up with *that?*"

"The gods work in mysterious ways." Mars took a long drink of lemonade, letting his hand drift into Venus's hair.

"The connection is lousy," Venus said, still annoyed, drinking some of her own lemonade but tilting her head into Mars's hand. "We've got bad phones or bad service or bad luck, I don't know. But when we go back, I swear I'll get that guy a laptop and smartphone and shove him into the current decade."

"He'll love that," Mars said, and Venus laughed, because they both knew that Dr. J, their boss, was a technophobe. She leaned against Mars, cradling her head on his shoulder.

"Do you have anything to do today?" She felt the hardness of his chest and laid her hand along his thigh, enjoying the play of skin and muscle.

"I have to get down to the diner pretty soon." Mars nuzzled her hair, breathing in the scent of her.

"Pity. Are you taking a shower first?"

"Yes." Mars sucked out the last drop of his lemonade and licked the last bead of moisture off the glass.

Venus rubbed his thigh, letting her fingers trail along his skin. "I could help you with that."

"That would be nice." Mars disentangled himself from her and stood, pulling her up with him and against him, where he held her close. His gaze melted her bones. "But I'm not giving you a pedicure until tonight."

Venus smiled. "I think my polish will hold up until then."

A SHORT TIME LATER, Mars, showered, shaved, and dressed in clean jeans and a crisp shirt, entered the diner, which was empty except for Ray Corkin, who sat at the counter next to the cash register eating a sandwich. Mars took a seat a couple of stools down from Ray. He heard dishes clattering from the kitchen, and pretty soon Peg saw him and came out to take his order.

"How's it going, Peg?" he asked, glancing at the specials on the blackboard.

"Big news, Mars," she said. "A Scottish policeman was in earlier today."

Ray sharply lifted his head, his sandwich poised in mid-air. "A Scottish policeman?"

Peg nodded, smiling. "Maybe you know him. It's a small country, right? Grayson Mochrie."

"Don't think I've had the pleasure." Ray turned back to his sandwich.

"Mr. Mochrie is far from home," Mars observed.

"He is," Peg agreed, taking out her order pad. "Now, what can I get you?"

"What's the soup today?" Mars asked, and proceeded to order his lunch.

DAMN! RAY SAT AT the counter and munched on his sandwich, now gone as tasteless in his mouth as haggis on cardboard. *The polis on their heels!* And they hadn't gotten rid of the goods yet. As soon as he was finished here, he'd let Ian know. They had to take some serious steps either to unload the diamonds or get out of town—and did they even have enough money to do that? Mickey had that job at the petrol station, but he hadn't been paid yet. Ian gave them twenty quid every morning, money he was taking off the top from that shop he went to every day.

But it wasn't enough. And he hated taking that money

from Ian, like he was a kid getting spending money from his daddy.

What could he do to help set them to rights? Perhaps the contents of the diner's cash register could help.

Peg went back to the kitchen to fix the big guy's lunch, and then the guy headed to the rest room. Otherwise, the diner was empty. *Now.*

He leaned over the cash register and punched a couple buttons. The drawer popped open, and he was glad to see that lunch business had been brisk. He reached in, his hand closing first around the crumpled stack of twenties, when suddenly somebody grabbed his other arm, pulling it up high and tight behind his back. A white-hot bolt of pain stabbed through this shoulder.

"I'd put that back," a deep, soft voice said. *Mars*, that's what Peg had called him.

Ray hesitated, and he felt his arm jerked higher. His shoulder socket gave a little, and Ray gasped from the pain. He let go of the money.

"That's better," Mars said. "Now close the drawer."

Ray closed the cash drawer. Mars lowered his arm somewhat, releasing the pressure on the shoulder socket, and Ray turned his head to see the big guy who just a second ago had gone to the rest room. He pushed Ray away from the cash register and shoved him against the stool.

"Sit," he said in a voice that you wouldn't want to contradict. Ray sat.

"How did you get behind me so fast?" he asked, rubbing his shoulder and flexing his arm. He'd have a strain tomorrow, maybe even a bruise, but otherwise, everything was fine.

"Magic," the big guy said. "Don't do that again. I'll know if you try."

Ray scowled. There was something about this guy, he didn't know what.

"I need money," he said.

"You guys are hopeless," Mars said.

Ray nursed his shoulder. He wished he knew what the big guy was thinking, and when he smiled, Ray got angry as well as worried. Who did this guy think he was, pushing him around?

"The Strodthoffs need a hand on their farm," Mars said. "They'll pay minimum wage and room and board. Tom's at the hardware store now. We'll finish lunch and go talk to him."

"I don't need a job."

"You need money," his abuser said. "And you're not getting it this way. You can do it my way, or you can accept some serious pain."

Ray thought about his choices. "I grew up on a farm," he said. "I could do that."

"I know," Mars said, amused.

Peg came out of the kitchen, holding a steaming bowl and a plate piled high with greens. "A bowl of split pea and a large garden salad, coming up," she said.

"Smells delicious," Mars said, sniffing the air and pulling a napkin out of the dispenser on the counter. "Finish your sandwich," he said to Ray. "Where you're going, you'll need your strength."

After lunch Ray and Mars walked almost companionably to the hardware store. When they got there, they found Tom Strodthoff talking to Ed and Alberto Medina about the prospects for next year's yields.

"The Farmers' Almanac has never let me down," Alberto said, his voice emphatic. "Twenty years I worked with Herman Scholz, and it was like magic. Everything that book said, happened."

"But does it account for global warming?" Tom Strodthoff demanded. "I'm telling you, in the *forty* years I've been farming, we've never had such a late summer as we've had this year. It's extending the growing season by *weeks*."

Mars cleared his throat. The three men turned to him.

"Tom, this is Ray Corkin," he said to Tom Strodthoff. "I heard you talking in the diner the other day about needing a hand around the farm, and Ray here grew up on a farm and

143

is looking for work."

Tom stared at Mars, startled. "I been thinking about whether I should hire a hand, that's true," he said. "I hadn't really decided yet."

"It's a big farm," Mars said.

Tom nodded. "Katrina's away at college and not any help except during school breaks, which you can't count on forever, and Elsbeth, my youngest, is busy in high school. But I don't remember saying at the diner that I needed a hand."

"You must have," Mars said.

Tom gazed at Mars for a long second before transferring his gaze to Ray. "Where was your folks' farm?" he asked.

"Not too far from a wee town called Thornhill, in the Scottish Lowlands," Ray said.

"Scotland, eh?" Tom said. "You're kind of far from home. What did your folks farm?"

"A few cows," Ray said. "Fodder crops. Some vegetable crops."

Tom nodded, and the other men peered at the floor, the walls, and out the door, while Tom thought.

"Can't pay much," he said finally. "Room, board, and eighty a week. Until we get the hay in."

Ray glanced at Mars, who crossed his arms. Ray turned back to Tom and nodded. "That suits," he said.

Tom stuck out his hand for Ray to shake. "Come on out tomorrow, if you've a mind to," he said.

"I'll do that," Ray said, shaking his hand. Then he and Mars nodded to Tom and the Medinas and headed for the door.

"See that you go," Mars said, once they were outside. "You won't regret it."

"I'll think about it."

"Remember what I said. You *don't* go, you answer to me. But you'll love it at the Strodthoffs." Mars grinned and slung his arm around Ray's shoulder. "You would not believe the scenery around there."

144

IT WAS NEARLY DARK when Maggie saw Ed's white pickup truck pull into the driveway and David hop out.

"He's home now," she said into the phone cradled against her shoulder. "Hang on a second. I want you to tell him." She opened the door and carried the phone outside.

"David," she said, "your father wants to talk to you."

He'd turned back to say something to Ed through the truck window, but he whirled when he heard her, his face breaking into a huge smile.

"Dad wants to talk to me?" he said, bounding up the stairs, grabbing the phone from her hand.

"Dad?" he said, going into the house. Maggie watched him go, a troubled expression on her face.

"Everything all right?" Ed asked through the window. He'd left the truck running, and she walked down the driveway to talk to him.

"It's John," she said, leaning her elbows on the window frame so she could see him eye to eye. "He's not taking the kids this weekend."

Ed kept his eyes straight ahead, his hands on the wheel. "Tough on them," he said.

"Yes." She sighed and glanced toward the house, but David had disappeared. "With Emmy, it's not a big deal. She wasn't even born when he left. But with the boys, it's heartbreaking." She shook her head. "I'm sorry. I don't mean to burden you with this."

Ed started to say something, but just then David came out onto the porch, looking a lot different than the boy who had gone into the house a minute before. His shoulders sagged, his feet dragged, his head was bowed. He trudged over to them in the driveway.

"We're not going to Dad's this weekend," he said, his voice flat.

"I'm sorry, sweetie," Maggie said.

"He said he'd make it up to us," David said.

"I'm sure he will," Maggie said, helplessly.

"Works out for me," Ed said. David and Maggie both

stared at him.

"I was going to ask you and your mom if it would be okay if you worked a few hours this weekend. We're going to be extra busy with the fall sale on Saturday and Sunday."

"I guess I might as well, now," David said, slumping against the truck.

"That's the spirit," Ed said.

"David, go in the house and get washed up for supper," Maggie said. "We're about ready to eat."

She watched David go into the house before she turned back to Ed. "Thank you for doing that," she said.

He shrugged. "We can put him to work," he said. "It will be better for him than brooding. And maybe after work we can all do something—go to the drive-in or a movie. Or bowling. If it isn't league night." He grinned at her, and she smiled back, feeling better.

"We'll see," she said.

He held her gaze a second longer, still smiling, and then shifted the truck into reverse, ready to go.

"Ed," she said. "Did you want to stay for supper?" she asked, feeling breathless. *What am I doing?* she thought *Isabel will kill me. I'm not ready yet. It's too soon. Forget about him. Forget about this.*

He shook his head, looking rueful.

"I wish I could," he said. "I promised my folks I'd drop by."

And I know what they want to talk about, Maggie thought.

"Saturday," he said, a gleam in his eye and his voice, low and husky, promising her secret things, lovely things. "Dinner. Something with the kids. And dessert. Count on it."

If she were ice cream, she'd have melted on the spot.

Chapter 14

Grayson Mochrie was jet-lagged, tired, hungry, bewildered, and irritated, and he needed a shave, a shower, and a break in the case. He'd come to what had to be the smallest town in the smallest state in America to track down the tail end of a far-reaching criminal syndicate. He'd expected to find Donald Nennig and the three couriers immediately, because how hard could it be to find the American boss of an international crime ring and three low-end Scots jewel thieves in a town this tiny?

He'd thought that the four crooks would leave a trail of stolen gems, precious metals, and laundered currency from one end of the state to another, but so far, he had nothing. Well, maybe not *nothing*—he had a sleep-deprived body, a food-deprived stomach, an intelligence-abandoned brain, a days' worth of stubble, and a crumpled suit. If you wanted to call that something.

The coordinating law enforcement agencies had been working on this case for almost two years, and since he'd been in the States, his colleagues back home had swept through the ring's Glasgow headquarters. Only Nennig and these three runners had escaped the dragnet. Somehow, they'd gotten away. They'd been lucky. They wouldn't be lucky twice.

But in a town whose population had to number in the

low thousands if not the high hundreds, he hadn't found them yet. Which made him feel about as clever as a cow patty at a national bakeoff. Grayson Mochrie wanted to find them before they found out that the ring had been smashed in Europe, before they took flight.

But first he needed lunch.

He drove his rental car to the diner and found a space right in front. Parking was never much of a problem in Cedarburg, but at three in the afternoon, the lunch crowd had long since moved on. The bell jingled as he opened the door, and he saw to his satisfaction that the small eatery was empty. Perhaps pretty Peggy Sontag could give him a few minutes for a wee chat.

He sat in a booth and leaned back, stretching out his long legs and closing his eyes. He was getting too old for this. He'd love to be able to stay at home, in his cool and misty highlands, and not chase crooks all over the world. He'd love to work in a small town like this one, where people knew each other and trouble came mostly in small doses. He'd love—

"Grayson?" Peg said.

He opened his eyes, smiling at her, seeing her eyes dark with concern, little crows' feet in the corners, her bonnie face flushed with the hard work she did.

"Peggy, love," he said.

"Are you all right?"

"Just tired." He closed his eyes again, knowing her concern didn't mean anything, that Peggy was the kind of person who would inquire about everyone, even lost and depressed Scots policemen.

"Tired, jet-lagged, irritable, and hungry," he amended.

"I can fix hungry," she said.

He opened his eyes again. "You can fix irritable, too, if you sit with me for a bit."

"I can do that. Let me get you something to eat first."

"I adore you, Peggy Sontag." He smiled at her, meaning every word.

"That's the hunger talking," Peg said, turning away.

PEG WENT INTO THE kitchen to fix a plate for him. She had to remember to keep a grip. To people from Scotland, calling someone "love" meant something like "you" or even "hey." It didn't mean love the way Americans meant love, all the mushy stuff. Like when he said he adored her. It meant nothing. Well—maybe it meant that he liked her. Or that he adored that she was bringing him his lunch. That kind of adoration was better than nothing.

He looked like he needed something sustaining, so Peg dished up a big portion of pot roast and mashed potatoes, covered it with gravy, and added side dishes of green beans and applesauce to the plate. Then she carried the food out to the booth, where Grayson's eyes opened appreciatively at the dish she set in front of him.

"You've saved my life," he said. He spread out a napkin in his lap and dug into the roast with a concentration she found appealing. His table manners were neat and tidy, almost dainty, for such a big man, Peg thought, who often judged people's characters by how they ate their meals.

He lifted his eyes only after he'd made serious inroads into his food.

"The pot roast is delicious," he said, setting aside his knife and fork. "And the potatoes. Everything."

"Thank you. There's more pot roast."

"Good to know," Grayson said. He went back to his meal.

"How's your investigation going?" Peg asked when he'd finished. "Would you like some pie?"

"Terrible," he said. "And yes. Please."

"Apple okay?" she asked, standing up to get it.

"What have I done to deserve food from the gods?"

Peg grinned. "With whipped cream?"

"As much as you've got."

"Coffee? I'm not sure my tea is up to your standards."

"Coffee, please," he said. "Someday I'll show you how

149

to make tea."

"I'd like that. Coffee coming up."

She brought over a piece of apple pie with whipped cream for him and poured them each a cup of coffee. When he'd finished the pie, he told her about the investigation and how tired he was of it all.

"You think Donald Nennig is a—*what?* Crime boss?" Peg asked in shock when he'd finished. "I know it's been a long time since he's lived in Cedarburg, but I can't believe he's a criminal! And Ian, Mickey, and Ray are *jewel thieves?*"

"You *know* them, then?" Grayson seemed to be as shocked as she felt.

"Well, of course, I know them," Peg said, feeling a little defensive. "They eat in here. They're staying at the Lay-Z Stay."

"They're *registered* there," Grayson agreed. "But I haven't ever found them there. And there's not enough manpower to watch the place round the clock."

"It's hard to imagine they're crooks," Peg said. "I mean, Ian's been helping out at Doris Perl's store since she had her heart attack, and I understand he's been doing very well. Mickey has the job at Denny's service station, and Ray is starting at Tom Strodthoff's farm. They all seem like nice guys. Well, Ian's a picky eater. But other than that."

Grayson stared at her. "You know where these chaps are, then?" he asked.

"Sure. A lot of people do. That new guy in town—Mars, Venus's husband? He told Ray about the job at the Strodt-hoffs' right here in the diner. But they've all been in here. I don't think they're trying to hide."

Grayson shook his head and then started to laugh.

"Peggy, love, if you knew all the time I've spent with American coppers, here and in New York, checking with immigration, following up leads that evaporated. I got a search warrant for their room at the motel, but found nothing. I've pounded on doors with photos that got me nowhere. Now it turns out that I would have moved faster if I'd just talked to you."

"Oh, well, photos," Peg said. "If they're anything like the photos on your driver license, your own mother wouldn't recognize you."

"They need you at Scotland Yard," he said. "Your talents are wasted here."

"I bet you say that to everybody who serves you pot roast," Peg said, but she smiled as she got up to clear the dishes.

MAGGIE KNEELED OVER her upended kitchen table and examined how the table's scarred legs joined the tabletop. Her eyebrows were knit in concentration; wayward wisps of her hair escaped the confines of her ponytail. Her hands were as steady as a neurosurgeon's as she applied Super Glue to one of the cross supports of her well-used and weary table and pressed it into place, leaning into it and letting the weight of her body hold the bond until it had set.

She'd wanted to strengthen the table for a while. The legs had always been wobbly, and this week a cross support had come loose. Tonight was a good night to get this job done; she was taking the kids out for pizza so they wouldn't need the kitchen table, and she was just waiting for David to come home from his job at the hardware store before they took off. The glue could set overnight and the table would be as good as new tomorrow when she needed it again.

She let up on the support and nudged it, checking to see if the bond would hold. It looked good, and she moved on to the next one. She squeezed out a ring of glue around the other end of the loose support, fitting it into the join of the tabletop, getting some of the glue on her hands. She should have worn gloves. Super Glue was incredibly strong and fast acting. She wouldn't be able to get that stuff off for days.

The back door shot open, and David came barreling into the kitchen. The draft blew the loose strands of her hair across her face, stinging her eyes. Maggie squeezed her eyes shut and reached up to push her hair away with both hands, tucking rebellious strands behind her ears. She brushed across her lids a couple of times to make sure all the hair was gone.

And she kept her eyes closed for a fraction of a second too long.

"When are we going for pizza?" David asked, dropping his book bag on the floor.

Maggie turned her head to face him. Tried to open her eyes. Tried not to panic.

She couldn't open her eyes.

The muscles in her eyes worked, but her eyes didn't open. Unbelievably, with her brain refusing to understand the concept, she couldn't open her eyes.

Somehow, when she'd brushed her hands across her eyes and squeezed them closed, she'd glued them shut.

She dropped the tube of glue and put her thumb on her cheek and her index finger on the ridge of her forehead, spreading her fingers to force the lids apart. She felt the skin stretch but the lids didn't open.

She tried it on the other side. Same results. Panic bubbled up and flooded her throat.

She tried again, pulling and prying downward on her cheek and upward on the lid. Still nothing.

"Mom? What are you doing?" David asked.

"Nothing," Maggie said. She stood awkwardly, her arms held out in front of her. Reaching for the sink, she held on to the counter with one hand and turned on the hot water with the other. Cupping the running water in her hand, she dashed it against her face repeatedly, then tried to pry her eyes open again. Nothing. Her eyes were as tightly shut as the proverbial barn door after the stolen horse.

Now, she thought. *Now it's time to panic.*

What could dissolve Super Glue that would be safe for the eyes? She knew she had nothing in the house, because she'd already tried everything on her hands from past spills. Nail polish remover, alcohol, gasoline, none of it worked. And none of it should go near her eyes, anyway.

"David?" she asked, still bent over the sink.

"What?" he asked. He had his head stuck in the

refrigerator door. Maggie hadn't heard the door open over the water running, but she could tell from the muffled sound from that end of the room.

"You have to do something for me now," she said. "I've managed to glue my eyes shut. You have to go back to the hardware store and ask Ed for a solvent that can dissolve it. Be sure to tell him it's my eyes."

"*What?*" David asked. Maggie heard the refrigerator door close. "You glued your eyes shut? How did you do that?"

"I used the special techniques of a highly trained specialist," Maggie said. "Could you go now, please?"

"Um, sure. Are you, I don't know, okay?"

"For now," Maggie said. "Go. Ed will give you something to dissolve this, then we'll head out for pizza."

"Okay." David went out the door again, letting it bang behind him. Maggie leaned against the kitchen counter, her back to the kitchen sink, and realized in the quiet just how helpless she was. She heard Emily playing in the next room; so far, that was okay. But if she couldn't open her eyes, it would be next to impossible to take care of her, cook any meals, drive the kids anywhere, do her crossword.

Not being able to see scared her, although she'd tried not to show that to David. What if her eyes never opened? Or what if the glue damaged her vision permanently? How would she cope?

Suddenly she felt very sorry for herself. She slid down the cupboard until she was sitting on the floor, her knees drawn up to her chin. If she was going to feel sorry for herself, she might as well be relatively comfortable.

Fifteen or twenty minutes later she heard steps on the back porch again. Twenty minutes of listening to Emily talk to herself, of listening to the clock tick, of listening to cars go by, driven by people who could open their eyes and see where they were going. Still, the steps on the porch were reassuring. Soon she would be delivered from the heart of darkness, and they could go out for pizza.

But then she realized there were too many footsteps.

David by himself couldn't be making that much noise. *Oh, good*, she thought. *David's brought someone home with him to share in my humiliation. That will be fun.* And then she heard the voices, David's and, yes, of course, Ed's.

"Mom, we're home," David said, coming through the back door.

"Yes, I hear that," Maggie said, embarrassed and feeling angry at feeling helpless. "Got the solvent?"

"No," David said. "There isn't any."

"You're out of solvent?" Maggie asked. "What kind of hardware store runs out of solvent?"

"We didn't run out of solvent," Ed said. Maggie heard him come into the kitchen behind David. "There isn't any solvent that's safe to use on your eyes. You just have to wait until the glue wears off."

If Maggie could have closed her eyes in despair, she would have. As it was, she sagged against the kitchen cupboard. "How long will that take?"

"A couple days." Ed cleared his throat. "Three at the most."

"Three days!" Maggie said, "I can't go around like this for three days!"

"Maybe four," Ed said.

Chapter 15

Four days. "How do you know it will take four days?"

"It's happened before."

Maggie couldn't see it, but she could envision Ed shrugging.

"It's not as uncommon as you'd think," he said. "People glue their eyes shut. The company has a web site up with a page on what to do if that happens. Basically the answer is, nothing."

"They're in the glue business," Maggie said. "That's what they would say. I'm going to call the advice nurse at the hospital."

"She won't tell you anything different," Ed said.

"David, bring me my phone. And dial the advice nurse."

David brought her the phone, speed dialing the advice nurse as he put it into her hand.

"I've Super Glued my eyes shut," Maggie said, when the connection was made. "What can I do?" and then the advice nurse laughed.

"It's not funny," Maggie said. "I really did this. What can I use for a solvent?" She listened, and when the advice nurse disconnected, Maggie held the phone out and David took it from her.

For a second, no one said anything.

"There are solvents," Ed said. "But nothing you can use on your eyes."

"A couple of days," Maggie said. "As many as four." She tried not to think about crying. What good would crying do, anyway? Her eyes were glued shut. Where would the tears go?

She needed to figure out what she could do. She couldn't take care of the kids for up to four days without help. If her mother weren't still in the hospital from her heart attack, she'd ask her to come over for the weekend. She didn't have any friends who weren't married with kids and husbands and jobs of their own. She could ask them for small things, but not for the kind of help she'd need for four days. That left only John. She hated to do it, especially since he'd already told her that he wasn't available this weekend, but this was an emergency. Surely he could help out in an emergency.

"David, hand me the phone, again, please, and dial your father's number," she said. "I need to talk to him."

"Why?" David asked.

"I can't keep Emmy for four days if I can't see," Maggie said. "There isn't anybody else. I have to ask him to come get you guys. It's an emergency. He'll come."

"No, he won't," David said.

"Sure, he will," Maggie said. "I know he disappointed you this weekend, but he loves you. When he hears that I'm laid up, he'll cancel his plans and come get you. You'll see."

"No, he won't," David repeated. "He's not home."

"Not home?" Maggie felt the breath squeeze out of her lungs. *What was she going to do?* "Do you know where he went?"

There was a moment of silence, and Maggie wondered what was happening between him and Ed that she couldn't see. She realized she missed a lot of information by not knowing what was flitting across the faces of her kids.

"No," David said. "He and Cindy were going somewhere. He might have said, but I don't remember."

John couldn't take his kids for a visit because he had to

have a romantic weekend with Wife Number Two. *Great, just great*, Maggie thought.

But self-pity would get her nowhere.

"Call him," she said. "I don't care if he's in *Antarctica*. You dial. I'll talk."

She heard David punch in some numbers and then he nudged her shoulder with the phone, and she took it, listening to it ring.

"Hello," his voice said, as clear as if he were in the next room.

"John, hi, it's me," Maggie said.

"I can't come to the phone right now," John's recording said.

"*Dammit*," Maggie said in frustration. "David, don't repeat that." When John's recording came to an end, she sighed.

"John, I'm having a medical emergency here. I apologize for ruining your plans, but you need to get the kids this weekend. I'll be laid up for four days. Let me know."

She disconnected and held the phone up in the air. Someone took it.

How could she make this work? She couldn't count on John to get her message or, really, respond, even if he did. Her mother was out. David was only twelve. She thought he was basically a good kid and would be willing to help, but she didn't think he could run a household for four days and take care of Emily. And anyway, for two of those days, he'd be at school.

She'd have to call all the babysitters she knew and schedule them to come over in shifts and babysit them for the weekend. They could prepare simple meals and take care of Emily without Maggie freaking out that she couldn't see what the little one was getting into.

Ed cleared his throat. "I could help," he said.

If Maggie could have stared at him, she would have.

"Thanks, Ed, but you have a hardware store to run," she said. "A hardware store that, I might point out, has yet to petition the Super Glue company to make a solvent that's safe and effective for use around the eyes. I'll schedule some babysitters to spend the weekend with us. We'll be fine."

"Don't call Mary Beth," David said. "She's boring."

"Okay, I'll call the others first," Maggie said. "But if we need Mary Beth, we need her. It's only for a couple of days."

"Or four," David said.

"It won't be four days," Maggie said, a grim edge to her voice. "I will take an ice pick to my eyes sooner, I promise you."

"No, really, I could help," Ed said again.

"You could?" David asked. "I'd rather have you than Mary Beth."

"David, stop," Maggie said. "Ed, you have to work. The store has a sale tomorrow. You asked David to work extra hours. You can't hang around here."

"Well, no," Ed said. "I couldn't hang around here 24/7. But if you and Em hang out at the store a bit, and David helps out, I can take some time here and there. We can make it work. It's just for Saturday. We're open on Sunday, but my dad takes Sunday."

Maggie felt the weight on her chest lighten, and then come back again. There was still probably Monday and, heaven forbid, Tuesday. Ed had a business. He couldn't babysit them for four days.

"Thanks, Ed," she said, "but—"

"For a person who's sitting on the kitchen floor with her eyes glued shut, you're awfully argumentative," Ed said. "Listen, it's pizza night. Let's go out. I'm hungry. We'll talk about it. We'll make a plan. I think it'll work."

"*Yes!*" David said. "No Mary Beth! I'll get Kyle," and he tore out of the kitchen and up the stairs to get his brother.

"Kyle! You missed it!" they could hear him yell. "Mom can't see, and Ed's going to babysit!"

"Oh, god," Maggie said.

"It'll be fine," Ed said. "Really." She heard him walk closer and then she felt his hand, comforting and secure on her shoulder. He slid it down her arm and took her hand, pulling her to her feet. He was standing much too close. The warmth of his body radiated to her chest.

On the other hand, it might be fun to have Ed around the house. Stimulating.

Stop that, Maggie thought.

"I need to get my jacket and Emily's shoes and jacket, too," she said. "How are my clothes? Do I have to change?" She probably should. She'd put on her worn jeans to fix the table—the ones that were torn at the knee and spattered with paint and other unidentified substances, probably Super Glue. She'd put on her turquoise and purple plaid flannel shirt because she liked the colors, but it, too, was faded and worn. But she didn't feel up to managing the stairs and figuring out something better to put on.

"You look great," Ed said, "and the clothes are okay for pizza. Just one thing." He pulled out the black scrunchie that had been holding her ponytail. The dark reddish mass of her hair fell free, and she raised her hands to run her fingers through it and shake it loose.

"Let me," he said. "You might still have Super Glue on your hands. It's dry by now, but it might still glomp your hair together." He put his hands on the back of her neck and then opened his fingers and let her hair sift through them, inching his hands up to let his fingers follow the curve of her head, always letting her hair stream through his open hands.

It was a tiny scalp massage. Maggie felt her head fall back and would have closed her eyes if they hadn't already been glued shut.

"That feels great," she moaned. "More. Please."

"Don't be shy, Maggie," Ed said. She could feel the smile in his voice. "Tell me what you really think."

"Okay," she said. "More. Harder. Please." She felt heavy with pleasure as Ed's hands worked over her scalp.

"Maggie? Is there glue on your lips?" Ed asked. She could feel his soft breath feathering her cheek as he leaned closer to see.

"I don't think so," she said. "Why?"

"I'm going to kiss you," he said. "Call me a daredevil."

He touched his lips to hers, tracing their outline with his tongue. She slid her hands up his arms, being careful to confine them to areas covered by fabric.

"So far, all systems go," he whispered into her mouth, and kissed her again, and she could feel him smiling as he nuzzled her nose and cheek before he let her go.

"Just checking," he said. "It would be a terrible thing if David and Kyle came down expecting to go out for pizza and found you and me doing our Super Glued act, joined at the lips."

Maggie laughed and backed up, smacking him on the arm. She tripped over the table still lying upended on the floor, but Ed caught her before she fell.

"Thanks," she said. "This is going to take some getting used to."

"Yeah, and it could be a difficult four days, because by the time you know where everything is when your eyes are closed is about when the glue will wear off."

"I've lived here forever. I know where everything is. Just watch me. I'm going to get Emily's and my coats now." She spread her arms wide and headed to the living room and the coat closet—and walked into the doorframe, smacking her forehead.

"Ouch," she said, rubbing the sore spot.

Ed steered her clear of the doorway and gave her one last, fast kiss as the boys clattered downstairs. "Like I said. You know, it's probably our destiny that you need somebody who knows about hardware and I need a place to practice my housekeeping skills. And you know what they say: you can't escape destiny."

How can I escape destiny? Maggie thought. *I can't even escape the kitchen.*

Ed and the boys got Emily dressed. Kyle steered Maggie to the door, but she went down the stairs by herself, clutching the railing. They took Maggie's car because that's where the car seat was, and Ed settled Emily into it while

David steered Maggie to the passenger side. Then Ed moved his truck to the street and parked it so he could get Maggie's car out of the driveway, and then he came back to Maggie's car and got in.

"All set?" he asked, as he adjusted the seat and buckled the seat belt.

Maggie felt exhausted, like she had followed Hannibal and his elephants across the Swiss Alps barefoot in a blizzard, and all she'd done was walk out of the house and get in the car with her eyes closed.

"This will never work," she said.

"Sure, it will," Ed said. He started the car and put it into gear.

"I don't want Mary Beth," David said.

"Ed's better than Mary Beth," Kyle agreed. "He can drive."

Maggie laughed, for the first time finding something funny in her predicament.

"Thanks, guys," Ed said. "A solid endorsement from the back seat."

"Well, you *are* better," said Kyle. "Can you take me to baseball practice tomorrow?"

"That's part of what we have to figure out," Ed said. "We'll make a schedule at the pizza place."

Getting into the pizza parlor was a mirror image of leaving the house, only Maggie got to feel more like the village idiot. She could hear that the restaurant was packed—well, it was Friday night, after all—and she knew every customer there would be watching her with Ed, who'd be leading her by the hand through the place because her eyes glued shut. But eventually they were all in the booth, with Emmy in a high chair in the aisle and David on one side and Ed on the other to feed her. It felt like the whole operation took four hours.

Ed opened a menu. "What should we get?"

"We always get pepperoni," Kyle said.

"Ed might not like pepperoni," Maggie said.

"I like pepperoni," Ed said. "What about Emily?"

"Emily doesn't eat pizza," Maggie said. "We order a banana for her."

"You can order a banana at a pizza parlor?"

"They have bananas for the ice cream sundaes."

"Of course, they do. What was I thinking?"

After the waitress had taken their order, Ed cleared his throat.

"Let's make the schedule," he said. "Maggie, I'm writing everything down so you know we won't forget anything. So what's first?"

It turned out to be easy. Ed said his father could open the store so he himself could get to work an hour or two late.

"That way I can help you and Emmy get up in the morning," he said.

Maggie didn't want to think about what it would be like if Ed had to help her get dressed. She certainly could put on her clothes without help. The big problem would be *finding* the clothes, or making sure that her top and bottom mostly went together. Maybe she wouldn't kill herself getting to the dresser and finding her underwear. Her underwear was a bit of an embarrassment.

"I'd like to go to the hospital to see my mother," she said. "If we can swing it."

"We can swing it," Ed said. The boys chipped in with what they needed to do, and after some skirmishes, everything got worked out. When the pizza came, Maggie burned her fingers trying to pull a slice onto her plate, so Ed helped her with that and then handed her some napkins to wipe her hands. But then she ate the slice without difficulty, thinking it was brilliant that they were eating food she didn't have to see to cut up.

"I don't feel so much like Helen Keller now," she said.

"I should hope not." Ed patted her leg under the booth. "You were hungry. That would make anyone cranky."

"That and gluing my eyes shut," Maggie agreed. She took another bite of pizza, carefully wiping her mouth afterwards. "I would make a much bigger mess of this if I had to cut anything up."

"We'll have casserole tomorrow," he said. "In bowls."

Maggie felt a rush of gratitude and then lust.

"Thank you, Ed, I'd appreciate that." She returned the pat on his leg, letting her hand linger there for a second, enjoying the play of muscle she felt under his jeans. "I don't know where we'd be without you."

WHEN ED HAD OFFERED to get to their house early to help them—but mostly Emily—get up in the morning, he hadn't counted on the surge of lust he'd feel. He couldn't dwell on what Maggie might look like in the morning, all tousled and dreamy from sleep. Of course, he wouldn't be able to see the sleep and longing—he wished—in her eyes, since those eyes would be glued shut. Still, tousled could work.

But when she put her hand on his leg and left it there, he wondered what she was thinking. He swiveled his head to assess, but of course she couldn't see his face. She must have felt the motion, though, because she turned her head, her face all soft, her mouth all tender, and her eyes all glued shut.

He swallowed. He lived in a town where people took care of each other. As a friend, as a neighbor, he wanted—felt obliged, even—to help her. But his desire to help went way beyond friendship. Not that he could say so here in the diner, in front of her kids, with the whole town watching.

"Stick with me, kid," he finally said. "Everything will be fine."

Chapter 16

Back from the pizza parlor, Maggie slipped off her coat and reached for the closet door, but rather than risk bumping into something, especially Emily, she instead waited for Ed. He said soothing things to the little girl—he really was good with kids—as he took off her jacket and put her down across the room.

"Kyle," she said as the boys clattered around her. "Ed's going to sleep in your room tonight, so move anything you want into David's room."

"That isn't necessary—" Ed said from across the room.

"Yes, it is," Maggie said. "And the boys won't mind, will you, boys? David's got bunk beds in his room for sleepovers."

"Yeah, it's okay," David said. "Can we stay up an extra half-hour?"

"Yes," Maggie said. "Go up now and get yourselves organized."

"Would you like me to give Emmy a bath?" Ed asked as he hung up her coat and the boys scrambled upstairs. "Daily bath time seems to be standard for my little nieces and nephews."

Maggie sighed. "I do usually give her a bath at night, but it's too much to ask."

"It's not a problem," he said. "I've had plenty of practice

with my sister's kids. Let's find something on TV for you to watch while I take her upstairs."

She felt the edge of the sofa against her leg and reached out for it so she could sit down.

"Why bother turning on the TV? I can't see it."

Ed clicked through the remote. "Comedy channel. Always good for a laugh, and you've probably had enough drama for one day. Ah. Here. You like M.A.S.H.?"

Maggie heard Alan Alda make a wisecrack, and she smiled. "Sure, that'd be good."

"Would you like a glass of wine or something?"

"I'd love a glass of wine," Maggie said. "The cupboard next to the refrigerator. There's no wine glasses, but I've got tumblers. One of those—two at the most—should do it. Thank you."

He chuckled. "Be right back."

When he returned, he guided her hand to the glass. Her skin jumped when she touched him. The back of his hand was smooth and soft, but his fingers were roughened from work. She wondered what it would be like to explore the bends and ridges of his hands—potentially a very hot Helen Keller experience.

The glass was full to the brim—thank you, Ed!—and a little spilled over when she took her first sip. She licked the drop away from the corner of her mouth, savoring the bouquet. This eyes-glued-shut thing was giving a whole new perspective to the concept of "blind taste test."

"I'm going now," he said, sounding a little hoarse.

"You okay?"

"I've got it," Ed said. "No worries."

Maggie felt relieved. Emily would have a bath, and she didn't have to give it to her sightless, and she didn't have to rely on David not to drown her. Finally something was going her way.

"Her pajamas are in the top right-hand drawer of her bureau," she said.

"I'll find them." They left the room, Emily chattering

unintelligibly but cheerfully the whole way. *She likes Ed*, Maggie thought.

She listened to the end of the M.A.S.H. episode, drinking her wine, and then the start of the next show, until she heard the clattering of what seemed like dozens of footsteps on the stairs.

"The boys have come to say goodnight," Ed said.

"Night, boys," she said. "Thank you for helping."

"It's weird you can't see," Kyle said.

"It's only temporary," Maggie said.

"Night, Mom," David said.

"To bed with you guys," Ed said. "Tomorrow's another day."

They said goodnight again and clattered back upstairs. Maggie could hear them talking and laughing as they went into their rooms and closed the doors. It all sounded very Walton-family-ish and comforting. She was glad the boys weren't giving Ed any problems. And then Maggie heard Ed's footsteps coming back down the stairs.

"I think I could use some of that wine myself," Ed said as he came into the living room.

"You've more than earned it," Maggie said. "I'm pretty sure there's more."

"There is, for which I thank the shopping gods and your excellent planning." When he came back from the kitchen, he sat on the other end of the sofa. She felt a little nervous, even though he was a relaxing kind of guy. Ed was spending the night—the next couple of nights, in fact, or until the glue on her eyes wore off. Did he have expectations that something would happen between them? She didn't know what to say to somebody she lusted for but wasn't sure she should get involved with. She hadn't had many opportunities to practice her dating skills since her divorce—Ian Strachan and Chuck Winkel notwithstanding.

And now she couldn't see, couldn't read in Ed's eyes what he might be thinking. Even if she could see him, she wasn't sure that she'd be able to tell if Ed felt the same. Why would he be interested in a woman with three kids? And even if she was sure *and* he was sure, they couldn't do anything as long as her kids were in the house.

He wouldn't even be here, sitting on her sofa, if she hadn't glued her eyes shut. Would he think she'd engineered it? To get him alone? The worst part was, she felt like an idiot for doing it. Feeling like an idiot did a lot to curb her libido, which had shown an annoying tendency to flare up in Ed's presence.

"Emily's already asleep," he said. "Cute kid."

"I like her." Maggie took a sip of wine into what had suddenly become a silence that went on too long.

"So I don't want you to take this the wrong way," Ed said finally. "But if the kids weren't here and you hadn't glued your eyes shut and I could look into your eyes and ask you what you wanted and if you agreed, I would totally jump your bones right about now."

Maggie laughed, choking on her wine. Ed refilled her glass, and she still couldn't stop smiling. And feeling happy, too, because if the kids weren't there, she'd totally want Ed to jump her bones.

"So maybe that's an idea for another occasion," she said. "Although—what would your parents have to say about that? I had a very scary conversation with your mother the other day."

"You did? I'm not sure I want to hear about it. And anyway, what *they* want doesn't really come into it. It's not their bones I want to jump."

"Really? Because I thought—"

"Nope. Sure, it'd be simpler if my parents approved all my choices and all my decisions, but when did they ever? Not saying that they'll be a bucket of laughs if we ever do actually date."

Maggie grinned. "Gotcha," she said. "Actually, my kids might not be all that ecstatic about the idea, either."

"So, since bone jumping is off the table, what would you like to do? It's still early. Listen to music? We could dance."

Maggie felt real regret. Dancing would be lovely, but not tonight.

"You know what?" she said. "I want to dance with you again, but now that I'm sitting down, I'm beat. I think the eyes-glued-shut thing is taking more out of me than I realized. I wonder—"

"What?"

"Well, I'm reading a book. It would be boring for you, because I'm in the middle of it, but—would you mind reading it to me for a little while? I think I'd find that soothing."

"Sure, I can do that, although I won't swear to my dramatic skills. It's this one right here, right? On the end table."

"That's the one. I've got a bookmark in it."

"I see that. Okay. Are you set? Have enough wine? Need any snacks?"

"I'm good."

"Okay. Then we can start."

He started to read, and Maggie leaned back, resting her head against the back of the sofa. His voice was soft and melodious, and she listened to its cadence almost more than she listened to the words. And she'd been right. It was very soothing. As he read, she found she leaned toward him until her head was on his shoulder.

After a while, he came to a stop. "Maggie? You awake?"

"I am, but I'm feeling very drowsy. Thank you, Ed. I enjoyed that. If that hardware gig doesn't work out for you, you could make your living reading for books on tape."

Ed chuckled. "I doubt that. Well, you're tired, and I am, too. Let's hit the hay."

"A man with a plan. I like that."

Ed took her hand and led her across the living room, and she shivered, the heat of it reminded her that she might have bone jumping sometime in her future. She hoped so, anyway.

"You need any help in the bathroom?" he asked when they got upstairs. "Take any prescriptions, or anything like that?"

She could still feel the heat of his hand, even though he wasn't touching her any more.

"Hand me the green toothbrush, will you? That one's mine." *What if he kissed her?* She wanted him to. So very, very much.

He lingered another second in the hall. *He could still kiss her. Or she could kiss him. Although that might be awkward. Where was he, exactly, in the hallway?*

"All right, then, Maggie. Good night. Sleep well."

He turned and headed down the hall. *Too late now.*

"Good night, Ed. And thank you for everything."

ED WOKE EARLY ON Saturday morning from a thin and restless sleep with his face smashed into the pillow and the blanket twisted around his legs. He'd slept poorly, in part because of the relentless onslaught and erotic qualities of the dreams that had haunted him most of the night.

That's the thanks you got for helping a neighbor.

He rubbed his eyes, trying to drive the sleep from them, trying to think more clearly. He wanted Maggie. He couldn't stop thinking about her. And she was right about one thing: his parents didn't like the idea of her, that was clear. Not the Anglo part, and not the three children part. And his family was close. If he brought someone home that they didn't like, there'd be trouble. He didn't need more trouble. *Maggie* didn't need more trouble.

But there was something about her strength and humor that went straight to his heart. Last night when he'd come down after putting Emily to bed and saying goodnight to the boys, he'd entered the living room to see her on the sofa, her face turned toward the television as if she could see it, and her face pale, lit by the bluish cast from the screen. He couldn't imagine what it must be like to be a single parent responsible for three kids and then lose your sight in one second. He'd wanted to scoop her up and take her home. And protect her from every pain and stumble she might encounter.

Of course, she'd get her sight back in a few days. But in the meantime, she was handling the stress like a trooper.

She'd said she was attracted to him, but she didn't want to have an affair. And why would she? They lived in a small town, and she had three kids to raise. The inevitable gossip would be hard on all of them, especially the kids, and family dinners with his folks wouldn't win him any points in the fun department. His parents were good people, they'd worked hard and he respected what they'd achieved, and like any parents, they wanted what was best for their kids. They just weren't afraid to push their agenda—and push hard—even if their kids had other ideas.

But nothing would get settled only by thinking about it. He kicked off the blankets that had a stranglehold on his legs and stood and stretched. It was still early; he might as well take a shower before anyone else was up.

Barefoot, he went down the hallway to the bathroom, stopping to check on the boys. They were both still dead to the world, their faces smooth and innocent in sleep, although Ed knew how deceptive appearances could be. They were both already a handful. Kyle had kicked his covers off, and Ed went in to cover him up. He'd admit it: he'd like to have children.

He took a towel out of the linen closet, then checked on Emily. She, too, was still sleeping, looking like a snot-encrusted angel with her blonde curls fuzzing into a halo around her head, her nose dried and clogged. *Little tyke must have allergies.*

Directly across from Emily next to the bathroom was Maggie's room, and Ed tried to pass it without glancing in, but opportunities handed to a person were made for taking. He didn't have a reason to go in there. He didn't have a reason to see her in her pajamas almost transparent from wear, her body all soft curves that moved gently under the thin fabric. He didn't have a reason to watch her or put his hands on her or hold her or kiss her—

Shit. He needed a shower, all right—a cold one, and the longer, the better.

He went into the bathroom, shaking his head to clear the

images from his brain, and turned on the shower. The pulsing water felt good on his skin, cleansing and refreshing. And when he was dried off and dressed, he felt like a new person. A person with options.

When he strode down the hall, Emily was awake, watching the door as though she were waiting for him, and when she saw him, she raised her arms to him and said "Da!"

His heart melted.

He went into the room and she kicked her feet and beat the air with her arms, and he picked her up and she threw her arms around his neck and laughed. She still smelled clean and sweet from the bath he'd given her last night, but this morning her skin smelled like sleep in a baby sort of way.

"Hey, Scout," he whispered to her, wiping her nose. "What do you say we go downstairs and make breakfast?"

He changed her clothes, taking off her teddy bear footy pajamas and putting on a white T-shirt with pink hearts and a pair of red corduroy overalls he found in her dresser. Socks and shoes followed, and he thanked his babysitting stars that he'd had so many younger brothers and sisters and nieces and nephews to practice on.

When Emily was dressed, he slung her over his hip and carried her downstairs. "It's just you and me, kid," he said. "Let's make the most of it."

He put her in her high chair and gave her a little bowl of cereal and poured some milk in a purple sippy cup for her.

"Your mom's got everything," he said to the baby, tying a bib under her chin. "Aren't you the lucky girl? Now let's see what the big people are going to have for breakfast." He surveyed the kitchen, checking for supplies, and then set to work.

MAGGIE WOKE TO the smell of coffee and something that smelled like pancakes. Was Ed cooking? She feared what the kitchen would look like if the boys had taken it into their heads to make pancakes.

She struggled into some clothes, finding everything with

difficulty and taking much longer than normal. She knocked something over in the bathroom while searching for her comb, but it sounded like it was plastic and hadn't broken. She fumbled around on the floor searching for it and was glad to learn the bottle hadn't leaked. She thought it was shampoo. She'd left that out.

She could hear the restrained chaos in the kitchen before she got there—Ed and the boys talking and Emily banging her spoon on her high chair and squealing. And when she got to the kitchen, there was hardly a break in the noise, but a strong hand took her upper arm, and Ed was there, pulling out a chair, guiding her into it with a nudge from his leg, and spreading a napkin into her lap.

"Pancakes this morning," he said into her ear as the boys argued about baseball and Emily kept up her own personal songfest accompanied by banging a spoon.

"Smells wonderful," she said.

"Here's your orange juice." She heard Ed pour some into a glass, and then he took her hand and placed the glass into it. His hand was big and warm, and Maggie felt her own disappear into it, like a caterpillar into its cocoon.

"Thanks," she said, feeling heat build in her blood. Even in the morning chaos, she wanted him. He was strong and kind and reliable and funny and a great dancer, and he had a body that she'd love to get her hands on.

"Want some coffee?"

She tried to control her wayward thoughts. "Please."

"You all right?" He poured her a cup and guided her hand to it, to show her where it was. "You're kind of flushed."

"Never better." But that was a lie. If anything, she felt her face get even hotter.

Breakfast was noisy and probably messy, and Maggie was glad she didn't have to see it, much less try to clean it up. After breakfast Ed loaded the dishwasher and then drove them to the hospital, where they all trooped in to see Doris. After a few minutes he took the boys to the hardware store, leaving Maggie and Emily to visit with Doris a while longer.

"That Ed Medina is a nice boy," Doris said. "Nice of him to stay with you while your eyes are glued shut."

"Yes. He's not a boy, though, Mom. He's thirty-eight." Maggie would have rolled her eyes if she could have.

"He's staying with you at the house?"

"I needed somebody, and you were busy. Some lame excuse about a heart attack."

Doris snorted. "It took my having a heart attack to get you on a date."

"I've been on dates," Maggie objected. "I went out with Chuck Winkel and Ian Strachan. Those were dates."

"Those were not dates. Those were exercises in poor judgment. I'm talking about your going out with Ed last night for pizza."

"That wasn't a date," Maggie said. "The kids were there, and I couldn't gaze deep into his eyes, since I can't even *open* my eyes. How did you find out about that already?"

"Cecelia Martin is an RN here, and her nephew's girl-friend works at the pizza parlor. I know the kids were with you. They'd have to be, since that loser ex-husband of yours dumps them whenever he can."

Maggie sighed. "He's not so bad, Mom. He pays his child support on time."

"There's more to fatherhood than money," Doris said. "Well, and sperm."

Maggie laughed. "I'm not going to argue with you," she said. "Ed's been wonderful about staying with us. I didn't have anybody else I could ask, and John couldn't take them. Heaven knows, he's got other fish to fry."

Doris looked confused. "John?"

"*Ed.* You're the one who wants to talk about him. Any-thing else?"

"Did you have fun?"

"Yes. Yes, I did." She'd had fun with him. And she hoped, in time, that she'd have more fun with him. A *lot* more.

Because the alternative suddenly felt very bleak.

Chapter 17

Ray Corkin stabbed his pitchfork into the dirty straw of an empty stall and tossed it onto the pile in the wagon that stood in the middle of Tom Strodthoff's barn. The Strodthoff's black-and-white Holstein cows, like the picture-perfect animals they were, stood outside in a lush green pasture next to the bright red barn under a deep blue sky chewing their cud like pampered resort guests. *All they need to make their stay more comfortable*, Ray thought, *is a chocolate on their pillow*, and then he spread out fresh straw on the floor and dumped a measure of grain into the feed trough.

Although cleaning out stalls could not be considered coveted work on a farm, Ray didn't mind it. The work was strenuous but not back-breaking—Ray could feel the flex of his shoulders and thighs as he found his rhythm pitching the dirty straw, and he worked quickly, kicking up a healthy sweat. The Strodthoffs kept a good farm, neat and clean, with healthy animals and well-tended buildings and grounds, and it was a pleasure to put in a hard days' work and see the results. Better than sitting around that bloody motel room all day, waiting for Donald Nennig to call them.

Working on the farm, the diamond gig now seemed far away. No more of Ian's endless pills, no more of Mickey's dissatisfactions, and most of all, no more waiting—for instructions, couriers, airplanes, or Donald Nennig. If—no, *when*—Ian sold the diamonds, Ray wanted his share. But until then, Ray didn't mind working in the barn. A man could do worse things with his life.

The fall weather had been glorious and the Strodthoffs were enjoying the fruits of their labor and the bounty of a plentiful harvest, which meant that Ray's work was plentiful, too. They were bringing in the hay this weekend, hoping to do it all in two days. Elsbeth, the Strodthoff's youngest daughter, the high school basketball star, would drive the tractor, and Katrina, the next youngest, who was away at college and playing basketball on a scholarship, was coming home to help.

Ray had thought that the girls wouldn't be strong enough to do the strenuous work, but Tom and Eva had assured him that Elsbeth and Katrina had been helping around the farm since they were wee things, there being no boys in the family to lend a hand. Ray had consequently revised his mental picture of Katrina, the college student, from a small, pretty blonde reading romance novels in class to a strapping farm wench practicing the latest in insemination techniques in a sterile laboratory. Katrina was expected any time, and when Ray was done in the barn and Tom had the mower oiled up, they'd start, and Katrina would pitch in when she got there.

When Ray had the stalls cleaned out, he let the cows back in and hooked them up to the milking machines. He had just set down a bowl of warm milk for the barn cats, squatting down to pet the nursing mother, when he heard footsteps approaching. The huge sliding door scraped open, and Ray was blinded by the sun streaming through the opening. He put his hands to his eyes and squinted to see who was coming in.

What he saw dazzled his vision, sending volts of electricity to his brain, rendering him speechless with wonder. It was a woman, taller than average, with pale blonde hair pulled back in two braids, from which tendrils had escaped and floated around her head, creating a halo in the sunshine that backlit her body and obscured her face. She wore overalls and a loose, colorful shirt and boots, and when she stepped into the cool, dim barn, Ray saw that she had skin as pale as alabaster, lips as pink as coral, eyes as deep and blue as lapis lazuli, and when she smiled at him, teeth as white and even as pearls. He gazed at her, so radiant and pure, fresh and wholesome, but yet of the earth, smiling down kindly at him, and suddenly and without warning, he felt his conscious will depart and destiny take over as he surrendered his heart to her.

Katrina Strodthoff gazed down at the new hand, who had an intense expression of reverence and longing on his face. He was strong and handsome, with broad shoulders and powerful thighs; his face was damp from exertion, and his T-shirt wet with sweat in a V down his chest that pointed to the waist of his jeans.

Nothing at college could compete with this.

"Hi," she said, reaching out her hand to help him up. "You must be Ray. I've been looking for you."

ED CHECKED OUT the busy store, customers coming in for their rakes and trash bags, pruning shears, mulch, weatherizing materials, furnace filters, and other needs for fall and winter. Every clerk was occupied, even Alberto and Isabel, as well as David, who was busy restocking shelves.

"I won't be gone long," he said to his father, glancing over at the sightless Maggie as she sat on a folding chair near the garden center check-out. "Forty-five minutes, maybe an hour, that's all. I'm going to make that delivery out to the Halford place and then run Kyle to his baseball practice and then I'll be right back. I've got Jason on the cash register in front. You'll be all right?" He was asking Alberto, but he was watching Maggie. He didn't like to leave her—especially since his father was suspicious, rightfully so—about his attentions to her.

"Why wouldn't we be all right?" Alberto asked, not quite

belligerently. "I've been busy before in this store without you."

"I'll be fine," Maggie said softly. "And Emily's asleep."

And what an unbelievable stroke of luck that was. They'd rigged a playpen out of decorative garden fencing for the little girl and given her a few toys. Ed didn't like to put kids in playpens at all, but he didn't see what choice they'd had while the toddler was in the store. Maggie couldn't see her, and the clerks and his dad couldn't watch her. But Emily had seemed to regard the playpen as a way to attract attention from the customers, and after flirting outrageously with every person who walked down her aisle, she was now taking a nap, exhausted from all the admiration she'd been getting.

Ed sighed, glancing at them all again for a minute. "One hour, tops," he said again. "Then I'll be back."

"Go," Maggie said.

He'd have to. And by the time he came back, either there'd be blood on the floor—Maggie's or Alberto's—or there wouldn't. Either way, he had to make the delivery and get Kyle to baseball practice.

"All right," he said, motioning to Kyle. "I'll be back soon." And then they headed out to his truck.

IN THE HUBBUB of the store, Maggie couldn't hear them go, but she knew an awkward silence when she felt it.

"I'm sorry I'm inconveniencing you on such a busy day," she said, turning to where she knew Alberto had to be standing by the counter.

"It is what Eduardo wanted," Alberto said stiffly. "It is fine."

"Is there anything I can do to help? I know I'm sort of limited, but—"

"No, no, there is nothing."

She heard Alberto move away to take care of a customer. Maggie felt acutely uncomfortable sitting there by the counter, on display like a potted plant. She and Emily, attention getters. At least Emmy was happy. She was a two-year-old rock star.

"Alberto!" Maggie heard a new, male voice at the back of the store. "Got a delivery for you!"

Alberto hustled out, and Maggie felt more alone than ever. It was one thing to have the glowering Alberto mere feet away, now she had no idea of who was standing there, maybe staring at her, saying hello, wondering why she was so rude not opening her eyes, then being nosy when she explained about gluing them shut.

A couple of minutes later, she heard banging and swearing as Alberto and the delivery man muscled something into the store.

"I'm not happy about this delivery," Alberto said to the driver. "You're almost a week late. If we can't get these shipments when we specify, we might as well not get them at all."

"You gotta talk to the boss," the driver said. "I just drive the truck. You want me to take 'em back?"

"No, no, I already said, and now they're here," Alberto said. "But tell him I said. And Eduardo will call."

"Sure. Sign here, Alberto."

Maggie heard paper rustle, presumably when Alberto was signing the invoice, and then the driver said goodbye and walked away.

"Can you believe that?" Alberto asked. "What am I supposed to do with these now?"

Maggie wondered if he was talking to her.

"What are they?" she ventured.

Alberto snorted. "Bulbs. For fall planting. We advertised them available this weekend. We were supposed to get them last Monday at the latest, so we would have time to repackage and display them. We got a good deal, we bought a bulk lot. But now they come five days late. It is Saturday, our busiest day, and they sit here in these crates. Like dead things."

"I could help," Maggie said, feeling tentative. "Maybe I could repackage them."

"No, no, impossible," Alberto said, snorting again. He

was crashing around doing something at the counter.

"Really, I think I could," Maggie said. "If you open the crates. And then you were going to repackage them in—what?"

"Little paper bags."

"Like in groups of five and ten?"

"And twenty."

"So I could do that. I mean, I can't *see*, but I can *count*. If you opened the crate, I could count them out, put them in the bags. Then—staple them shut?"

"Yes," Alberto said, unwillingly.

"And then if you had something right here—a big box? A nice, decorative planter? I could just drop them in. And the customers could pick out the bags they wanted."

"No, no, impossible," Alberto said, but he sounded more thoughtful.

"And I could write the number of bulbs on the bag. And maybe the kind of bulb? I don't have to see to do that. I mean, it wouldn't be neat. And I wouldn't go fast. But it could get done. At least, I could make a decent start."

Alberto didn't respond.

"And then I'd keep busy, and you'd get the bulbs out. Do you have a sign of some kind?"

"We made one up," he said grudgingly.

"Okay. If you put up the sign, stick it on the container and put the container right here, it could be like an impulse purchase. I could do that." Maggie waited, hoping Alberto would let her help. It wasn't particularly that she wanted Ed's folks to think well of her. She wanted to *do* something, not just sit here on display like a glued-eye freak.

"Please," she said. "It would be a favor to me, if I could help."

The silence seemed to stretch forever as Alberto pondered her offer.

"Okay," he said. "Let me fix it up."

And in a few minutes, it was done. Alberto ripped open a crate of crocus bulbs, heaped a stack of small paper bags by Maggie's elbow, put a Sharpie pen in her hand and an open barrel on the floor, and set her to work.

"When you're done with the crocus, tell me, I'll open the daffodils," he said.

I can do this, Maggie thought as she fumbled her way to a paper bag, scrawled "10 crocus" partly on the bag and partly on the counter, and counted out ten bulbs, dropping them in the sack. She stapled it closed, felt for the barrel, and dropped it in. *Done.*

In the next hour, Maggie filled the barrel with small bags of bulbs. Customers came by, laughed and joked, asked her about her eyes, and picked up some bulbs. By the time Ed came back, Maggie had emptied a couple of shipping crates of bulbs, and the barrel had been emptied twice.

"Dad's got you working?" he asked.

Maggie nodded. "Bagging bulbs. Alberto got an unexpected delivery."

"We're gonna fire those suppliers," Alberto said, coming around from the back.

"Yeah," Ed said. "Seems like you got it under control for now, though."

"*Si*," Alberto said. "Maggie helped." He hesitated. "It was her idea. If she wants to stay, she can stay."

Maggie would have wept with relief and happiness, if tears could have escaped her eyelids.

"Thank you, Alberto," she said. "I'm glad to help. I could come back tomorrow and finish the job."

"Okay, tomorrow. If there's any left to do." He went to help a customer choose a rake, and Maggie felt Ed move closer, bend down to her year.

"So you're sucking up to my parents now? You think that's going to work?"

"I'm not sucking up! I—"

"Good job," he said, laughing softly. "Keep it up."

IT WAS LATE AFTERNOON when Mars glanced over the top of his newspaper and watched as Venus twitched aside the drape in the living room and peered down the street for what must have been the twentieth time. "Who are you expecting?" he asked.

"The postal carrier. He usually comes about this time."

"Is this for Maggie?" Mars shook out his newspaper. "Because I have to tell you, I don't see it."

Venus let the curtains fall into place and plopped down in a chair across from him. "I don't either," she said, shaking her head. "But Dr. J was very specific. 'The man who brings mail to the door,' he said."

"Have you seen this guy?" Mars asked. "Too buttoned down for Maggie."

Venus nodded. "He wears a uniform. Now, I like a uniform. A uniform lends distinction to a person's physique. But in Maggie's case, I think a uniform is not the way to go. People in uniform don't seem to be ideal mates for people who glue their houses together. Not to mention, their eyes."

"Too much spit and polish," Mars agreed.

Next door the front gate squeaked open, and Venus jumped up. "Gotta go!"

Mars enjoyed the vision of long legs and clouds of hair leaping down the stairs while he leisurely folded the paper, set it aside, and followed her out the door. By the time he got outside, she was already talking to the mail carrier.

"Hi," Venus said, smiling radiantly at the postal worker. She gazed at him and then at Maggie's house. "Isn't it a beautiful day?"

"Yes, it is," the carrier said, gazing at Venus with a stunned expression and then up at Maggie's house with a soft yearning. "Lovely for this time of year."

Mars assessed the mail carrier. He was a sprightly sixty, and he wore that uniform—all crisp and pressed, the shirt tucked in—and a wedding ring.

"Do you think Mrs. Jorgenson is home?" the carrier asked, his gaze never wavering from Maggie's house. "She's such a nice person."

Ed came out of Maggie's front door and seemed surprised

to see so many people gathered at the front steps. "Hi, Venus, Mars," he said. "Clarence. Got any mail for Maggie?"

Clarence looked crestfallen. "Two catalogs, a grocery flyer, and an appeal for funds from a national charity," he said. "I think I should hand it to her personally."

"I'll take it," Ed said. "Maggie's tied up right now."

Clarence ignored him, holding the mail, peering over Ed's shoulder at the door. "I'm supposed to put it in the box, or I could hand it directly to the addressee."

Ed raised his eyebrows. "I'll take Maggie's mail, Clarence," he said again. "I'm going right in. Thanks."

Clarence sighed. "All right," he said sadly, surrendering the mail. "Nothing for you folks," he said to Venus and Mars, and retracing his steps down the walk, opened the gate, glanced back at Maggie's door as the three of them watched, and trudged down the street, his shoulders stooped.

Ed shook his head. "That was weird. Maybe Clarence needs to think about retiring. Well, see you." He went back up the porch steps, and, as he went into the house, they heard him say, "Maggie! It's all junk mail, you want it?"

Mars and Venus went back indoors.

"That wasn't right," Mars said, shaking his head. "Clarence isn't the only one losing it, if Dr. J thinks that he's a good match for Maggie. Clarence is married. Did you see the ring?"

"I did," Venus said. "The phone connections have been atrocious, but Dr. J said 'the man who brings mail to the door.' Who else could it be?"

"And what's going on over there?" Mars asked. "Ed Medina is spending a lot of time at Maggie's house."

"Nothing's going on over there. I'm sure of it. Ed's just helping out."

"Whatever you say, babe," Mars said, putting his arm around Venus. "But take it from a guy who knows military tactics. Ed's got her surrounded. And I ought to know. I'm the guy who used to wear a uniform."

HOURS LATER, LONG after supper had been cleared and the dishes washed, Maggie sat alone in the living room waiting for Ed, who was upstairs putting laundry away and making sure that David and Kyle had turned their lights out and Emily was tucked up for the night. Ed had been wonderful all day, putting in his time at the hardware store, but also driving them around, taking care of them all. He'd made dinner—casserole, served in bowls, like he'd promised—and then they'd all played Twister, of all things, because Maggie didn't have to see much to do that.

They should put age restrictions on that game, she thought, *nobody older than twelve allowed to play*, thinking about how it had felt when Ed's leg had intertwined with hers and then how his face had pressed against her side. Thinking of how they'd been wrapped around each other and how her heart had pounded, Maggie's mouth went dry.

So now here she was, feeling grateful that he was doing them this huge favor, and also really, really turned on. She had lain awake most of last night fantasizing about what Ed could do to her with her eyes glued shut, and that was *before* they'd played Twister, and she felt warmth pooling in her lower belly just thinking about it.

ED CAME DOWN the stairs determined to hold out against Maggie's appeal. He wouldn't make any moves on her while her kids were in the house—he had plenty of self-control about stuff like that—but he felt like a randy teenager. It was a weird space to occupy.

"Everybody's asleep," he told her. "When you were taking your bath, I checked out movies for us to watch. Do you want to do that? I thought maybe *His Girl Friday*, with Rosalind Russell and Cary Grant."

"That's an oldie but goodie," Maggie said. "I love those screwball comedies."

"Me, too," Ed said. "And I thought something with a lot of dialogue and not much scenery. Not important scenery, anyway."

"Good point. Ed—" Maggie stopped.

He hoped she'd say something simple, like, "Let's have oatmeal for breakfast," or "What time is it?" He really didn't want to get tangled up in a discussion about a "relationship" they weren't having. Not that he didn't want to get tangled up anytime, anywhere with Maggie. That Twister game had made it clear to him.

"What?" he asked, feeling wary.

Maggie smiled. "I like you, Ed. You're a good person."

"Yeah, yeah, yeah. Are we going to watch this movie now, or what?"

"Could we have popcorn?"

"Good idea," Ed said and went into the kitchen to make it.

A short time later, Maggie heard the microwave beep and the popcorn spill into a bowl. It smelled wonderful.

"You know, I could have made the popcorn," she said when Ed came back into the living room. "There's a separate button for popcorn on the microwave, so I wouldn't have to see to set the timer. I'm afraid I was taking advantage of your kindness."

"Well, I can see, so I can do it faster. You did a great job in the garden section today, by the way. Dad said so."

"I wanted to help. And that's a lot different than taking care of four people for four days. That's *huge*."

"Yeah, I worked up a sweat making this popcorn. Ready to watch the movie?"

"Ready when you are."

"Move over a little, why don't you? You can't see anyway. Why should you have the good spot?"

"Did you bring two bowls?" Maggie moved over, reaching out for the popcorn.

"No," Ed said. "We're sharing this batch. One less bowl to wash."

"If we're sharing, I get to hold it."

"Greedy," Ed said, but she could tell he was smiling. He gave her the bowl and sat down beside her, leaning into her more than was necessary to get a handful of popcorn.

"Ready?" he asked.

"You've got the remote. You're asking?"

"A mere formality." Ed clicked the movie to start and they settled down to watch.

Chapter 18

Early Monday morning Ed stood in Maggie's doorway, watching her sleep. She lay on her side, as tousled as he'd imagined that she would be, her face flushed, dead to the world. He felt weird watching her—a little bit like a voyeur, a little bit like her keeper. But there was no doubt he wanted her. Every time he looked at her, he felt his blood quicken.

He didn't know when or why he'd decided that he'd defy his parents' hopes for his future. But he had. After only one long weekend with her and her kids, he couldn't think about anything else.

It wouldn't be easy. Not just his folks, but her kids, who might not accept him if they thought he was taking the place of their dad.

Eventually he'd—*they'd*—have to face those were problems, but he wasn't in any rush. He could give her time to figure out how things would work and the kids time to get used to him. But he knew what he wanted. He wanted Maggie—and her kids—for a lifetime.

He hated to wake her. He thought that having her eyes glued shut was taking more out of her than she was letting on, but it was time to get moving. The kids had to get to school and he had to get to work. He entered the room and knelt by the edge of the bed, smoothing a strand of hair off her face.

"Maggie," he whispered. "I'm sorry, but it's time to get up." He watched her come awake and smiled when he saw her try to open her eyes.

"Damn," she said, and he laughed.

"Good morning to you, too," he said. "It'll be soon now, Maggie. Today's the third day."

"I know," she said. "I didn't mean to sound grumpy." She stretched, her arms high over her head, her legs rigid under the covers, and when she relaxed and brought her arms down, she hit Ed on the shoulder.

"Sorry," she said, but then she didn't move her hand. The weight of it burned through his cotton shirt and her breathing hitched as she stretched her fingers across his shoulder and stroked down his arm.

"You're doing a great job of making up for being grumpy," he said, his voice raspy, as she curled her hand around his arm and pulled him toward her.

"I can do better." She pulled him closer until Ed was pressed against the edge of the bed, leaning over her. He didn't—couldn't—resist. He smelled her lavender soap and heard her soft breath quicken, and then he lost track of all senses but touch as she stroked back up his arm, across his shoulder until her hand was holding the nape of his neck, her fingers entwined in his hair.

"Come here," she said, pulling him down to her, and he went, like a sailor to the siren's call.

Her mouth was soft and giving as Ed kissed her. She was drowsy but yielding, tasting him, nibbling on his lower lip, reaching up for him. He opened his mouth and breathed into her, their lips and tongues tangling in a lazy dance of parry and thrust that turned him dizzy with want.

He slid one hand under the covers, finding her waist and settling on the warm skin of her stomach where her pajama top had rucked up. She was wearing ridiculous flannel pajamas, pink with ice cream cones printed on them. She looked like a teenager at a slumber party, and he wanted to be the boy who saw to it that she didn't get any sleep. He absorbed her heat through his hand, feeling it warm his entire body. She shivered as he stretched his fingers to cover her rib cage, his thumb sliding under her breast.

She pulled away from his kiss, reaching up for him until her lips almost touched his ear.

"*Now* it's a good morning," she said.

"It can be better," Ed said as he buried his face into her neck, licking the place where he felt her heartbeat. He traced the curve of her shoulder and along her collarbone, enjoying how her skin jumped whenever he hit a sensitive nerve.

He moved his hand up from her rib cage, stroking her breast, until he heard her breath catch in her throat. Maggie arched into him, pressing against his hand, holding onto his shoulders, and Ed felt his blood pound with the need to touch her everywhere, explore all her most sensitive places. When she shifted her legs under the covers, Ed closed his eyes, feeling desire surge through him. *One day*, he thought, *when the house isn't full of kids and no one has to be somewhere, we'll have a really good morning, but that morning isn't today.*

He pulled his hand out from under her pajama top and leaned back. "No one is sorrier about this than I am, Maggie, but it really is time to get up. If you want a shower, you have to get in the bathroom."

Maggie sighed, but then somewhere an alarm clock buzzed, and Ed gave her one last, hard kiss.

"Rise and shine," he said, getting to his feet. "Do you need any help?"

"I can do it," she said. When he turned around to get the kids up, he saw David standing in the open door watching them.

"HOW AM I SCREWING UP?" Venus demanded into the phone. She stood in the middle of the backyard, and until a few minutes ago, she'd been pleased with what she saw. But it needed only one phone call from an irate boss to dim her appreciation of her flourishing garden.

"I'm doing everything you tell me," she said. "'The guy who carries the mail,' that's who you *said*, so that's who I *got*. *What?* I can't hear you. *No*. The mailman was *not* the right guy. The mailman is *married*. Even if he were otherwise right for Maggie, which he *isn't*." She paused for a minute and then rolled her eyes to an inscrutable heaven. "*Fine*. Whatever you say. *Soon*." She disconnected the call and threw the phone against the kitchen door, nearly hitting Mars as he came out.

"Problems?" he asked, grinning.

"Dr. J is an arrogant, ignorant, complacent jerk who does nothing but complain," she complained.

"That's our boss for you." Mars picked up the phone and slipped it into his pocket before joining her in the yard. "Want some lunch? I picked up some things at the deli. Double chocolate mousse pudding," he tempted. "The chef said it was better than sex."

"And you believed her?" Venus snorted in contempt. "You've been spending too much time alone."

Mars slipped an arm around her waist. "I told her we'd put it to an empirical analysis. Results due tomorrow." He pulled her close and nibbled her ear. "Or maybe day after tomorrow."

"That reminds me," Venus said, pulling back to gaze into gray eyes gone warm. "Dr. J had a message for you, too."

"Not when there's test results due," Mars said, pulling her close again and kissing her. "Anyway, I know what the message is. I'm almost done here."

"Well, I'm not, and you're not leaving without me."

"Dr. J might feel differently."

"Well, he can just go weed my azaleas for all I care," Venus sniffed.

"Save me a seat for *that* showdown." He licked her shoulder, which was completely unfair, because he knew she was sensitive there.

"Stop that! I have work to do!" She jumped away,

heading for the house.

Mars laughed, going after her. "I'm coming, and I'm bringing the double chocolate mousse pudding. A man of science never sleeps."

MAGGIE WASN'T LOOKING forward to David's getting home from school, when they'd have to have a Talk that she wasn't ready for. Worse, The Talk would be about Ed, too, and Ed would be there, and she wasn't sure that Ed would be any more ready for The Talk than she was. Maybe even David wouldn't be ready for it. But they would have to have it nonetheless.

At least she and Ed hadn't been having sex. Ed thought that David hadn't seen anything more than that last quick kiss. It wasn't the Oedipal scene, not quite. But it was bad enough. It was sort of a pseudo-parental-unit-living-together-without-doing-it Oedipal scene.

What got into me? she wondered now in shock. *I am not the kind of person who drags men into bed first thing in the morning. And we're not even going steady.*

And yet, there in the early morning quiet, when she'd awakened to find Ed kneeling next to her, she'd been all over him like gravy on mashed potatoes. The thought of it, of Ed's mouth and hands on her and how she'd wanted to get hers on him, made her restless even now, even knowing that David and Ed would be home soon and that they'd have to talk about It.

David got home first, coming through the back door, ignoring her, before going up to his room. That seemed to be about as good a place as any to have The Talk, so she edged through the kitchen and living room to make her way upstairs. Kyle was at his after-school program. Ed was bringing Emmy from day care. It would be only the two of them. *Oh, joy,* she thought.

"David?" she asked, knocking on his closed door. "We have to talk."

No answer.

"David," more firmly now. "I'm coming in."

She went in. His music was on, and she hoped he was doing homework but thought it unlikely. She edged over to the bed and sat down, crossing her legs. She decided to go with the best-case scenario.

"You saw Ed kissing me this morning," she said.

"It wasn't my fault!" David said, his voice shrill. "The door was open!"

"I'm not blaming you, David," she said. "We left the door open because there wasn't anything you shouldn't see, there was nothing to be ashamed of." Well, nothing to be ashamed of unless your eleven-year-old son had gotten up five minutes earlier and had X-ray vision and could see through bedding.

"It was *gross*." He sounded disgusted, and Maggie had to laugh.

"Next time don't look," she said.

"I couldn't help it. You were right there." He kicked the leg of his chair.

"Besides being gross, does anything else bother you about Ed and me kissing?"

"I don't want him to move in here."

"That's not the plan," Maggie said. "He's here until my eyes open up. That could be any time now."

"But he *could* move in here," David said. "Like Cindy moved in with Dad."

"We're not exactly dating, either," Maggie said. "So far, pretty much every time we've done something together, you and Kyle and Emmy have come along." She thought for a moment. She knew that wasn't David's point.

"Try to think about Ed not as somebody you saw me kissing," she said. "Just think about Ed. Do you think he's an okay guy? When we played Twister and went out for pizza, was that fun? When he teaches you stuff, do you like that?"

"I guess. I still don't want him to move in here."

"Tell me something," Maggie said. "Do you feel shut out at your dad's?"

David was silent.

"I can see how you might feel that," Maggie said. "Your dad loves you. You're his son, and that's a special bond. I'm sorry he's not showing that to you better."

She heard the front door slam and knew that Ed was home with Emily. *Please let me get through this okay,* she thought.

"Your dad didn't want to be married to me anymore, and he wanted to marry Cindy, so that meant he moved out of the house," she said. "You might feel that he picked her over you, but that's not how it is." *Please let that be true,* she thought, *or I will push John Jorgenson into a deep black hole myself.*

"I'm not picking Ed or anybody else over you," she said. "I will always have just as much time and love for you as I do right now." She heard footsteps climbing the stairs. *And pretty soon I'll have to explain to Ed how I'm not picking my son or anybody else over him.*

"I think Ed and I do want to go out on dates," she said. "But we will try not to be gross, at least in your presence." She heard the footsteps stop outside David's door. "Anything you want to add to that, Ed?"

"I have a question for Ed," David said, his voice hostile and aggressive. "Are you marrying Mom?"

This is what happens when you try to help a friend and neighbor who glued her eyes shut, Maggie thought. *You get grilled about your matrimonial intentions by an eleven-year-old.*

"I heard what your mom said about going out on dates," Ed said. "We do want to do that."

Excellent, thought Maggie.

"Sometimes dating leads to marriage," Ed said.

I'd be willing to think about that, Maggie thought.

"But in the case of your mom and me, it's too soon to think about that."

Really? Maggie thought. *Because I'm thinking of it.*

"But however long your mom and I date or whether we

ever get married, I want you to know that I wouldn't try to take your dad's place. I'm not your dad. I couldn't be him, even if I wanted to. You and I have a separate relationship."

"Okay," David said.

"What you and I have is different," Ed said. "So if you want anything or need anything that I could help you with, then I'm there, whatever happens between your mom and me. And I'm counting on you to keep coming to the hardware store. I need your help with that."

What did I do to deserve this guy? Maggie wondered.

"Okay," David said again. Maggie imaged how the boy and the man must be measuring each other. Even without her sight, she could see the edges of the man her son would become.

"Are we square now?" Maggie asked. "Because I'm hungry, and Ed has to make dinner."

"I'm okay," David said.

"Me, too," Ed said. "Come on down and help me. That's part of the special relationship I was talking about. You get to help me cook."

Maggie heard David laugh tentatively, and she felt herself warm to the bond these two men in her life had begun to forge.

"David thought our kissing was gross," she told Ed as they all headed down the stairs.

"He thought *that* was gross?" Ed asked, astonished. "Wait until he sees what we're having for dinner."

THAT NIGHT MAGGIE hummed as she washed her face in the bathroom before she went to bed. She was feeling cheerful and optimistic. The Talk hadn't been so bad, David had been hostile to begin with but seemed to relax as they talked, Ed had acted normal, and Kyle and Emily had been oblivious. The best part was, Ed said that they were going on dates. Maggie felt her breath quicken as she thought about dancing with Ed or sitting in a dark movie theater with Ed and maybe making out in the back row. *I wonder if he'll want me to go all the way?* Maggie thought with a smile. *I hope so.*

She turned off the water and wrung out her face cloth, feeling around until she found the towel rack. She draped the face cloth over it and grabbed a towel, which she hoped was still presentable. *Having your eyes glued shut gives a person a whole new take on cleanliness,* she thought, and patted her face dry. And then she did what she did every night since last Friday when she'd glued her eyes shut: she put the fingers of one hand on her upper lid and the fingers of the other on the lower lid and tried to pull her eyes open.

Tonight they opened.

It wasn't easy. As she pulled on her right eye, Maggie felt like she was prying an oyster open. The lids peeled apart only reluctantly and left the edges red, inflamed, and tender and her eyes watering. But she could see! *And,* she thought, *let's hope I get the other one open, or instead of channeling Helen Keller, I'll be channeling a one-eyed pirate.*

Feeling excited but nervous, she pried open the second eye. And peered at herself in the mirror.

Her eyes were bloodshot, her eyelids puffy and red with white gunk flaking all over them, and she was blinking like an owl in daylight. She'd never looked so good.

She washed her face again, using cold water this time to bring down the puffiness, trying to get most of the dried glue flakes away from her lids. Then she went downstairs to share her thrilling news with Ed.

She peeked in on the sleeping kids as she went downstairs, and never had any image been as welcome as the sight of their flushed faces, mouths open, drool and snot leaking out. *Imagine how Ed's going to look*, she thought, and felt her heart kick up a notch.

The only light in the darkened living room came from the reading lamp at the end of the sofa, where Ed sat engrossed in her book. The light cast shadows on his face, turning his cheekbones into illuminated planes. One hand, capable and gentle, held the book open while the other was buried in the inky thickness of his hair. Maggie had never seen anyone more beautiful.

"Ed," she said, smiling at him.

He glanced up, and then his eyes widened and a grin spread over his face.

"Fantastic! You're among the seeing."

"Isn't it great?" she said. "It happened just now while I was washing my face."

"Come over here and let me see." He put the book down and watched her cross the room.

"You didn't walk into anything," he complimented her.

"It's a lot easier when you can see what's in front of you," she said, sitting down next to him and tilting her head to his.

"Sit in the light so I can see," he said. She leaned into the light and he leaned into her, putting his hand on her face and running his thumb gently over her eyelids. "They look sore. How do they feel?" He took his hand away and Maggie, feeling the loss of gentleness, opened her eyes.

"Sore. But they open. And better yet, if I close them, I can open them again if I want to."

Ed laughed. "That's great. I guess the Super Glue people knew all along." He paused for a minute. "It's time for me to get going."

"What?" Maggie said. "Why?"

Ed's eyes were dark and unreadable. "I was staying until you could see. Now you can see. I don't want David to think I'm moving in because I'm still here when you don't need me anymore."

I'm pretty sure I need you, Maggie thought. "Stay until tomorrow," she said.

"No offense, Maggie, but Kyle's bed isn't all that comfortable."

So that was it? He'd just go, and that was it? What about those dates he'd talked about? He didn't make a move on her, and she thought, *I'm not jumping you again, I did that this morning, now it's your turn, buster,* so when nothing happened, she got up, and he stood up with her.

"Okay." They moved to the front door and the coat closet, where she reached for his jacket. "You know there's nothing I can say, Ed—" she said as she turned to hand him his coat.

He took the jacket from her and dropped it on the floor, grabbed her around the waist, pulled her tight against him, and buried one hand in her hair.

"I don't care if all your kids wake up and come down here and line up on that sofa and watch us," he breathed into her ear. "I'm kissing you now."

He moved against her until she could feel the full length of his body against hers, thigh to thigh, hip to hip, her breasts crushed against his chest. And then he brought his lips to hers with such a tender ferocity that Maggie thought she would melt from the force of it. Everywhere he touched her, her skin burned, and he touched her everywhere, running his hands through her hair and down her back, over the soft curve of her backside and over her hip and up her side to her breast. She put her arms around his neck to hang on, thinking she would faint from dizziness and want.

When he pulled back, he buried his face in the curve of her neck, tasting the salty sweetness of her skin, inhaling her scent.

"You drive me crazy," he said, lifting his head, smoothing her hair back, lingering to feel its softness. "And we don't get out of the house enough. When are we going on that date you promised me?"

"Friday." Maggie stood on her tiptoes to nip his ear, nuzzling his neck along the way.

Ed pulled away. "Stop that, or I'll never get out of here." He held her against him with one hand and put the other against her face. "I have to work Saturday," he reminded her.

"I'll get you home before curfew." Maggie rubbed her head against his shoulder.

Ed grinned. "God, I hope not."

Chapter 19

Doris Perl sat up in the hospital bed, fully dressed, her jacket on, her white curls combed, her shoes neatly tied, and glared balefully at her daughter. "Get me out of this dump," she said to Maggie. "The food stinks and room service is slow. I want to go home."

"Mom," Maggie said.

The nurse laughed. "It's always a good sign when the patients are ready to leave. Now remember, Doris, do your exercises every day and follow the diet we gave you. I've got some information sheets for you to take home, and we've got your first out-patient visits scheduled."

"Yeah, yeah, yeah," Doris said.

"*Mom*," Maggie said again. "Thank you for everything," she said to the nurse, and then they were out of the hospital.

"Should we stop at the grocery store for you?" Maggie asked once they were on the road. "We could read this nutritional information and make a list."

"Let's go out for lunch," Doris said. "I feel like celebrating."

They went to Peg's diner for a late lunch, where Peg cleared a booth for them and fussed over Doris. After they'd given their orders, Doris settled back in the booth, leaning her head against the edge, and closed her eyes for a second.

Mom looks tired, Maggie thought, gazing at Doris's lined face, *and old,* and she felt a sudden rush of alarm. When had her mother gotten old? And how would she get by if she lost her?

Doris leaned forward and opened her eyes. "I'm going to Europe next spring," she said to Maggie, whose vision of a weak and ailing mother evaporated faster than steam from an Italian espresso machine.

"What?"

"I want to give up the shop," Doris said. "I'm going to retire."

"What?"

"I want to travel more," Doris said. "I want to have more fun. I don't want to be tied to the store any longer. I contacted Road Scholar, and I'm making plans."

"Road Scholar?" Maggie asked.

"You know, the educational travel company for the older set," Doris said. "Are you getting this? I'm not sure you're getting this."

Maggie felt stunned. "It's so sudden. You want to retire?"

"Yes," Doris said. "People came to visit in the hospital and everybody said what a good job that Ian Strachan was doing in there—and I'm telling you Maggie, I think it's strange that he just took over. Good, but strange."

"I didn't know he took over," Maggie said. "I guess I should have checked. I never thought about it when my eyes were glued shut. I wonder why Ed didn't tell me."

"It doesn't matter," Doris said. "The point is, Ian's doing a good job, everybody says, and I realized I don't miss it. I had fun with it for a long time, but when I was in the hospital I didn't miss it, and now I don't want to go back. And there's no point in getting sentimental over it, but a heart attack is a wakeup call, Maggie. There's still things I want to do in my life. I'm going to do them."

Maggie wondered what things her mother still wanted to do. "Good for you, Mom. What do you plan to do with the shop?"

"Sell it to Ian Strachan, if he'll take it."

"Oh." Maggie thought about Ian's many pill bottles and hoped that he'd have a broader view for the shop than he had for his health.

"I'm going to talk to him about it tomorrow," Doris said. "Can you take me over there sometime?"

"Whenever you want," Maggie said, feeling the under-pinnings of her life give way.

DAVID WALKED HOME after school, dragging his feet. His dad was picking him up for the weekend, but he didn't want to go. Cindy was boring and weird, and his dad acted kind of weird, too. But he didn't want to stay here, either. Ed and his mom were kissing, so probably they wanted to get married, too. That sucked, on top of everything else. Everything was wrong, and he didn't belong anywhere. Not really.

He was passing Denny's service station when he saw a new guy labeling the trashcans with giant markers, the kind of markers he'd stolen from the hardware store. He wondered what the guy was doing—if he was tagging the trashcans. He seemed kind of old to be into graffiti. Plus it was the middle of the afternoon.

David walked up silently on the concrete driveway. "What are you doing?" he asked.

Mickey jumped, and the marker skidded up the side of the trashcan.

"Now see what you made me do," he growled. He grabbed a rag and tried to rub the magic marker streak off, but all he did was smear it.

"You're making a mess of it," David said.

"So you fix it."

"What are you doing?" David asked again.

"I'm labeling cans for recycling."

David nodded, scrutinizing at the trashcan. It said GLA, but the A had skidded up.

"It was going to say GLASS," Mickey said.

David saw that there were already other cans marked

PAPER and CANS.

"Okay," he said. This would be easy to fix. He took the black magic marker from Mickey and extended the L to the top of the can to match the A and then added two elongated, serpentine S's and then took the red marker and added an outline with flourishes, and when he was finished, the can looked more decorative and only a very critical person would have thought that the A had been a mistake.

"Hey, kid, that's pretty good," Mickey said. "Want to do the rest? What's your name? I'm Mickey."

"Sure," David said. "I'm David." He checked his watch. He still had more than an hour before his dad would come.

He finished decorating the trashcans and Mickey offered to buy him a soda, so they each got a soda from the vending machine, and Mickey grabbed a bag of potato chips from a cupboard. Then they pulled two rickety aluminum lawn chairs out from behind a storage bin, set them up in the driveway, and drank the sodas and ate chips as they watched the cars drive past. It was nice being quiet. Mickey didn't seem desperate to talk all the time, unlike most grownups.

"I stole some markers like those," David said after a while.

Mickey gazed out at the traffic. "What'd you do that for, then?"

"I don't know." It was puzzling, in fact, like an episode from another life. "I wanted to. It was easy."

Mickey nodded. "That's how I got started."

"Started? With what?"

"My life of crime," Mickey said, laughing at himself.

David wasn't sure whether to believe him. "You've committed crimes?"

"Aye," Mickey said. "And I started just like you. Thefts. Then robberies, car stealing. Like that. It seemed easy."

"Did you ever get caught? Have you been in jail?" This guy seemed so normal, but he was *fearsome*.

"Aye. One night, Glasgow jail. Never want to repeat it. Place stinks, I mean, it really stinks, guys pissin' everywhere, food is terrible, everybody in there is a loser, drunk, stoned, vicious. Awful place. Couldn't wait to get out."

David stared in shocked silence. He'd never known anyone who'd been to jail. Not anyone who admitted it, anyway.

"I was a bit of a ned tosser," Mickey said. "Didn't go to school. Didn't have much of a home life. Me dad ran off when I was five, me mum drank all the time until she lost her job. I'm not blamin' them for my own mistakes, but it was easy to get into trouble with all that."

They sat, drinking their sodas, watching the cars.

"I have to go see my dad this weekend," David said.

"Where's your mum, then?"

"She's here. They're divorced. My dad's remarried. I think my mom wants to get married, too."

"Mmm." Mickey bit into a potato chip.

David took another sip of his soda. "I don't want her to."

"Does she get drunk on the weekends? At night?"

"No."

"You're lucky, then," Mickey said. "Your dad?"

"Him neither," David said. "I don't know. It's weird when I go there now. It's so different. I want it to be the way it was."

"Yeah, old ways often seem best," Mickey said. "They're familiar, anyway. What about your dad's new wife, then? What's she like?"

David shrugged. "She's always laughing even when nobody tells a joke, and she's always fussing over me. I hate that."

Mickey nodded. "She's nervous."

"What?"

Mickey nodded again. "Sure," he said. "She wants you to like her, and she wants your dad to see that you and her can get along. That makes your dad nervous, too. You said he's weird now when you go there, right? That's why."

David looked at Mickey. "I make her nervous?"

"Not you," Mickey said. "The situation makes her nervous. Do they do stuff you like to do?"

"Sometimes," David said. "Sometimes we have to do stupid stuff."

"Yeah," Mickey said. "That happens."

They sat some more, and David reached for the potato chip bag. Mickey handed it to him.

"What's the bloke like then that your mum wants to marry?" Mickey asked.

"Ed? He's okay. I work at his store after school and on weekends sometimes. But I don't want him and my mom to get married. It will make the house too crowded."

Mickey shook his head. "It must be tough, you being such a lucky lad," he said.

David jerked his head around. "Huh? What do you mean?"

"Well—I know it ain't easy with your mum and dad not being together anymore. That happened to me, too, and I hated that."

David nodded.

"But now, look what you got out of it. Something you didn't have before. Your mum's boyfriend gave you a job, so you can earn real money that you can spend how you like. You can buy a car when you're older, so you'll be able to drive around on your own and make out with girls in it. That will be great. Would your dad give you a job?"

"No," David said. "He's a lawyer."

"See?" Mickey said. "What else does your mum's boyfriend do for you?"

"He teaches me stuff." David thought about it. "Like how to fix things. He plays baseball with my brother. He took care of us when my mom glued her eyes shut."

Mickey blinked. "Kinky. And your dad's new wife, what's her name? What does she do for you?"

"Cindy." David grinned at the sudden memory. "Once she took us to the TV station where she works. She let us sit in front of the camera."

Mickey raised his eyebrows. "Sounds like fun."

David nodded. "It was pretty cool."

"So now instead of two parents, you've got four," Mickey said. "You've doubled your chances of doing new stuff, of having more fun."

"I guess so."

"I know so. I had only me mum, and then I lost her to drink when I was ten, and I can tell you, having four parents who want to do stuff with you makes you lucky."

"I guess so," David said, feeling more sure. He finished his soda and tossed it into the trashcan marked CANS. "I've got to go and meet my dad. Thanks for the soda."

"Thanks for marking the cans," Mickey said. "Don't tell your mum what I said about buying a car and making out with girls. She'll have a fit. And while you're working at Ed's store, save some of your money for art stuff. Then you can come and paint a picture of me here hard at work."

David laughed. "Okay," he said. "See you." Maybe his dad would want to do something fun this weekend. Maybe they could go to a baseball game. Kyle would like that, too.

Mickey watched the boy run down the street. The kid seemed all right, and he did a damn fine job with the trashcans. Then he stood up and tossed his own empty soda can in the new recycling bin. He felt good. The trashcans spruced the place up, and maybe he'd helped steer a kid away from a life of petty crime. Not bad for sitting on a lawn chair, drinking a soda, and watching the cars go by.

MAGGIE BORROWED Venus's turquoise dress again for her Friday date with Ed because Ed had seemed to like it. Venus had offered something different, but Maggie thought that if she planned to have a long courtship with Ed, she might need to call on Venus's wardrobe more than once, and she didn't want to push it.

She showered and washed her hair and left it in loose waves. She put on her strappy high-heeled sandals and some makeup, happy that she could see to get her mascara on without poking herself in the eye. She was ready.

Just as she got downstairs, the doorbell rang. *Ed*, she

thought, feeling her heart kick up a notch, and she opened the door to see him standing there, relaxed and handsome. He was wearing all black—black slacks, shirt, and jacket.

He looks like a pirate, Maggie thought. *I'd let him kidnap me.*

"Hi, Maggie," he said, his eyes lingering on her. "You look great. I love that dress. Are you ready?"

"Where are we going?" Maggie asked as they got into his truck. But Ed refused to say, and she was surprised when he drove into the parking lot behind the hardware store.

"Did you forget something?" she asked.

"Come with me." He opened the truck's door for her with a flourish and led her up the stairs to his apartment, motioning for her to go first as he flipped on the light switch.

She gasped when she saw how he'd transformed the place. He'd turned it into a tropical paradise, with an elegant table for two set in the middle of the dining room.

Tropical flowers in festive pots crowded the floor and every available surface. Birds of paradise, bougainvillea, gardenias, and other flowers Maggie couldn't identify bloomed in colorful abandon and lent their heavenly fragrances to the warm air. A small fountain in the corner splashed into a mosaic ceramic bowl, and streams of vivid fringed paper flags hung overhead. In the background, Maggie could hear waves crashing on the shore and the soft strains of a Latin jazz group. Over the top of it all, rich, spicy smells from the kitchen let her know a delicious meal was waiting.

"This is wonderful," she said, turning to him. "I can't believe you did this for me."

"Props, compliments of Medina Garden and Hardware," Ed said. "You mentioned that you hadn't traveled much."

Maggie felt her chest tighten and tears film her eyes. No one had ever done anything so special for her. For a moment she couldn't say anything.

"Maggie?" Ed asked. "Are you okay?"

"Yes," Maggie said, her voice shaky, and Ed tilted her

face so he could see into her eyes.

"It's still not traveling," he said kissing her. "But we couldn't make it to Madrid and be back in time for work tomorrow."

Maggie laughed.

"That's better," he said. "No weeping on the first date, it's a bad omen. So—okay. I thought, we can't travel yet, but we can make a start. Welcome to Casa de Medina de la Hardware," he said with a flourish.

"Gracias," she said, smiling.

"Talking like a native already." Ed took her coat and poured her a glass of wine, and then he handed her a bowl of something to snack on while he finished the meal preparation.

"Try this," he said. "Sort of a ceviche."

"Ceviche? Doesn't that mean raw fish?"

"It means delicious oysters in lime juice. Try it."

The oysters were so good—briny and fresh, tasting of the sea—that Maggie could have eaten nothing else. *No wonder they say oysters are an aphrodisiac,* she thought. *If somebody gave you these, you'd be putty in their hands*, and then she realized that Ed *had* given her those. Well, she was pretty much putty even before the oysters, just by seeing him all dressed up. She leaned on the counter and watched him work, warming to the food, wine, music, and the effort he'd put into entertaining her.

They sat down to a bountiful meal set at a beautiful table in the midst of the floral miracle.

"I hope you're hungry," Ed said.

"When did you have time to make all this?" Maggie gazed at all the steaming dishes. "This food is amazing."

"Don't give me too much credit, *dulcita*," Ed said. "My mom helped with the cooking."

"Really? That seems, ah, surprising."

Ed grinned. "We had a full and frank discussion of the issues. It's too soon to say she's pro-Maggie, but evidently, the talk you two had, which I don't know about and don't *want* to know about, gave her food for thought. And dad was impressed with your work ethic."

"Well, repackaging those bulbs was really more of a favor to me. I was embarrassed just sitting there in the store like a wart on a pickle."

"Nice analogy. I told mom that tonight was a special occasion, so she decided to help out. It's a peace offering, sort of, expressed through good Guatemalan home cooking. Now, do you know what all these things are?"

"I don't know what any of it is, but everything smells delicious," she said. "I'll have to call and thank her."

"She'll be pleased if you do. And I'm sure she'd be happy to give you any cooking advice you want. Or don't want."

Maggie laughed, pointing to a pretty red floral bowl filled to the brim. "I know what that one is, basically. It's chicken. What did you call me? *Dulcita?* What's that?"

Ed laughed. "Specifically, that dish is chicken in green sauce. The green comes from chipotle chiles and tomatillos. Don't worry, it won't scorch your tongue." He waited a beat. "Think it through."

Maggie thought. *Dulcita,* she thought. *Dulce means sweet. Plus the "ita." Little sweet one.* She smiled and he grinned at her, looking like he'd eat her for dessert right now.

"This is a potato and green bean dish," Ed said, handing her the bowl. "What makes it uniquely Guatemalan is the squash seed sauce." He waited until she'd served herself and then he handed her another dish.

"Here we've got tamales negros, or black tamales," he said, and laughed when she winced. "I think you'll like it. You get the dark color by adding chocolate to the sauce."

"It smells wonderful," Maggie said. *First oysters, then chocolate. So far, the aphrodisiac thing is totally working.*

"And to round everything off, a traditional radish salad made with oranges and mint. Let me fill your glass."

Sometime later, Maggie regretfully put down her napkin.

"If I eat one more thing in the next week, I'm going to burst," she said.

"There's banana cake," Ed said.

"In a little while," Maggie said optimistically. "Does your mom cook like this all the time? It's incredible."

"She enjoys an occasion." He grinned. "We always have very schizophrenic holiday meals. For Thanksgiving, we'll have turkey and tortillas, with plantains and cranberries."

"Mixing the old with the new," Maggie said.

Ed nodded. "Blending is good," he said. "Multiculturalism is the wave of the future."

As they talked, the candles tucked around the flowerpots cast a wavering glow of lacy shadows across the walls, and a tape of waves crashing against rocks sounded like the real thing. She wondered if she'd have as much fun traveling to a tropical paradise as she was having in Ed's apartment over the hardware store.

"We could dance," Ed said after a while, and Maggie said, "Let's," so they went into the living room. Ed had banked flowers here, too, and they slid into each other's arms, Maggie nestling her head against Ed's shoulder and Ed resting his cheek on the top of Maggie's head. When the music stopped, they stood there, nestled against each other.

"This is the best date I've had *ever*," she said, and Ed kissed her. His lips touched hers like butterfly wings at first, skimming across her mouth as gently as air, but as Maggie gave herself up to the moment, Ed pulled her closer, sinking one hand in her hair and tightening the other around her waist. She felt his heat through the turquoise dress, her arms resting against his strong ones. Her mouth opened to him and her tongue tasted wine and the spices of the food they'd eaten.

After several long moments he pulled away, his eyes dark with desire. "I've been thinking about nothing but you for days," he said. "Please tell me you're staying with me tonight."

"I want to stay, you're not the only one who's been thinking," Maggie said with a shiver. Ed slid his hands down her back and lifted her, wrapping her legs around his waist and carrying her into the bedroom, where he sat down on the edge of the bed with her still on his lap.

Ed lowered his head to kiss her, and Maggie arched her back against the pressure of his hands and the demands of his mouth, wanting more. He nuzzled her neck as he moved his fingers under her skirt, seeking the heat and silky softness of her inner thigh.

This should be good, Maggie thought through a haze of mindless lust. *I'm not wearing any underwear.*

SHE'S NOT WEARING any underwear. Ed's brain almost shorted out over that one last detail in the mind-blowing picture of Maggie in his bedroom sitting in his lap with her incredible legs wrapped around him kissing him. He moved his fingers higher up her thigh, until his fingers nudged her core and she gasped—but didn't pull away. Drawn by her heat and the softness of her skin he stroked her gently at first and then with increasing urgency as he felt her arms tighten around him and her legs squeeze his waist. Then she cried out and surged against him, clinging to him, nuzzling his neck, whispering soft things against his skin.

Ed held her close to his heart, stroking her back, thinking how maybe that lucky star that followed his family from Guatemala was still shining on him after all.

MAGGIE CLUNG TO Ed, feeling her pounding heart meld with his, gradually coming back to earth, feeling his hand make circles on her back, feeling his arm hold her against him, feeling liquid to her bones and radiant with happiness. She felt him shift against her, turning his head so he could kiss her shoulder, and she leaned back to look at him.

"We're not stopping?"

"I wasn't planning to." Ed nudged her off his lap and, when they were standing, helped her pull her dress up over her head and off. And then she stood before him, naked as the day she was born. She felt her skin glow, like it was a beacon in the candle-lit room, and her dark hair tickled down her back.

"I have fantasized about you all week," Ed said. "You're more beautiful than I had ever imagined."

"What else was in your fantasy?" Maggie asked. "Maybe I could do it, if it isn't too complicated. I didn't bring any props."

"Help me take my clothes off," Ed said.

"I can do that." Maggie stroked her hands across his chest, feeling the smooth cotton under her fingers, the strength of his chest, and began to unbutton his shirt.

"When you picked me up tonight, I thought you looked like a pirate," she whispered, opening his shirt and running her hands under it, up his chest and around to his back, leaning into him and nipping his shoulder before kissing it.

"What do you think now?" Ed pulled the shirt off as Maggie went to work on his belt buckle.

"I feel like I'm sailing in dangerous waters," she said. "With a pirate."

"Let me steal you away." He shrugged out of the rest of his clothes and pulled her onto the bed with him, wrapping his arms around her and kissing her until she was breathless and desire lapped in her belly again. She leaned into him, half sprawled across his chest, as he touched her, holding her. His hands were sure and demanding, stroking her everywhere, causing her nerves to tingle and the tightness in her belly to spiral.

He rolled away, leaving her for a second, and then he found the condom and came back, his hands sliding under her, pulling her hips to his, kissing her mouth, her neck, her shoulder, until she felt the ache down into her toes. And then he was inside, pushing into her, thrusting against her, and she rocked against him, finding their rhythm, feeling the spiral start low and build, feeling him against her, hot with desire, seeing him want her, and she felt the tension build and the desire mount and the heat cascade and she felt him push harder and higher and still the heat and the tension and the desire built until there was nothing but Ed and his hot, dark eyes, holding her hips, holding her gaze, and when she peaked against him, Ed came with her.

They lay, limp and spent, not moving until their minds came back, and then Ed put his arm around her and pulled her close, kissing her a couple of times before he curled against her.

He's a cuddler, Maggie thought, feeling lucky. "Ed?"

"Maggie?"

"We didn't get to your fantasy, did we?"

His arm tightened around her as he laughed, a low, re-laxed rumble deep in his chest.

"If you mean, did we complete my fantasy of getting you naked and having mind-blowing sex, I got that," Ed said. "If you mean, did I have an idea I wanted to try and have we tried it yet, well, no. But there's plenty of time. We have all night. And tomorrow."

All night, Maggie thought, and *tomorrow*, and then, *more fantasies*, and she felt very, very lucky.

HOURS LATER, ED sat up against the headboard, eating a piece of banana cake, watching Maggie sleep. He'd dozed off but, unused to having anyone in his bed, had awakened when Maggie had thrown an arm over him. Then he remem-bered the banana cake and tiptoed out to get some. He thought about all the kinds of hungers he was having with Maggie and wondered if they'd ever be satisfied.

"Hey." Maggie opened her eyes, her voice groggy. "What's going on? Banana cake?" She stretched, smiling at him, re-laxed and sleepy and as boneless as a cat. Her tangled hair spread out over the pillow, and he could see one breast peek-ing out from the sheet that didn't quite cover her. His groin tightened and heat spread down through his legs.

Ed broke off a piece for her. "Want some?"

"Mm." Maggie raised herself up on one elbow, which exposed her other breast, and Ed felt his mouth go dry. She licked the cake from his fingers. "Good."

When she'd swallowed the morsel, he swiped his finger across the cake's frosting and smeared it over her nipple, and then he smeared the other one before he bent his head to lick it off her. *I'll never look at banana cake the same way again*, Ed thought before he gave himself up to seeing how many places on Maggie's body he could crumble cake and then lick it up.

IN THE MORNING, a barefoot Maggie sat across from Ed at the dining room table, dressed in one of Ed's clean white T-shirts and a pair of Ed's coveralls with the legs rolled up, and, surrounded by the flowers and fountain and palms, ate her Cheerios. She felt radiantly happy.

"You could have brought a change of clothes," Ed said, rubbing her feet under the table with his own. "Not that I mind your wearing mine."

"I didn't want to seem too slutty," Maggie said. "What if you didn't invite me to stay?"

"Like there was any chance of that." Ed grabbed two pieces of toast from the toaster and handed one to her. "You're pretty cute the way you are, but I don't know what you're going to do about shoes."

"I'll wear my heels," Maggie said, inspecting her strappy, spike-heeled sandals.

"A slutty vibe," Ed said, looking interested, and Maggie felt her blood heat up. *I'm hot,* Maggie thought, *Ed's hot for me. Yes.*

Ed had promised her pancakes in the morning, but then they'd decided to shower together and that turned out to take longer than they'd expected, saving neither time nor water. When they emerged from the steamy bathroom, Maggie had asked, "Was that your fantasy?" and Ed said, "Not yet." With no time for pancakes now, since Ed had to get to the hardware store, they got dressed and sat down to Cheerios, their bare feet touching under the table.

Then Maggie remembered what her mother had asked her to do that day.

"My mom wants to sell the shop and retire," she told Ed.

Ed glanced at her as he poured a second cup of coffee.

"When? To whom?"

"Soon. To Ian Strachan."

Ed added milk to his coffee and stirred it. "Why not to you?"

Maggie stared at him. "To me?"

"Why not? You don't like your job. You like her store. You'd be great in retail. Your mom would give you a payment plan."

"It couldn't support me and the kids," Maggie said, her mind refusing to acknowledge the sudden rush of hope she felt.

"No? That was quite a birthday party she threw for herself. Ask to see the books. It's worth a shot."

Maggie felt happiness, wonder, amazement, pleasure, and mind-numbing joy radiate from her face and leak from every pore.

"What?" Ed sipped his coffee.

I love you, Maggie thought.

"That's a great idea, Ed," she said. "I'll ask her about it."

Chapter 20

As soon as the last customer departed the garage at six that evening, Mickey pulled out one of the tattered lawn chairs from behind the storage bin and set it up on an oil stain between the hydraulic hoists, falling into it with a sigh of bone-weary exhaustion and putting his feet up on a stack of tires. Thank God it was Saturday. The garage was closed tomorrow. He'd never been so knackered. *If I'd known how much work it was to go straight,* Mickey thought, *I never would have done it.* Then he remembered Mars and that fierce death grip on his throat and thought, *well, maybe I would have.*

Denny Carlson came out of the office carrying a bottle of single malt Scotch whisky and two tumblers and handed them to Mickey. He retrieved the mate to Mickey's shabby chair and set it up on the other side of the tire stack. Then he took the bottle back, poured two fingers into each glass that Mickey was holding, took one glass for himself, and set the bottle on the floor between them.

"Here's mud in your eye," he said, lifting his glass to Mickey.

"Cheers." They each took a sip, and Mickey savored the smooth glide of the liquor as it went down. That was a mighty fine distillation, and having a drink at the end of the day with the boss was a mighty fine tradition.

Denny settled back into his chair, shifting a bit.

"So," he said.

Mickey reached into his pockets, looking for his smokes, wondering what his employer wanted to say.

Denny shifted again, and Mickey lit up, inhaling the smoke deeply into his lungs. He usually never smoked on the job, but Saturdays were long days, and he was overdue. He got up to get the tin can he used for an ashtray.

"I was wondering," Denny said when Mickey sat down again, balancing the tin can on his knee.

"Uh," Mickey said, to encourage him.

"What are your plans, down the road?"

Mickey glanced at him in surprise. "Dunno," he said, "exactly." Frowning, he gazed out the garage door, still open to the balmy fall weather. "I'm thinkin' that me partner will finish his business here, and then we'll go back."

Denny nodded. He took another sip of Scotch.

"How long do you think that might take? To finish your business?"

Mickey shook his head. "No telling. We've been here, what—two weeks already? And nothing's happened so far."

Denny nodded again. Mickey smoked.

"I was thinking," Denny said.

Mickey tapped his ash into the tin can.

"I could use some help," Denny said. "Permanent, like."

Mickey jerked his head to stare at his boss. "What?"

Denny shrugged. "You can see how busy we are. There's plenty of work. You're a good mechanic. You could stay." He paused. "If your other situation doesn't work out."

Mickey marveled. He'd been at the garage for less than two weeks, a criminal— even if not a convicted one—and this innocent wanted to hire him.

"Thanks, Den," he said, "but I don't think so."

Denny nodded, as if in agreement. "It's a lot of responsibility, taking on half a garage," he said. "I don't blame you."

"What?"

"Partnership," Denny said. "Taking on half the garage. It's a lot of work."

"Partnership? You'd give me half the garage?"

"Well, I wouldn't *give* it to you. I'd *sell* it to you. But yes, I think you'd make a good partner."

"Why's that?" Mickey felt like he'd been hit sideways in the head.

Denny shrugged. "You know cars," he said. "You give a fair day's work, and you're good with the customers. I've been looking for somebody to come in with me. I've got too much work and I'm not getting any younger. Nobody I've talked to about it is right."

Partner? Mickey had never owned anything in his life. He could be his own boss. No more following Ian around like a bloody servant to the king. He could make his own decisions, earn his own money.

Then he thought of the diamonds. There was a lot of money in diamonds, more than in a garage. A lot more.

But the likelihood of going to prison for stealing diamonds was high. He'd hated the one night he'd spent in jail. Mickey thought about small, enclosed, barred spaces. He thought about bad food and vicious drunks. He didn't want to go to prison.

He studied the garage and its organized chaos. He scanned the cars driving down the wide street, the trees casting their shade on the sidewalk, the other neat businesses he could see.

Okay, he'd thought Cedarburg was a prison, too. But that was before he was offered a partnership. Before he talked to the kid. Maybe he could fit in here after all, build a place here in this town. Put down roots. Be a guy who owned a garage. Half a garage, anyway.

"Maybe we could put in a car wash," he said. "Do body repair."

"Good idea," Denny said. "Detailing, painting—there's a lot of things we could do."

Mickey took a sip of Scotch, putting out his cigarette. Denny took a sip from his own glass.

"I don't have any money," Mickey said.

Denny shrugged. "Didn't figure you did. We could have Timmy Hedrich or Henry Wusterbarth work something out so you pay your share through wages or profits."

Mickey contemplated the stained concrete floors, the hydraulic hoists, the tires, the tools, the shelves, the displays, the torn calendar, the garage door with its cracked and peeling paint. *Half of this could be mine*, he thought. *Maybe, in time, all of it.*

"The first thing we do is paint that door," he said.

"Okay." Denny cracked a smile for the first time. "Partner." He leaned forward and reached his hand out to Mickey, who leaned forward to shake it.

"Okay," Mickey said, saying goodbye forever to Ian, diamonds, and a life of crime and hello to oil spots, business ownership, and broken-down cars.

"I'LL PICK YOU UP as soon as I close the store," Ed said to Maggie on the phone. "Ten minutes, tops." He waved goodnight to two of the clerks as they left for the evening.

"You could stay over here," Maggie said. "But then, you'd be stuck wearing my clothes in the morning."

Ed was loving this conversation. When they'd parted in the morning, they'd agreed they wanted to spend Saturday night and Sunday together. Now here they were, having a mundane conversation about where. *We're a 'we' already,* Ed thought. *We're an 'us.' I think.*

"But I have all those leftovers," Ed said. "Think tamales negros." He lowered his voice. "Think *banana cake*." He let his voice linger on the words.

"What are you doing sitting around at the hardware store?" Maggie said. "Get over here and pick me up."

Ed laughed. "Be there soon, *querida*," he said, disconnecting.

"Me esperas?" Alberto said, right behind him, relaxing into Spanish now that all the customers and other clerks had left.

Ed jumped. How did his father sneak up on him like that?

"Si," he agreed. He *had* been waiting for his father. "Es

tarde," he said. "Son las seis." Six o'clock. Closing time.

"Were you talking to that Maggie Jorgenson?"

"Yes." He hated that his father said *that Maggie Jorgenson*, as though that were a bad thing. But he didn't want to start an argument now when Maggie was waiting for him.

"The one who helped me package the bulbs the other day. The one your mother cooked for. The one with three children."

Ed nodded, feeling like he was fifteen again.

"Did she like the meal?"

"She said it was delicious." *Especially the banana cake.*

"She has good taste, then," Alberto said.

Ed was so relieved, he laughed. "You don't mind that she's not my brother's wife's cousin? That she might not exactly fit in with the family? She doesn't speak Spanish."

Alberto shrugged. "Your mother is not precisely happy about it, but she is resigning herself. And she says, by now you are old enough, you should know what suits you. Although I must warn you, she says it with a sniff."

"And you, Papi? What do you think?"

Alberto smiled. "Of all our kids, you were the headstrong one. I hope you know what you're doing."

"I'm going to need your advice with her kids," Ed said before he stopped to think about it.

"Children keep you young. David will turn out okay, I think. The others—you like them? They like you?"

"I like them. The baby, a little girl, she likes me. The boys will need more time."

"Better get going, then," Alberto said. "I'll lock up here. You don't want to keep Maggie waiting."

"No," Ed said. "Thanks. I'll see you Monday."

"I'll tell your mother," Alberto said ambiguously.

GRAYSON MOCHRIE sat across from Peg Sontag in a booth at the diner, now closed late on Saturday night. Peg had turned off the neon sign outside and dimmed the interior lights, but anybody driving down Main Street could see them, sitting in a booth in the window, leaning toward each other over pie and coffee, talking.

He'd been sitting there for some time. He'd come from the latest fruitless search for Donald Nennig and the diamonds that he was sure were hidden somewhere in this town. Driving down Main St. toward the diner and something to eat, he'd seen Mickey Adair and Denny Carlson come out of the garage, lock the door, shake hands, and part ways, each heading in opposite directions. He'd thought about stopping Adair for another chat, but then he hadn't. He'd questioned the man multiple times already, and the results were always the same: Adair didn't know anything. Didn't know Nennig. Hadn't seen him. Grayson believed him. The whole situation was very strange.

Now he was sitting with Peg in the diner eating berry pie with cream. In the diner, the only crime was not doing justice to the meal.

"So Peggy, love," he said when he'd finished the pie, "tell me—have you ever been to Scotland? It's a lovely place."

"I've been," Peg said, her voice rueful. "But it's a sad story."

"Scotland's a place for tragedy," said Grayson. "Tell me."

So Peg told him about her vacation.

"I've always had this thing about Scotland," she said, embarrassed. "I've read all kinds of histories and novels and guidebooks, and I know it's shallow of me, but I've always loved the accent. I could listen to a Scots accent for hours."

Good news, Grayson thought.

"I'd always wanted to go there, and then three years ago my best friend from college and I decided we'd go for three weeks," she said.

"Sounds like a dream come true." Grayson got up to get them more coffee. "Where's the tragedy?"

"It *was* a dream come true." She paused. "This is embarrassing."

"No worries," Grayson said. "A copper's heard it all."

Peg drew in a deep breath. "Well—the accent, the history, the castles, the legends—okay, I've already said I'm shallow. I'll admit it. I always had this fantasy that I'd marry a Scot and go to live in Scotland."

Hallelujah, Grayson thought.

"It sounds crazy and juvenile," Peg said.

"No, it doesn't." Grayson stirred milk and sugar into his coffee. "It shows that you are a woman of distinction and discernment, as well as very high intelligence."

"Oh," Peg said, coloring. "Well, thank you. So anyway, Teri—that's my college friend—and I went to Scotland, and we had a marvelous time. We signed up for one of those guided tours on a bus. The tours were localized, we enjoyed the sights, and the guide brought everything to life."

"I'm getting a bad feeling about this," Grayson said.

"I thought you might," Peg said. "The guide didn't just bring history to life. He also brought Teri to life. They fell in love, and she stayed behind and now they're as happy as two stoats in heather, from what I can tell. She's expecting their first baby in January."

"Ouch."

Peg laughed. "I don't begrudge Teri her happiness. Well, maybe a little. But somehow it doesn't seem fair that she got to have my fantasy."

"There's other Scotsmen who'd be willing to fulfill your fantasies," Grayson said, watching her.

"Yes," Peg said. "I've thought of that."

ED SAT AT THE END of his sofa, his arm around Maggie, who had her feet tucked up and her head on his shoulder. They'd finished watching the 1941 film version of *The Man Who Came to Dinner*. Maggie had seen it once before, but she loved the hilarious story of the crotchety man whose unexpected sojourn in the house of strangers causes the family members to fulfill unexpected destinies. Sort of like Ed and her, when her eyes were glued shut.

She felt warm and content, full of leftover chicken in

green sauce and tamales negros. She'd been disappointed when Ed had served her banana cake on a plate, but she'd caught a twinkle in his eye, so she hoped for a different fantasy from him soon.

Ed clicked the remote to close the system and then leaned over to kiss her until she felt almost dizzy.

"Are you ready for bed?" he asked. "Because the night's still young. And I have plans for you."

Excellent, Maggie thought.

"Is this the fantasy?" she asked, following him into the bedroom.

"One of many." He bent to kiss her, running his hands up her arms. "I need you to agree to something," he said. "Nothing painful."

"Okay." Maggie tilted her head so he could kiss her shoulder.

"You don't want to know what it is?"

"Yes. But as long as it doesn't hurt, I'll do it."

Ed laughed and licked her earlobe, drawing it into his mouth.

"I want you to wear something for me," Ed said, sliding his fingers through her hair.

"What?" Maggie held onto his arms and let her head fall back into his hands, her eyes closed. "Fishnets? Garters? Teddy? Lace thong? I have to warn you, I won't look that good in a lace thong. Not to mention, they itch."

"A blindfold," Ed said.

"What?"

"All that weekend when your eyes were glued shut, I kept thinking what it would be like to make love to you when you couldn't see where I'd be touching you next."

Maggie thought about what that would be like, and she felt her blood quicken.

"Okay," she said.

"You don't know what temptation I faced." Ed went to a dresser drawer and opened it, pulling out a pink paisley bandana. "This is you, I think." He advanced toward her, and

Maggie thought of him as a pirate again.

"Ready?" he asked. "Close your eyes." Then she felt the soft cotton against her face and the band snugged up against the back of her head. And then everything was dark and she felt disoriented. She reached behind her and felt his thigh.

"Can you see anything?" he asked, and when she said no, he said, "I'm going to undress you now." But then nothing happened. It was still in the bedroom and Ed didn't make his move. Maggie tensed up.

Why doesn't he start? she wondered. She knew he was still standing behind her, she still had her hand touching his leg for balance. But he wasn't doing anything, not even touching her. Ages seemed to go buy. Her nerves stretched. Her breathing seemed to fill the room.

Then a feather light touch, so light she almost wasn't sure she felt it, whispered across her breast. She gasped, instantly aroused.

And Ed stepped away. She couldn't touch him anymore.

"Ed," she said.

"*Querida,*" he said, off to her side, and then she felt a finger tracing circles behind her knee. Liquid heat pooled through her legs. Slowly he traced a line up the inside of her thigh. She was still wearing Ed's overalls and the T-shirt, spike heels, and no underwear that she'd started out wearing that morning, because Ed had seemed to like the look. The overalls were so big that they'd fall off her if Ed opened the snaps, but he didn't seem to be in any hurry. *And I'm not either*, Maggie thought, wondering if her heart could pound any harder.

Ed stopped his exploration well short of where Maggie hoped he'd been going.

"Hold your hair up for me, please, *dulcita*," he said, and she twisted her hair into a roll and held it to the top of her head. And then Ed let his hand trail up over her bottom and around her waist and inside the bib of her overall while Maggie let her head drop back against his shoulder and then his hand went lower and still lower until he'd reached the soft triangle where her legs met and then he slipped his finger inside her and she jerked against his hand.

"I like this no underwear thing," Ed breathed into her ear. "Very sexy." He was holding her tight against him, and his fingers were doing delicious things to her. And then his hand was gone and she felt abandoned, until she felt him undo the hooks on the bib and the coverall fell to her knees, and then he pushed the T-shirt up and then it was over her head, and she stood there wearing only her high heels and a pink paisley bandana blindfold.

"You are so beautiful." Ed's voice was husky, his breath stirring against her skin, but Maggie could hear him smile. "And you're at my mercy."

"Don't forget I'm wearing high heels," Maggie said, breathlessly. "A woman can do a lot of damage in high heels."

"I like to live on the edge," Ed said, and then he stepped in close to her and put his hands on her waist and lifted her up; she wrapped her legs around him, and he carried her to the bed and lay down with her.

"The reality is so much better than my fantasy," he said, kissing her, running his fingers over her cheeks and across her nose, over her lips, around her ear, down her neck. And then his hands were everywhere, hot and strong and sure, and his breath sent chills and heat across her skin, setting her on fire, and his mouth and tongue surprised her and then inflamed her until he went inside of her.

Afterward, she lay languidly in his arms, feeling his strength enclose her, feeling the wild beating of his heart as it slowed. Feeling that she could lie in Ed's arms every night and tell him anything, and he would get it, get *her*.

"I talked to my mom today," she said. "We think that I can take over her store."

She could feel his smile against her hair. "That's great, Maggie. I'm proud of you."

He pulled the pink bandana up over her head and smoothed her hair back, kissing her again, and she turned her back to his chest, taking his hand with her so that he cradled her against his chest, like spoons in a drawer.

"Good night, Ed."

"I love you, Maggie," he said, half asleep.

Maggie felt herself go very still. *Please don't say that unless you mean it,* she thought. *I couldn't bear it if you didn't mean it.*

Chapter 21

S o that's it? You're *staying* here?" Ian turned from Ray and gazed down the dusty driveway of the Strodthoff farm. Other than the array of vehicles that no doubt had depressing practical uses, Ian could see nothing out here but the red barn, the white house, the fences, and the cows. Ray had a stubborn tilt to his chin as he leaned against Ian's red compact rental.

"I like it here," he said simply. "I love this girl. We plan to marry."

Ian shook his head at the foolishness of youth.

"Keep my share of the diamonds," Ray said. "I don't want them." He leaned over to shake Ian's hand, who dropped it quickly and got in the car.

"Ta then," Ian said. That was it. You bring a jewel thief from Europe on a tricky mission and lose him to love on an Iowa farm. It showed you how the world had gone mad.

He'd had much the same conversation with Mickey. He'd found him at the petrol station, where he was spending all his time these days, scraping the garage door after hours, two gallons of pristine white paint stacked in a corner.

"I'm going to be a partner," he'd said to Ian. "I'll own half. I won't have to be watching over my shoulder for coppers all the time."

"You're a city rat from Glasga," Ian had said. "What are you going to do in the country?"

"Don't know," Mickey had said. "I might have to go to Chicago and steal a car now and then, just for practice."

"You won't make any money in this," Ian had said.

Mickey had shrugged. "Won't make a lot, but it'll be steady," he'd said. "You can't spend any money in jail."

So now Ian was back at the Lay-Z Stay, packing. He laid his folded clothes in the open suitcase lying on his bed, secured the internal elastic straps to hold everything in place, closed the lid, and snapped it shut.

He was heading back to New York. He'd never hooked up with Donald Nennig, who'd shown an unbelievable indifference to fencing a small fortune in stolen diamonds. Un-effing-believable! But Donald Nennig wasn't the only fence in the world, and if he didn't want to do business with them, their crew boss would find somebody else who did. If they couldn't make a quick connection in New York, Ian would go back to Glasgow and take the diamonds with him.

The stones were the last thing to pack. He picked up the goldfish bowl and carried it into the bathroom, where he scooped out the little fish to toss it into the toilet. But the fish had a sixth sense about survival and didn't want to leave the aquatic confines of its bowl. It wriggled. Water spilled out of the bowl, and the bowl slipped out of Ian's hands. It smashed on the sink, scattering broken glass and pretty pebbles everywhere. The fish went into the toilet after all.

Ian cursed and then he began picking up the pebbles and dropping them into a small plastic bag. Only the small, grayish-pink, quartzlike ones.

Only the diamonds.

He left the motel, closing the door behind him. The Lay-Z Stay had been adequate for his purposes. Still, he'd be happy to see the end of the place. He had tossed his bag into the trunk of the rental when somebody grabbed him from behind, jerking his arm up behind his back, shoving his face hard against the roof of the small car.

"Hey!" Ian said.

"Just checking," a man's voice said, and then a hand was patting him down, searching for weapons, which Ian never carried. The hand pulled out Ian's wallet and found the small bag of diamonds pinned to the inside of his shorts.

"You can have those," the voice said. "I'm not interested in diamonds."

The hand that had patted him down jerked him around and Ian saw his attacker. He was tall, with cold gray eyes and dark hair. He looked like he could handle himself in a fight. But Ian could, too, even if he was smaller.

"Who are you, and what do you want?" Ian asked. He squared his feet to get ready for whatever was coming.

"I'm a friend of Doris Perl," Mars said, seemingly relaxed. "You owe her some money."

"You're daft," Ian said. "I worked in her store for her after she had her heart attack. If anything, *she* owes *me* money."

"I don't think so, mate," Mars said. "Seven-eighths of the till every day isn't the going rate. Anyway, she needs the money and you don't." He flipped open Ian's wallet and counted the bills in it, taking out all but three of them.

"You don't know what you're going on about." Ian's anger grew as he saw how much money the bruiser was taking out of his wallet. "I *earned* this money."

"You earned *some* money. What I took"—Mars held up the folded notes for Ian to see—"is what you stole. That's what I'm giving back to her."

Ian's frustrations about his failed weeks in Cedarburg boiled over.

"Go to hell," he said, punching his fist into Mars's abdomen with all the considerable force he could muster.

Mars absorbed the blow without flinching and in a response so fast that Ian was never sure how the bruiser did it, slammed the edge of his open hand down on Ian's wrist like a kung fu master breaking a brick. Ian bellowed in pain. He leaned against the rental car, glaring at Mars.

"You didn't have to hit me that hard," he complained,

cradling the injured arm.

Mars shrugged. "You might want to have that checked out before you leave. And when you *do* leave, Ian?" He spoke softly, but with the threat clear in his voice. "Don't come back." He pocketed the wad of bank notes he'd taken from Ian's wallet as Ian unlocked his car. When he turned back, the bruiser was gone. How could he have disappeared so quickly and silently? Although he was relieved the encounter was over. Ian got carefully in the compact and drove himself to the hospital.

An hour later, Rosario de Moya pushed her cleaning cart down the covered walkway of the Lay-Z Stay Motel and stopped in front of room number nine. Benny had told her this guest had checked out.

She knocked and said "housekeeping," and when no one answered, she took out her ring of keys, unlocked the door, and went in.

The bathroom was a mess. Broken glass everywhere, water everywhere, little polished stones everywhere. When she checked the toilet, she saw a goldfish swimming around. He seemed okay, maybe a little bewildered.

She unwrapped one of the plastic water glasses they put in the rooms, scooped the little fish out of the toilet, and took him out to the cleaning cart. The container was so small he barely had room to fan his tail, but she'd stop by the Medinas' hardware store on her way home and get a bigger bowl for him. And then she pulled out some trash bags, paper towels, and cleanser and went back to the mess inside.

Thirty minutes later the bathroom looked clean, but she decided to do one more sweep before she declared the room finished. Broken glass was dangerous and hard to see. She wouldn't want a child to go in there barefoot and cut his foot on a sliver.

She wiped up the floor and then the counter one more time, and as she swept the towel around the sink fixtures, she felt a hard scrape against her hand and was glad she'd checked again. A good-sized chunk of glass had been hidden there.

She examined it more closely. It wasn't glass, after all. It was one of the pebbles that she'd found, one that had been at the bottom of the fish bowl. It didn't look like the others, though. The other pebbles had been brown and blue and gray, polished smooth. This one was a grayish pink and much rougher; it looked sort of like quartz.

She tucked it into her pocket. She'd show it to her geology professor tomorrow in class, along with the other pebbles she'd saved. He'd know what it was.

GRAYSON MOCHRIE was heading out. He'd learned that Ian Strachan had checked out of the Lay-Z-Stay, bound for New York. He'd give chase another day or two in the Big Apple, coordinating with the New York detectives, but if Ian stayed Stateside, then he'd head home and leave the case to the New York side of their bust and be happy to do it.

He had only one thing left to do, but first he had to call Joe Nennig, the local jeweler, at his home. The detective had abandoned the idea that Joe was working with his brother Donald in the crime business. That solution would have been so easy, but it hadn't panned out. Nothing about the three Scottish jewel thieves had panned out. With luck, they might catch the diamonds on Ian Strachan in New York, but Ray Corkin and Mickey Adair were staying in America, and their criminal days, if not over, would soon be the Americans' problem. Off his plate, ta very much.

So he was going back without the three jewel couriers, but if luck held and the gods were kind, he wouldn't be going back alone. But first he needed to get Joe Nennig to come to the shop, even if it was an official day of rest.

"Mr. Mochrie, it's Sunday," Joe Nennig protested. "Come into the store tomorrow. I'll help you then."

"I canna," Grayson said. "I have to leave today. And it's very important. The lives of two people are at stake."

There was a pause as Joe Nennig considered whether saving the lives of two people justified leaving his Sabbath nap and newspaper.

"Very well," he said. "Anything I can do for humanitarian purposes. Say, fifteen minutes?"

Grayson was pacing in front of the store in ten when Joe Nennig entered the shop from the back and opened the door from the inside.

"I need a lady's ring," Grayson said. "A nice ring. An expensive ring."

Joe Nennig blinked, and Grayson understood why Donald had never brought his brother into his jewel thieving racket, even though the setup of Joe's owning this shop must have been tempting. Joe didn't seem smart enough for a life of crime. In fact, Joe barely seemed smart enough for a life of honesty. The entire village by now had to know that the Scottish policeman had been courting Peg Sontag.

"Well, let's see," Joe said, moving behind a display case. "We have a nice selection. Is there anything you were interested in particularly?"

"Diamonds," Grayson said, "if you have them."

Joe Nennig had just the ring—a beautiful, old-fashioned, square-cut stone set in a gold band—and Grayson paid for it with his credit card, hoping he wouldn't have to return it. Then he drove across the village and stopped his car outside Peg's inviting, one-story bungalow, with its bright yellow door and smoke drifting from the chimney. Suddenly nervous, he approached the house and rang the bell. Peg looked surprised when she opened the door for him.

"Do ye have a minute, Peggy, love? I'd like to have a wee chat with ye, if ye can spare the time."

Once inside and seated on a comfortable overstuffed chair next to the cheery fire, he didn't know how to start. Peggy Sontag was a talented, independent woman who owned her own home and ran her own successful business, and she didn't need anyone to take care of her. The last thing she wanted was an old, ugly bachelor who had a brutal job and lived an ocean away. What had he been thinking?

"I'm leaving tonight," he said. "Ray and Mickey are

staying here, may the good people of Cedarburg never live to regret it, but I'm following Ian Strachan. He's headed to New York, and so am I."

"I'll miss you," she said.

That was something, at least. *Now or never,* he thought. Mustering his courage, he dug into his jacket pocket and pulled out the small jeweler's box. He closed his eyes. *Please let me do this right,* he thought. *Please let her say yes.*

He got down on his knee next to her chair and opened the box, showing her the diamond ring.

"I'm not an eloquent man, but I love you, Peggy Sontag. We've not known each other long, but I feel that I've been searching for you my entire life. And now that I've found you, I hope you'll make me the happiest man on earth by becoming my wife."

Peg smiled at him, her eyes soft, and put her hand against his face. "Yes," she said. "Yes."

Relief and joy flooded through him. "That's brilliant, love, brilliant," he said. "I'll do everything in my power to make you happy. But we have a bit of a problem now, and I'm hoping you'll give in to me on this one wee thing. I'll never ask for another thing, I promise."

"You'll never ask me for another thing?" Peg asked, laughter in her eyes.

"Never," Grayson vowed. "Well, maybe for the correct time now and then, but only if my watch has stopped. I promise."

"What do you need?"

"Do ye think ye could live in Scotland?"

"Are you kidding?" Peg asked. "It would be a dream come true."

Grayson felt his breath go out in a whoosh. "Peggy, lass, my love, my heart, everything I have is yours, everything I am is yours."

Peg took Grayson's ring from the box and slipped it onto her finger. It fit perfectly.

"Your plane doesn't leave for hours yet," she said, standing up and reaching for Grayson's hand. "Come with me. I have some etchings I've been wanting to show you." And she led him to the back of her house, to her bedroom.

THAT NIGHT ED, wearing a towel, and Maggie, wearing Ed's bathrobe, stood over Ed's sink and brushed their teeth. Maggie grinned at him in the mirror, feeling drunk with happiness, and realized how goofy she looked with toothpaste foam smeared over half her face. Good thing Ed didn't seem to mind that she was smeared with weird substances most of the time.

"Godda fpit," she said, and bumped him out of the way to lean over and spit out the foam and rinse her mouth and face.

"By durn," Ed said, when she came up dripping, and he bumped her back and rinsed his own mouth, and then they toweled off and headed into Ed's bedroom.

"Alone at last," Ed said, which was a joke since they'd spent the whole day together. Now he untied the sash of her robe, sliding his hands over her waist and around her back, drawing her closer.

"I wish tomorrow weren't Monday," Maggie said as he pulled her onto the bed and rolled her on top of him.

"Fulfills another of my fantasies," Ed said, nuzzling her neck.

"How can that be?" Maggie asked. "Tomorrow's *Monday*."

"I've been imagining what it would be like to live with you," Ed said, sliding his hand up her back under the robe and smoothing her hair back with the other. "What it would be like brushing my teeth with you every night. Getting up with you to go to work in the morning."

Maggie felt her blood thicken as her breath left her body.

"Now you know," she said.

"Not yet," Ed said. "Not really. Maybe in a few years. Fifty or so." He kissed her then, and she tasted peppermint on his breath.

Sometime later, after a few more of Ed's fantasies had

been fulfilled, they lay entwined, their fingers tracing idle patterns on each other's skin.

"So what's your plan, Maggie?" Ed asked, kissing the top of her head, which was nestled against his shoulder. "About your job and your mom's store?"

She smiled. "Tomorrow I go into the law office and give two weeks' notice. Then in two weeks I have a garage sale and get rid of all my navy-colored clothes."

Ed laughed. "And your mother's store? Are you taking that over in two weeks? Will she be ready to get out that quickly?"

"She says yes," Maggie said. "There's the matter of buying for the Christmas season, though. She'd been planning to go on that cruise, but she's not sure if she's strong enough yet, and she doesn't want to buy anything for my store anyway, so I'll have to figure something else out."

He was silent a moment, while he traced figure eights on her arm. "Does she still have the ticket?" he asked. "Maybe you could go in her place."

"Maybe," Maggie said, snuggling closer.

"Maybe I could go with you," he said. She lifted her head, startled.

"*Would* you? I'd love it if you'd come. That would be *great*, Ed."

"Maybe it could be our honeymoon."

Maggie closed her eyes. "Ed—"

Married. He wanted to get married. He'd wanted to dance and then go out and now he wanted to get married, and he liked her kids and they liked him. She felt lightheaded and dizzy with lust and love. What could she say to a man like this?

"Or not," he said, his voice a little strained. "A vacation would be great, too. I don't want—Maggie, you're crying. What's the matter?"

She realized she was crying, as well as clutching his shoulder. The better to hang onto him with.

"What's wrong, dulcita?" he asked, sounding very

worried now. "I didn't mean to make you cry. I take it all back. Tell me what's the matter."

"You can't take it back." Maggie sniffed. "You said 'honeymoon.' That's what I want, a honeymoon," Maggie said, a hiccup in her voice. "A honeymoon would be even more fun than a vacation."

"That's good then, right?" Ed asked, handing her a tissue. "Because that's what I thought, too. No cause for crying. Although I didn't ask you to marry me the right way. I should have had a ring. We should have been at a romantic dinner somewhere. You could have worn the turquoise dress."

"No, Ed, this was perfect."

"I pictured it all different, though. That I'd ask you at a nice restaurant, with a view and a ring and a speech. But you were standing there at the sink in my robe covered in toothpaste gunk, and I couldn't stop thinking about how I want you just like that every night, all the time. I couldn't stop myself."

"I'm glad about that," Maggie said. "Nobody has ever loved me covered in toothpaste foam before."

"I think the cereal mush set me up," Ed said. "I've always been a pushover for cereal mush."

"I love you, Ed," Maggie said, and kissed him.

"I love you," Ed said. "So we'll get married when? I can wait until your kids are ready, however long that takes. But if you think they're ready now, and if we want the cruise to be our honeymoon, we've got some time constraints."

"It's a lot to think about."

"There's no pressure, though. No matter what, we'll take the cruise and you can make it a holiday merchandise buying trip. Maybe some of my relatives could meet us at the ports. My uncle Esteban will love you."

"That sounds great," Maggie said. "We can talk to the kids tomorrow, but I think they'll be fine with our getting married."

"I think so too," Ed said. "And then we can set a date. Sooner or later, depending."

"Sounds like a plan," Maggie said.

He pulled her closer and adjusted the flannel comforter around her shoulders. "The weather's changing," Ed said as they snuggled. "Feel it? It's getting colder."

"Colder weather can have some nice side effects, you know," Maggie said, resting her head on Ed's shoulder and tangling her legs with his. "But that reminds me I should have someone look at my furnace."

"I can do that," Ed said, "but not right now." Then he bent his head to hers and focused on kissing her.

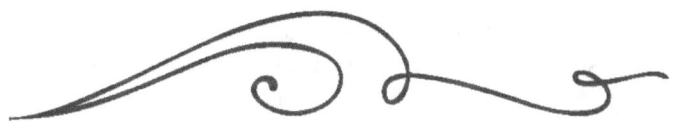

Chapter 22

T his Cedarburg job went well," Mars observed as they prepared to leave town on a bright Monday morning.

"Maybe for you." Venus sniffed as she composed a note for their next-door neighbor. "I can't believe how Dr. J messed me up. *First* he tells me Maggie is supposed to date the guy who's headed to the slammer and rotten to the core, so I set her up with that Ian Strachan."

"Hard to believe anybody thought *that* was a good idea."

"Yeah, well, who knows *what* our fearless leader thinks, right? Now it turns out, it was just our horrible cell service provider garbling our messages. No wonder there were so many mistakes."

Mars finished his coffee and rinsed out the mug. "But in the end, it all turned out okay. No harm done."

Venus glanced up from her note. "We were lucky. I plan to speak to Dr. J when we get back, because if he wants to send us to places with no cell service, we have to get a better communication system."

"That's a good idea, because Ian Strachan wasn't the end of it. Who was next? I forget. There were so many."

"You never forget." Venus glared at her consort. "You know perfectly well that when Ian Strachan didn't work out, Dr. J said to fix Maggie up with the financial planner who's a terrible bore. At least, that's what it *sounded* like."

"So you set her up with Chuck Winkel," Mars said. "Makes sense. In a Dr. J kind of way."

"Chuck Winkel was all wrong for Maggie." Venus signed her name with a flourish and tucked it into an envelope, ready to be dropped off. "I told Dr. J, but he didn't believe me. And then the next thing I heard was it was the guy with the quiet manner who carries mail to the door."

"Clarence. *That* was never going to happen."

"What Dr. J was *trying* to say was that Maggie was supposed to meet the guy who uses a hammer and runs the hardware store. But not even a linguistics expert would have been able to understand that."

"I told you Ed had her surrounded. And the best news? They didn't need us at all."

"*Despite* Dr. J's interference. I'm so glad for them. Maggie and Ed are made for each other."

"And Dr. J has to like how you got Peg Sontag and Grayson Mochrie together," Mars said.

"He does," Venus said complacently.

"You're a miracle, babe," Mars said, kissing her in the doorway. "Without you, the world wouldn't go round. You almost ready? We've got to rumble."

She hadn't packed, because she'd decided against taking anything with her. She wouldn't need it where they were going. She had no regrets except for the turquoise dress, but Maggie—and especially Ed—loved it more than she did.

They went out the back door so Venus could deliver the note for Maggie. She gestured to her garden on her way over to the shabby house next door.

"The garden looks especially nice," she said, noting the bright flowers that crowded the flourishing beds, the vines sinuously curling around Bacchus's legs.

"You did excellent work this trip," Mars said, "even if a lot of it was accidental." And hand in hand, they walked down the driveway and out into the bright fall sunshine.

WHEN MAGGIE GOT home from the office, she went into the kitchen to figure out what to make for dinner. A note lay on the kitchen floor by the back door. Without putting Emily down, she picked up the envelope and tore it open.

"'Dear Maggie,'" she read aloud. "'I'm sorry we have to leave town in such a rush. Mars got a big job that will last so long that I decided to go with him.'"

Emily mewled, and Maggie went to the cupboard to get her some Cheerios. "There, Emily," she crooned. "I know just how you feel."

She went back to the note.

"'I'll miss you. I had so much fun with you trying on clothes, I feel like you're the sister I never had.'"

Maggie smiled down at Emmy, who was gumming cereal onto her navy blazer. "Isn't that sweet, Emmy? Venus thought of me as a sister."

Maggie continued reading.

"'We're going to a much warmer climate, and none of my clothes are right for the new place, so I left our back door open and all my stuff in the closet. Please take anything you want and give the rest to charity. Think of me when you wear the turquoise dress. Better yet, think of Ed.

"'Best of luck, sister of mine! Maybe we'll meet again at the crossroads of the universe. Venus.'"

Maggie blinked. She hadn't known Venus very well, but she'd been kind and friendly, and what a gift! The turquoise dress! And all those other lovely clothes she'd tried on. How very generous of Venus to leave them for her.

She gazed out the window toward Venus's house. The light was fading, but the house was dark. Venus and Mars had gone.

Maggie peered harder. The yard looked deserted already, too. The ivy around the little Bacchus was turning brown, and the coneflowers were dry and brittle. Fallen brown and yellow leaves blew across the pathways, where the grass had lost its luxuriant green color and seemed to be flattened and dull. Everything seemed more shriveled. Of course, the weather had turned quite a bit cooler. Winter was finally on its way.

Maggie turned away from the window when she heard footsteps stamping up the front steps. The boys and Ed were discussing the finer points of the World Series contenders with a vigor and enthusiasm that Maggie wished her sons would apply to their homework.

"They're home, Emily," Maggie said to the little girl. "Our guys are home and they're talking about sports. Are you going to be a baseball fan, too?"

"Ma-ma!" Emily said, patting Maggie's face. "Ma-ma! Da!"

"I can't believe you're talking! Emmy, say 'ma-ma' again."

She went into the living room, excited with the new development. David turned to her.

"Ed says you're getting married," he said, but he didn't sound hostile. Thank heaven.

Maggie's eyes flew to Ed's.

Ed shrugged. "He asked."

"Ed says we're moving into a new house!" Kyle shouted.

"What?" Maggie said.

"I said *maybe*," Ed said.

"Now you've done it," Maggie said.

"If you're getting married, and we're moving into a new house, can I have my own computer in my room?" David asked.

"*No*," Maggie said.

"We'll have a second one, though," Ed said. "I use a computer at home for work. You or Kyle can use that one, too."

David brightened. "Cool!" he said. "Come on, Kyle," he said, grabbing his younger brother. "Let's go upstairs until dinner's ready."

"No video games," Maggie said.

"Do your homework," Ed said, trying it out.

"Yeah, yeah," David said, pushing his younger brother

up the stairs.

Maggie turned to Ed, who engulfed her in a welcome-home hug.

"So about a new house," Maggie said when she came up for air.

"I said *maybe*," Ed said. "Let's go in the kitchen and I'll show you how to make chicken in green sauce. You like that."

He took Emily from her as they headed toward the kitchen, and Maggie noticed that some of the cereal mush that had stuck to her shoulder had transferred to his.

"Look," she said, smiling at him, pointing to the mess.

Ed grinned. "It's a cross-cultural exchange."

"A blended family."

Ed brushed Emily's hair back as the boys squabbled upstairs. Maggie watched him, feeling a forever glow deep in her heart.

"A blended family," he said. "And a mighty fine one, too."

ABOUT THE AUTHOR

Kay Keppler was born and raised in Wisconsin and now makes her home in northern California, where she lives in a drafty old house with a wonderful fireplace. In addition to fiction, she writes regularly for the *Writers Fun Zone* web site and other popular and scholarly publications.

www.ingramcontent.com/pod-product-compliance
Lightning Source LLC
Chambersburg PA
CBHW051429170626
46809CB00006B/2379